For His Pleasure

ALSO BY SHELLY BELL

At His Mercy

His to Claim

For His Pleasure

A Forbidden Lovers Novel

SHELLY BELL

FOREVER

New York Boston

Copyright © 2019 by Shelly Bell

Cover design by Elizabeth Turner. Cover image © Shutterstock. Cover copyright © 2019 by Hachette Book Group, Inc.

Forever
Hachette Book Group
1290 Avenue of the Americas
New York, NY 10104
read-forever.com
twitter.com/readforeverpub

First Edition: June 2019

Forever is an imprint of Grand Central Publishing.
The Forever name and logo are trademarks of Hachette Book Group, Inc.

The publisher is not responsible for websites (or their content) that are not owned by the publisher.

The Hachette Speakers Bureau provides a wide range of authors for speaking events. To find out more, go to www.hachettespeakersbureau.com or call (866) 376-6591.

LCCN: 2019932462

ISBNs: 978-1-4555-9603-4 (pbk.), 978-1-4555-9602-7 (ebook)

Printed in the United States of America

LSC-C

10 9 8 7 6 5 4 3 2 1

This book is dedicated to all the survivors.

Acknowledgments

There would be no Cash or Dreama if it weren't for the people who inspired this series. Aliza Mann, MK Schiller, Heather Novak, and Sage Spelling, you are the Sam to my Dean. I'd never be able to do what I do without you cheering me on. I can't wait for our next 3:00 a.m. conversation over tea.

Thank you to Jessica Alvarez at BookEnds for being the agent of my dreams. You always know the right thing to say.

To Madeleine Colavita for your endless patience and your wisdom. I might write the words but you make them shine.

A shout-out to everyone at Grand Central Forever. From start to finish, there are dozens of people who worked on this book. I appreciate each and every one of you.

To the readers and bloggers, I want you to know I don't take you for granted. There are so many wonderful books out there, and it means the world to me that you take the time to read mine. I hope you love Cash and Dreama as much as I do.

I'd like to thank Brooke's Legacy Animal Rescue for all

the good that you do in the community and for giving me a way to get my cat fix.

Last but never least, to my family. You've supported me throughout my journey without complaint. Now it's my turn to support yours.

For His Pleasure

ONE

Dreama's bones ached as if she'd spent the last twelve hours hog-tied by a Dom to an unforgiving steel punishing bench. Not that any Dom she knew would commit such an egregious act. In her circles, leaving a sub bound like that for twelve hours would violate the BDSM principles of engaging in safe, sane, and consensual activity. Therefore, she'd never been hog-tied for more than minutes at a time. But she imagined if she had been, her bones would ache like this.

She thought back to the night before. The sexy Dom she'd scened with had worked her over with a flogger pretty hard, but it wasn't her first rodeo at the end of a whip—or even the hundredth. And she wasn't hungover; she hadn't drunk a sip of alcohol. Granted, she'd only gotten about six hours of sleep, but that wasn't unusual for her.

On a sneeze, she rolled over in bed and shut off her alarm clock.

Three more sneezes followed. *Ugh.* Her head felt as if it were stuffed with cotton.

Damn it.

She could not afford to get sick right now. Not while she was in the running for the supervisor position that meant a ten-thousand-dollar-a-year raise and the ability to have more of a voice in the parole office she currently worked in. Equally qualified, Meg was the only other person being considered for the job. Since the day she and Dreama had begun working together, Meg had treated Dreama as a competitor rather than a coworker. Meg had rejected every one of Dreama's attempts at friendship. If Meg got the job, Dreama would have to constantly watch her back because Meg would fire her ass the moment she got the opportunity.

Naked and shivering, Dreama threw off the covers and got out of bed, grabbing a hooded sweatshirt and a pair of sweatpants from her dresser and putting them on. Even the simple act of dressing exhausted her. This was more than a cold. She'd bet anything she'd caught the flu that had been going around her office.

Maybe if she medicated herself enough, she could see her morning clients and make alternative arrangements for her afternoon ones. She snatched a tissue from its box and opened her bedroom door, intent on searching the bathroom for something that would make her feel halfway human.

Even with the blinds covering the windows, it was way too bright for her eyes as she stumbled out into the family room. She blinked, realizing she wasn't alone.

Her roommate, Jane, placed a blanket over her baby, Maddox, who was babbling happily in his car seat. Beside them stood Maddox's father, Ryder, who, until recently, had been out of the picture. Dreama's heart warmed at the sight of the three of them together. She hoped this meant Ryder and Jane were working through their issues.

"Oh. I thought you'd be at work," she said to Jane. Normally, Jane would have dropped Maddox off at day care by now. She acknowledged Ryder with a short wave and asked her roommate, "Do you have any cold medicine? I ran out."

"Yeah. It's in my bathroom, underneath the sink." Jane's expression morphed into one Dreama recognized as motherly concern. "You look terrible."

Just what she needed to hear. She looked as bad as she felt.

"I feel terrible." Dreama blew her nose and when she stopped, the room started to spin. *Forget the medicine.* She needed more sleep. "I think I have the flu. I'm calling in to work and going back to bed."

Starting toward her room, another wave of dizziness crashed into her and she held out her hand to steady herself. Suddenly, Jane was beside her with an arm around her waist. Rather than take her to her room, she led her into the bathroom. Jane flopped the toilet lid down and pointed at it. "Sit."

Dreama was too tired to argue. She collapsed onto the seat and held on to the sides for balance.

Crouching, Jane opened the cabinet below the sink and riffled through it, standing up with a full bottle of cold medicine and a thermometer in her hands. She turned to Dreama and dangled the digital stick in front of her mouth. "Open."

Dreama plucked the thermometer from Jane's fingers and slid it under her tongue. Ten seconds later, it made a fast beeping noise. Jane pulled it from Dreama's mouth and frowned as she read it. "One hundred and three degrees."

Dreama's teeth began chattering. "I'll be fine. I just need to get some rest." She watched Jane pour the orange liquid into the tiny measuring cup, thankful to have such a kind friend. "Things looked pretty cozy between you and Ryder. I have a feeling I'm going to need a new roommate soon."

Jane handed her the medicine. "We're taking it slow."

As sick as she felt, she couldn't suppress her smile. "You forget how thin these walls are. I heard how slow you were taking it last night." She knocked back the liquid as if she were doing a shot.

"Yeah, well, sex isn't one of the problems between us," Jane mumbled. She folded her arms and pursed her lips. "We were going to go to the community center to get a picture of Maddox on Santa's lap, but maybe I should stay here. I don't want to leave when you're this sick."

Shaking her head, Dreama stood, which was a bad idea because now the room was spinning again. She leaned against the wall to keep from tumbling to the floor. "No. I want you to go. I want a copy of the photo for my nightstand." She loved Maddox as if he were her own. She'd hit the jackpot when Jane had answered her ad for a roommate and moved in. Other than her cousin Isabella, she didn't have a closer friend. "I'm really happy for you, you know. Ryder's a good guy. He might have his head up his ass right now, but he'll come around. Mark my words. By this time next year, you and Maddox will be living with Ryder. You'll have everything you ever wanted."

Jane's eyes shone as if she was about to cry. "I love you. Promise me that no matter what happens, we'll always be friends."

The thickness in Dreama's throat had nothing to do with the flu. "Promise."

Jane helped Dreama back to her room, where Dreama got back into bed and called in to work. By the time she hung up, she'd drained every remaining drop of her energy. And her cell's battery. She must have forgotten to charge her phone last night. Coughing, she eyed the charger sitting across the room by her sewing machine. It was *soooo* far away.

Placing her dead phone on the nightstand, she decided she'd charge her phone after she took a nap and closed her eyes. She heard the front door close and drifted off sleep.

The next thing she knew, her body jolted awake.

She was no longer freezing. In fact, she felt sweaty and overheated, and her heart was pounding much too rapidly. How much time had passed?

She eyed her clock and did some math. She'd only been sleeping for about twenty minutes. *Weird.* Normally if she was sick and took that medicine, she'd sleep for hours.

A loud crash in the family room had her holding her breath.

Had Jane and Ryder come back already?

She was about to call out to them, but a strange sense of foreboding sat heavily in her gut, warning her to stay quiet.

Attempting to suppress the need to cough, she swallowed repeatedly. For once, she agreed with her mother's motto: *Better to be safe than sorry.*

Eyeing the charger, she grabbed her dead phone and slid out of bed. Why hadn't she plugged her cell in before she went back to sleep?

Her hands shook as she connected her phone to the charger. The red light appeared on the screen, indicating there wasn't enough juice yet to even make a call.

She was probably under some medicine-induced paranoia, but her instincts were screaming to get out of that apartment.

And she never ignored her instincts.

Problem was there was only one exit to her apartment and that was the front door. If there was a burglar in there, she couldn't get out without him seeing her.

As her phone charged up, she pressed her ear to the door. There was a moment of silence before she heard the slam of a drawer and an unfamiliar male voice swearing.

Okay, okay. okay. Not medicine-induced paranoia.

She needed a weapon.

She quietly opened her closet and pulled out a baseball bat, grateful her mom had told her all those terrible news stories about what happened to single women who lived alone. Her mom had intended those stories to change Dreama's mind about moving out of her parents' house, but instead, it had served to remind Dreama to keep something in her apartment to protect herself. She didn't feel comfortable with a gun, so she figured a baseball bat would have to do, at least until she could get to the kitchen and grab a knife. Never in her wildest nightmares did she ever think she would have to use it.

She returned her ear to the door and checked her phone again, but it still hadn't turned on. The intruder's footsteps grew louder. She was running out of time.

Maybe she should hide in her closet?

She didn't get the chance to decide.

The footsteps stopped and the doorknob turned.

Arm cocked with bat in hand, Dreama took a step back.

Her phone lit up with energy.

But it was too late.

The masked intruder filled her doorway.

TWO

With every step Dreama Agosto took, pain blasted through her right coxal bone and femur. A year ago, she didn't even know what a fucking coxal bone was (turned out, it was the hip), but after spending months in the hospital and then a physical rehabilitation center, she could probably pass the damned medical board exams. It was information she would rather not have learned if she'd had a choice.

Which of course, she hadn't.

Because a guy wielding a baseball bat and a temper had taken the choice from her.

And her body never let her forget it.

Most people wouldn't consider the walk from the parking lot to her office a long one.

But those people weren't her.

Those people hadn't spent hour after hour in surgery,

having their shattered bones repaired with metal screws, pins, rods, and plates.

Those people didn't suffer from constant swelling and pain.

Those people didn't have to look in the mirror every day and see ugly surgical scars all over their bodies.

No one had ever told her that scars could hurt.

But they could. And hers fucking *did*.

The doctors didn't believe her at first.

Later, after much debate and numerous tests, they'd labeled it as scar neuropathy. Nerve damage. Already she suffered from continuous pain, but when she walked more than a few feet, the pain elevated to a fifteen on a scale of one to ten. It was like her nerves were being stabbed by a butcher knife.

Physical therapy, biofeedback, antidepressants, psycho-therapy, creams, injections…nothing diminished the pain.

And so, she'd learned to live with it.

Hard to believe a little more than a year ago, she'd enjoyed a bit of pain at the hands of a Dom.

But erotic pain was quite different from the kind she'd come to know. This pain had taken away her control and stolen her ability to feel physical pleasure.

Inside the one-story brick building, Dreama nodded to the young security guard as she placed her purse and winter coat on the conveyor belt to be X-rayed.

He was new, at least to her, since she hadn't set foot in this building since her attack. For all she knew, he could have been working there for months.

She ambled through the metal detector, hoping to make it through without drawing any attention to herself.

Any hope of that deflated when the light on top of the machine flashed red and a triple beeping alerted the guard.

"Take out everything you have in your pockets," the guard said, stopping the conveyor belt from moving. "Keys, cell ph—"

"I don't have anything in my pockets," she explained to him. Hell, her conservative black pants didn't even *have* pockets. "The metal is inside my body."

"Ma'am," he said, speaking as if she were ninety-two rather than twenty-seven.

Really? She'd left the workforce for a year and was considered a *ma'am* now? She couldn't be more than a year or two older than him.

He continued. "An implant or small amounts of metal inside the body will not set off the alarm. Please go back and walk through the detector again."

She wasn't going to cry.

She didn't do that.

Ever.

And she wasn't about to start just because a long line of people was waiting behind her or because taking an extra ten steps to her would be like running an extra ten miles for anyone else.

No, she wouldn't cry. But she would make a scene that was likely to end with him crying for mercy on his knees and her getting thrown out of the building. And if she couldn't be in the building, then she couldn't work, and if she couldn't work, she couldn't pay for her new apartment, and if she couldn't pay for her apartment, she'd have to move back in with her parents, and if she moved back in with her parents, she'd go insane over her mother's incessant hovering.

"Listen, I'd really rather not have to go through the detector again," she said, flashing her pearly whites and batting her eyelashes at him. "So maybe could you just...I don't know...use a wand on me?" She gestured to the parole office sign in front of them. "I work here—my badge is in my purse—and since we're going to be seeing a lot of each other, and this is likely to happen every day because I practically have enough metal inside me to make me the star of *RoboCop*, we should find an alternative arrangement to the metal detector."

As if considering her request, the guard tipped his head to the side. "Again, ma'am, *employee* or not," he said, the emphasis on the word *employee* making it clear he didn't believe it, "you are not permitted inside the building unless you successfully clear the metal detector."

The people standing in line started to get restless, their whispers and frustrated groans reaching her ears. She stared at that damn metal detector wishing she had the ability to melt it with her eyes.

"Excuse me, sir?" said a man from behind her. "As an employee of the state's parole office and this building being her place of employment, the lady is entitled to reasonable accommodations under both federal and state law in light of her disability." At the guard's blank look, the man added, "She indicated she's setting off the detector because of the metal inside her body and if you had observed her walking through the detector instead of checking your cell phone, you would have noticed her slight limp."

Damn. And here she'd thought her limp wasn't that noticeable.

"Furthermore," he continued, "she's asked for those reasonable accommodations. Denying her would violate the Americans with Disabilities Act. If you don't have a wand, I'm sure the security guard manual you keep quoting says something about alternative methods in lieu of the metal detector." He kept going, calmly reciting all the specific federal and state laws the guard was violating.

Her jaw dropped.

And if she'd met this guy at a play party, her panties would have too.

He was tall. Like, seriously tall. Probably a good foot above her five-five frame. And broad shouldered, filling out every inch of his black Henley perfectly. His dark brown hair was shaved close to his scalp in an almost military fashion, accentuating his sharp, high cheekbones. His nose was a bit off center with a slight bump on the middle as if it had been broken a few times, but somehow it worked for him. Gave him a dark and dangerous edge that she used to find physically attractive.

And his lips... *Oh man, those lips.* His bottom lip was plumper than his top. It was another slight imperfection that somehow worked on him.

Yeah, he was fucking gorgeous.

Not in the movie-star, pretty-boy kind of way, but in

a Dreama-falling-to-her-knees-and-kissing-his-feet kind of way.

She couldn't stop herself from zeroing in on his lips, not because of their unique shape, but because of the way he spoke with them. Quiet, but commanding. A voice you couldn't help but obey. Like top-shelf whiskey, hand-rolled cigarettes, and dirty, kinky sex all rolled into one. Three of her favorite vices. It had been far too long since she'd indulged, months since she'd even been tempted.

This man was temptation personified.

Her gaze dropped to his hands. They were a working man's hands. Large...blunt fingertips...a little dirt under his nails...*large*.

What could she say?

Some girls got off on a guy's chest or their eyes, while others liked their butts.

Large hands pushed all her buttons.

Large hands and all the wicked things they could do to her. At least what they *could* have done if she could tolerate a man's touch.

She realized the stranger had stopped speaking.

And the guard was looking like a kid who'd just learned there was no Santa Claus. "Sorry, ma'am," he said sheepishly. "After my shift, I'll speak with my superior about finding an alternative to the metal detector." He stepped out from behind the conveyor belt. "I don't have a wand, so for now, I'll just pat you down and you can be on your way."

"Don't touch me!" she shouted, losing her balance and falling to her knees as she recoiled from him.

All the oxygen expelled from her lungs. Her chest felt as if it were being crushed by a heavy weight and her heart jackhammered behind her breastbone.

The room spun and the edges around her vision blackened.

She had to get it together.

Couldn't allow the fear to drown her.

Breathe, damn it. You're better than this.

Focus.

"Back up," said a firm male voice.

Not to her, but *for her*.

"Focus on my voice," he said in her ear. "No one's gonna touch you. You're safe."

Her eyes were closed, but she recognized the speaker. It was the man with the large hands. He was crouched beside her. Not touching her. Just talking in that low, calming voice of his. A voice that both demanded and crooned.

Following her old therapist's advice, she breathed in through her nose and out through her mouth. She smelled something citrusy, reminding her of the time she went to an orange grove in Florida. Her heart rate slowed from a gallop to a steady pace, easing the pressure in her chest and vanquishing the vertigo.

She opened her lids to the sight of concerned gray eyes.

Her entire body flushed warm.

God, how embarrassing.

"Thank you," she whispered to him. "I'm good now." Still a bit shaky, she got up from the floor and turned to the security guard. "Maybe you could call my supervisor."

She sensed her rescuer standing right behind her as if he was there to catch her in case she fell again. "Meg Wilson can verify—"

"That's okay," the young guard blurted. His throat worked over a swallow. "No need to call her. You can go on ahead."

Ah. Apparently, he was familiar with her boss. Dreama wouldn't have wanted to call her either.

Collecting her purse and coat from the end of the conveyor belt, she gave her gray-eyed giant one last nod to show her appreciation. His expression was stony, almost severe. Another time, another life, she would've flirted with him. Now all she wanted to do was run from him.

Her hands shook as she pressed the buzzer to be let inside the employee entrance of the parole office. She looked up at the camera in the corner of the ceiling and waved. Upon hearing the click of the lock, she pulled open the door and stepped into the hallway beside the receptionists' area.

Suddenly, Candice barreled into her, knocking her backward onto her heels before wrapping her arms around Dreama and squeezing. Fire shot down her right leg, and it was all she could do to keep from crying out. Her friend had no idea how much a hug like that hurt her.

And she never would.

"It's so good to see you," Dreama said. And she meant it. Although Candice was twenty years older, they'd started working at the parole office around the same time and had developed a friendship.

Candice took a step back. "Even better to see you, darlin'.

I know you probably don't want to talk about it, but we have all missed you around here. I tried to see you in the hospital but—"

"I wasn't up to seeing anyone but family." Or more to the point, her family hadn't allowed her to say no to their visits. Dreama squeezed Candice's hand. "But my mom made sure to pass along your well-wishes."

"I'm glad to hear that. Now that you're back, we'll have to catch up. Wait until you see how much my grandbaby has grown this year."

"We'll do lunch." Dreama smiled, ignoring the phantom ache where her womb used to be. "Is Meg in her office?"

"She is and she's expecting you." Candice mouthed, "Good luck," and bounced back to her desk.

Dreama focused on not limping as she walked down the hall to her supervisor's office. The last thing she wanted to do was give any more ammunition to Meg Wilson to use against her. It had been hard enough to convince Meg to rehire her.

Had this hallways always been this long?

In front of Meg's closed door, Dreama gritted her teeth and massaged the tight muscle in her thigh. This might have been Dreama's office if not for her attack. She knocked on the door and opened it upon hearing Meg's forceful "Enter."

For such a no-nonsense, never-let-them-see-you-sweat kind of woman, Meg was unusually short and petite, reaching only Dreama's nose when standing—and Dreama was five foot five. But Dreama had learned not to underestimate her boss. Because she managed to compact a giant amount of meanness into her tiny frame.

"You wanted to see me?" Dreama asked from the doorway.

Not bothering to look up from her computer screen, Meg waved her in.

Dreama closed the door behind her and waited for Meg to acknowledge her. To tell her to take a seat. *Something.*

Clearly, nothing had changed in the year Dreama had been gone from work. Meg was as passive-aggressive as ever. It irked Dreama that Meg was still competing with her. Didn't she realize that she had already won? She'd gotten the job Dreama had wanted and was now the boss. Couldn't she let go of whatever petty jealousy she had for the good of the office?

Five minutes later, Dreama's right thigh was cramping, and sweat was trickling down her jawline. She eyed the empty chair in front of Meg's desk, almost desperate to take the weight off her legs. But she wouldn't give Meg the satisfaction.

Finally, Meg raised her gaze from the computer and looked at Dreama, pursing her lips and wrinkling her nose in distaste as if Dreama were something smelly on the bottom of her shoe. "I'm going to be honest with you," Meg said. "I looked over your employee file, and while previous supervisors praised your work, I expect more from my employees. If I had my choice, I wouldn't have preserved the position for you. But fortunately for you, the law was on your side. Do you understand what I'm saying?"

That you're a patronizing, sadistic bitch?

Yes, she understood. As a state employee, Dreama had been able to take a yearlong medical leave and still have a job to return to. If she hadn't been, Meg would've fired her. Which was bullshit because despite Meg's claim, Dreama had been more than adequate at her job. *Stellar* was the word her regional manager, Meg's present boss, had used to describe her work. Meg knew that if the attack hadn't happened, this office might have belonged to Dreama. And Meg hated her for that.

Dreama literally had to bite her tongue to keep herself from responding the way she wanted to. "I do. And I won't let you down."

All she wanted was the chance to get some part of her old life back.

"I hope you won't allow your"—Meg's lips twisted into a sneer as she zeroed in on Dreama's legs—"*imperfections* to prevent you from doing your job duties. Being a field officer might prove too much for you now. Due to budget cuts, we've had to eliminate several positions, which means your caseload will be a bit larger than it was. I'm not certain you'll be able to keep up with it. Of course, if you need accommodations, I'd be happy to find you a suitable position within the office. Maybe the front desk would be more comfortable for you."

There wasn't a chance in hell that Meg gave one fig about Dreama's comfort. This was all an attempt to intimidate Dreama into taking a demotion and eliminating the perceived threat to her own job as supervisor. Meg had never cared about the parolees. They were all just ex-criminals and case numbers to her. Maybe it was because Dreama earned her degree in social work rather than criminal justice like Meg, but Dreama saw the men and women beyond their criminal histories. She did whatever she could to help ensure they successfully completed their parole and became a productive member of their community, whether that meant requiring them to go to group therapy, anger management classes, or twelve-step meetings, or having them work at a soup kitchen. Every client—she preferred the more dignified word *client* over *parolee*—was unique and required different interventions to put him or her on the path to success. Meg hadn't bothered to get to know her clients, which meant she'd been able to fit more parolee appointments into the day.

Dreama gave Meg one hell of a smile and ignored the burning cramps in her thigh. "My *imperfections*, as you call them, will in no way affect my ability to do my job. But thank you for your considerate offer. Now, unless you have anything else to say to me, I believe I have a full caseload today and I'd hate to start the day already running behind."

Meg returned her attention to the computer screen, silently dismissing Dreama.

Okay, then.

Dreama got out of there before Meg could think up some other way to insult her.

The parole administration was set up almost like a square with the office staff up front behind bulletproof glass and three hallways of offices surrounding it, with the longest hallway in the back. Currently, they only had a staff of thirty or so, including supervisors, officers, and support staff, for the entire county. Dreama's office was the last one in the back to the right. Normally, she relished having the office farthest from Meg's, but right then, every step was agony. By the time she made it to her desk, the back of her neck was wet with sweat.

One glance at the clock on the wall told her she was going to run late today thanks to the fiasco at security and Meg wasting time with her attempt at intimidation. It was already past nine, and she had a waiting room filled with people waiting to see her, but she at least needed to go through her morning files to quickly familiarize herself with her clients.

Rather than making appointments, the parolees were seen on a first-come, first-served basis, scheduled only for a morning or afternoon on a certain date of the week or month. She met with more than a dozen clients every day, in addition to her responsibilities of documenting the visits and other paperwork, making phone calls, doing home and work visits, and going to court and the prisons for hearings. Unlike Meg, she didn't believe in rushing through her client meetings. They deserved her full attention and respect. If that meant working more hours, then that's what she'd do.

After hanging her coat on the back of the door, Dreama spent a few moments in her chair and turned on her computer, reacquainting herself with the office's software and checking that day's calendar. Thankfully, there were no internal meetings scheduled. She wasn't ready to see the collective pity in her coworkers' eyes or answer their questions about her welfare.

She popped a couple ibuprofen into her mouth, swallowing them down with the help of a bottled water she'd brought in her purse, and then turned to her morning's pile of files. Glancing at the check-in screen, which alerted her to those who were currently waiting in the lobby and to the order in which they'd arrived, she pulled her first client's folder from the stack.

Cash Turner. Thirty years old. Spent the last eight years in prison for involuntary manslaughter. She read through the pages, the facts of the case hitting her hard. An intoxicated Cash had lost both his wife and unborn child in a car accident when he'd plowed into the highway's concrete wall and flipped the vehicle twice. In lieu of a trial, he had pled guilty and had been a model prisoner during his time behind bars.

It wasn't her job to judge his past actions, but it wasn't always easy to avoid, especially when children were involved. Still, Cash Turner had served his time and deserved a second chance.

His previous parole officer had visited him in prison a month ago to make sure Cash had arranged a place to live and employment upon his release.

At half past nine, she stood up from her desk and made the trek down the long hallway. Tomorrow, she'd make sure not only to take her ibuprofen before work, but also to arrive extra early. At the end of hall, she opened the door to the waiting room and called her first client of the day.

"Mr. Turner," she said, resting her back against the door.

A closely shaved head immediately snapped up at the call of his name, and she gasped as startled gray eyes met hers. Hunched over with his large hands spread out wide on his knees, the man slowly uncurled his body and stood to full height.

Her sexy stranger from the lobby.

Well, shit.

THREE

Cash should have been surprised that the woman from the lobby would wind up being his parole officer, but then again, when had anything in his life turned out the way he'd expected?

He'd started the morning off with the same goal that he'd had every day for eight years: to keep his head down and stay out of trouble. Bad things tended to happen to those who brought attention to themselves in prison.

But for some reason, he couldn't keep himself from getting involved in that little situation out in the lobby.

He'd observed her walking into the building when his sister had dropped him off for the appointment, and his eyes had gone directly to her backside.

He couldn't help himself.

Sure, there was a limp to her gait and she was wearing a long navy winter coat that covered her ass. But, man, that woman worked it with every step she took. Like a metronome, her hips swayed from side to side. He'd been mesmerized.

He hadn't planned on doing anything about it. He certainly hadn't planned on coming to her defense when that kid who called himself a security guard denied her entry into the building. Or that he'd find himself crouched on the floor beside her to bring her back from the edge of an apparent anxiety attack.

She was attractive. He'd give her that. Just the type that got his blood revving. Curvy with those sexy wide hips and small waist. Almond-shaped eyes with dark lashes. Shoulder-length hair that started out black at the roots and progressively turned to light brown at the ends. It was neither straight nor curly, but somewhere in between. Long enough to hold on to and play with but short enough not to get in his way.

Except her looks had nothing to do with why he'd opened his big mouth. Truth was, he never could resist a woman in need. Hell, that was exactly how he'd found himself married to Maddie at the ripe old age of twenty-one, and look how well that had gone.

He couldn't go down that road again. In the end, not only had he failed to save Maddie, but also his reckless actions had killed her. He might have served his time in the eyes of the law, but that didn't mean he forgave himself.

He crossed the waiting room and strode toward the woman, noting the way her eyes greedily ate him up as he moved closer and the spasm of her slim throat as she swallowed hard.

The force of his desire to see this woman on her knees in front of him in submission nearly bowled him over.

Back in the lobby, she'd seemed brazen and confident but at the same time a bit fragile. Exactly the kind of woman he'd preferred to top in the past. But those days were over. After making the mistake of confusing fragile for broken in Maddie, he no longer trusted his instincts to know the difference.

The woman let him pass her before closing the door, and he caught her scent, a tease of strawberries and sunshine in this frost-covered state of Michigan.

As the door clicked behind them, she looked up at him. Even with her womanly curves, she was petite. Probably a good foot shorter than his six-three frame.

"Mr. Turner?" she asked in a businesslike tone, completely ignoring their previous encounter. At his nod, she continued. "I'm Dreama Agosto. Your new parole officer."

"You're a woman," he blurted before stopping himself. His last parole officer had been a man. He had just assumed the parole office made assignments along gender lines. Wasn't it dangerous for her to work with male parolees, especially the rapists and murderers? He didn't like the thought of her risking her life every day.

"Thanks for pointing that out." She gave him a weak smile. "Let's go to my office."

Shit. He'd offended her. Not a great way to start with the person who had the power to send him back to prison.

That was twice now he'd worried about her well-being, and he didn't even know her. Normally, he had more control over his mouth, but something about her made him forget to stay quiet.

He walked beside her down the hall and noticed her limp was more pronounced than out in the lobby. "I just...I thought I'd have a male parole officer since I'm a—"

"Man?" She shook her head. "We don't have enough male officers to cover the caseload. Each of us has more than a hundred parolees assigned to us at any given time." She brought him to an office and waved him inside. "Have a seat, Mr. Turner."

Right. He was Mr. Turner, her parolee, and she was his parole officer. Not a potential lover. Not even his friend. From this point on, he had to remember that.

"Yes, ma'am," he said, seating himself in front of her desk. He noticed it was angled so that she was closer to the door than him. *Good. Harder for some deranged parolee to trap her in here.* Hopefully she had a panic button too.

"You don't have to call me 'ma'am.' I'm Dreama Agosto. Call me Dreama. Do you mind if I call you Cash?"

Yes. Because his name on her lips sounded way too good. "That's my name."

Dreama. Reminded him of the song "Dream a Little Dream of Me."

Unusual name for an unusual woman.

He scanned his surroundings, a habit he'd developed in prison. And just like prison, her office space was pretty bleak. Fading whitish walls that probably hadn't seen a fresh coat of paint in years. A scratched-up oversized brown desk with a couple wire baskets on it that people used for mail. An old computer monitor that looked as if it had been around since the twentieth century.

Nothing on the walls. No photos or plants or anything that screamed life and individualism. This office could belong to anyone.

It certainly didn't fit the unusual woman named Dreama. He didn't even know her and he could tell *that* much.

"How did you know all that legal stuff about disabilities?" she asked.

He shrugged. "Took an online Intro to Law class through Edison University while I was in prison." To fill up his time behind bars, he'd taken more classes than was necessary to earn his bachelor's degree in zoology. He'd only been two classes away from earning a second bachelor's degree in sociology when he'd gotten word he would be released this month.

She took the chair across from him and picked up a manila folder that had his name typed on the label. "Oh. Well, thank you for your help out there."

He caught the underlying embarrassment in her tone, and he didn't get it. What did she need to be embarrassed about? So, she'd had some kind of panic attack. He'd witnessed men twice her size having them behind bars.

She opened the folder. "I understand you got out of prison two days ago. Any problems with your transition?"

She sounded like a shrink rather than a parole officer. It was none of her business if he was having a hard time adjusting.

So maybe he'd had a difficult time sleeping. The house was just too damned quiet. He'd grown accustomed to the various noises in prison.

But he wasn't about to tell her that. The last thing he wanted was someone messing around with his head... especially her.

He leaned back and stretched his legs out, uncomfortable from the hard chair that was way too small for his body. "No problem at all."

Pursing her lips, she didn't speak as she stared at him with an intensity that put him on edge. He got the feeling she was trying to figure out if he was lying. "I'm glad to hear that, because leaving prison can be overwhelming for some. There's exposure to temptations such as alcohol and drugs and old friends or family members who may have caused problems in the past. It's my role as your parole officer to help you readapt to society and to stay informed on your conduct and condition. I just wanted to make sure you were okay with it so far."

In other words, she was his keeper, his babysitter, and his prison warden all rolled up in one sexy package. His terms of parole included weekly drug and alcohol testing for the next month and then at random for five years. He understood why it had been included. His drunk driving had led to Maddie's death. Problem was he had no recollection of drinking at all that night, and he'd never had a problem with alcohol or drugs. In fact, he'd pretty much stayed away from both once he'd gotten married.

"I'm fine with the transition so far, ma'am," he said.

Her eyes narrowed a bit at his referring to her as *ma'am* again. She obviously didn't like it, but too bad. She'd just have to get used to it. Here in this office, she had power over him. And calling her *ma'am* rather than *Dreama* would help remind him of that fact.

"You're living with your sister. Is that going to be your temporary or permanent residence?"

"Temporarily permanent," he said, staring down at his shoes and realizing there was a hole near the toe. He hadn't worn these particular sneakers in more than eight years, and he was suddenly hit with the memory of Maddie nagging him to buy new ones. "We haven't really discussed how long I'll be staying."

Or rather, they hadn't agreed on how long he'd be staying. Rebecca had already thrown her neck out for him. The last thing he wanted to do was burden her with his shit.

"At some point, I will be making an unannounced home visit to confirm you're living where you say," Dreama said. "I'll also be checking in with your employer to make sure you're showing up for work. You'll be working at the county animal shelter?"

"Yeah."

Just one more item on a long list of what Rebecca had done for him.

Dreama looked up from the file, her dark brows arched high. "It says here you worked with dogs in prison. Can you tell me about that?"

He shrugged, uncomfortable. "I trained a dog or two."

"You did more than that." She beamed as if he'd done something worthy. As if she was proud of him. "Apparently, you started the county's PAWS program. Can you tell me about it?"

Prison wasn't much different than the animal shelters. Both lacked an air of hope. Especially for those labeled violent offenders. Hard enough to find qualified people to adopt a dog. But for one with a history of aggression or biting? Most of the time, the animals were written off. That was why Cash had started PAWS.

His previous parole officer hadn't given a shit what Cash had done behind bars. He'd simply run down some checklist, telling Cash what he needed to coordinate before his release and had reported back to the parole board.

PAWS was none of Dreama's business. He didn't need her reading any more into it than it was.

He drummed his fingers on his thigh and looked at the corner of the room. "Every four months, select prisoners were assigned a dog to rehabilitate. They spent hours each day walking the dog, taking it to obedience class, and retraining it. Gave us something to do."

The last thing he needed was for his parole officer to think he was some kind of hero, because he wasn't. That's why he left out the part that the idea of the program was that the inmate and the animal would learn to trust each other and bond. Once the dog graduated, it was usually adoptable, giving prisoners a sense of accomplishment.

Bad enough that he was attracted to the woman sitting across the desk from him. If she actually *liked* him, it would make it that much harder for him to remember that within these walls, he wasn't anything more than an ex-con.

Serving eight years in prison for manslaughter had flushed his dreams of ever becoming a veterinarian down the drain. He liked animals. Always had. But starting PAWS wasn't anything he should be commended for. Didn't make up for all the lives he'd ruined.

He waited for a follow-up question that never came. Instead, the room remained quiet. Against his better judgment, he pulled his gaze from the wall and looked at Dreama.

Shit.

Her lips were tugged up into a wistful smile and her eyes shone with something that resembled admiration.

He had a flash of her on her knees for his pleasure, that same look on her face. Pupils dilated and fixed on him. Crimson lipstick smeared around her mouth and evidence of tears in the form of black mascara running down her cheeks. Naked except for the leather collar around her neck.

Fuck, he hated the way that smile lit up her eyes, making her even more beautiful. He hated it even more because he wanted to be worthy of it. But he wasn't. And the sooner she realized it, the better.

He didn't deserve her admiration.

For two days, he'd had no problems with his transition from prison to the outside world. Not a single thing had tempted him.

Not until Dreama.

Suddenly, the walls of the room seemed to shift inward, swallowing the space in the room. It was as if he were back in his prison cell, trapped and restless. "You think I'm a good guy because I played with a few dogs in prison? You don't know me. Don't fool yourself into thinking otherwise." She certainly wouldn't think he was a good guy if she knew the kinds of things he wanted to do to her.

"Contrary to what you might think, I'm not the enemy," she said softly, speaking to him as if he were one of the dogs in the PAWS program. "I'm here to help you."

How many times had he heard that line? From the firefighter at the scene of the accident who'd cut his seat belt to pull him from the wreckage to the defense attorney who'd convinced him to take a plea deal, everyone allegedly wanted to help him. But no one other than his sister had believed him when he'd sworn he hadn't been drinking the night of the accident, especially since the evidence stated otherwise.

And this slip of a woman with a limp and a panic disorder wanted him to believe she was on his side. What could she do for him other than remind him of who he could no longer be and what he could no longer have?

"Help me," he parroted. "Lady, I might be new to this parole thing but I'm not stupid. You may think you're not the enemy, but you have the power to put me back behind bars. That certainly doesn't make you my friend."

"Listen, we're going to see a lot of each other over the next few months. I'm not here to judge you. I don't care whether you were guilty or innocent of the charges that sent you to prison. As far as I'm concerned, you paid for your crimes. You're entitled to a fresh start."

How he wished that was true. He might not have been intoxicated the night of the accident, but it was still his fault. If only he could remember what had happened that night after he'd asked Maddie for a divorce.

"Ninety-six months behind bars for killing my wife and son," he ground out. "You think I've paid? Who are you to decide that? You know nothing about me or my crimes."

She tilted her head as if she was considering his words. "You're right. All I know is what's in your file and the kindness you showed me out in the lobby."

"Just did what anyone would do."

"Bullshit," she said, shocking him with her coarse language. "You got involved. Most people run *from* conflict. Not *to*. That told me more than any damned file could." She gave him another one of her smiles and he was done for.

He gripped the arms of his chair as if they were glued to his palms. He needed to get out of there before he did something stupid...like kiss her. "We finished here?" he asked gruffly.

Her smile melted from her face. He wasn't sure if he was pleased or pissed to see it go. She snatched a paper off her desk and slid it across to him. "This is your lab order for drug and alcohol testing. The address is on the top of the order. It's just a mile from here. Make sure you go today so that I have the results before we meet again next week." She winced as she jumped to her feet. Her fingers dug into her thigh as if she were in pain. "I'd like to remind you one of your conditions for parole is to avoid any establishments that serve alcohol and that includes your sister's home."

He picked up the order and stood. "Won't be a problem. I haven't gotten drunk or high since my sophomore year at college." Despite what everyone thought. She frowned and rested her back against the wall with one leg outstretched as if she was trying to keep her weight off it. He wasn't sure if the frown was due to her leg or his comment about not drinking. A part of him hoped it was the latter, but he was a realist. No one had believed him before. He doubted now would be any different.

"If Monday mornings work for you," she said, "I'll put you on the schedule for the next three months. After that time, we'll probably move to bimonthly appointments. If you ever need to reschedule, you can call me at the office or if I'm not here, you can call my cell. But remember, you have to make up your appointment within forty-eight hours or it's considered a parole violation."

She swiped a business card off her desk and held it out to him with her arm fully extended as if trying to keep as much distance between them as possible. That he understood. She was thinking about her safety. But what confused him was the unnatural way in which she held the card, pinching a corner of it between her thumb and pointer finger. And her hand was shaking. It reminded him of one of the prisoners in the PAWS program, a guy who'd signed up to help himself get over his fear of dogs, and the way he'd given a treat to his dog for the first time.

He took a step closer to her and slid his own fingers down the card until his thumb and hers practically touched. On a gasp, she quickly released her grip and shrank back, flattening herself against the wall.

He looked up to see her slim throat working over a swallow and noticed that her pupils were dilated. What the hell had happened?

"You scared of me, Dreama?" he asked her, concerned. No *ma'am* this time. He couldn't help rolling her name on his tongue again. It was the closest his tongue would ever get to the woman.

She shook her head and let out a breath, her body relaxing. She gave him a smile, but it was nothing like the one before. This one was a mask. "No. I'm not scared of you, Cash."

If he hadn't scared her, then what had? Because he recognized fear when he saw it. She hadn't gone into a full-blown panic attack as she'd done in the lobby earlier, but she'd panicked just the same.

As if the last few seconds hadn't happened, she limped across the room and opened the door. "I'll walk you to the front."

He wanted to order her to sit down. Tell her he could walk himself out. Her leg was obviously bothering her. She needed to take better care of herself. That much was clear.

But he didn't have the right to tell her what to do.

And he never would.

FOUR

By 6:00 p.m., Dreama had met with ten parolees. Convicted sex offenders. Drug dealers. Murderers. She'd made seven phone calls. Completed all her reports. Read through the files of her next couple of days' clients during lunch. But as busy as she'd been, she couldn't stop thinking about Cash.

With those soulful eyes and beautiful hands, he'd shaken her to the core and knocked her entire world off-kilter.

He'd accused her of being scared of him.

Still at her desk, she laughed quietly as she snatched his file from the bottom of the pile.

She'd lied to him. He *had* scared her. Not because he was a convicted felon or because she worried he'd intentionally hurt her. It was such a simple act. Handing him her card. And yet, her throat had seized up and she could barely breathe. Her heart had felt as if it were going to jump out of her chest. All because of the possibility that their fingers might connect.

It was ridiculous.

The attack had left her fearful of a man's touch.

She wasn't scared to sit in a room with a murderer, but she was deadly afraid to shake his hand. It was such an ordinary thing to do, a standard procedure of hers whenever she met a new client. She knew before she returned to work that she'd no longer be able to shake hands, but she hadn't considered all the little things she did that had the potential to put her in direct contact, things like giving someone her business card.

That wasn't the only thing she feared now.

Shadows and creaking noises played havoc on her imagination. Unfortunately for her, she had an awesome one.

Bogeymen hid under her car and would slice her ankles to incapacitate her. Monsters waited in her closet with sharp knives and jagged teeth. Men's fingers were laced with poison that would burn her flesh and snap her bones.

All of it was irrational.

She knew that.

But she couldn't change it. Not since some freak had used Dreama's own baseball bat to beat her within an inch of her life. That wasn't even an exaggeration. Her heart had literally stopped beating for two minutes on the operating table.

Now she made sure to check under her car and inside it before getting in. Searched her apartment whenever she arrived home. She even moved to a more secure apartment building complete with an armed guard at the front. These were things that kept her safe.

But she missed a man's touch. A gentle caress down her

arm. Naked flesh sliding against hers. Large hands that pinched and slapped and squeezed.

It was all a huge part of who she was as a woman.

A submissive.

A masochist.

A sexual creature.

Gone. Gone. Gone.

It had been a year since she'd hugged her own fucking father.

Cash reminded her of everything she'd lost, and how fucked in the head she'd become.

More than that, Cash had scared her because she'd never been attracted to a client before. He inspired thoughts of whips and ropes and gags and large hands spread wide on her inner thighs.

The visualization of it had been so clear in her mind, she could almost feel the imprint of his fingertips digging into her skin like a brand. But even if she didn't have her phobia, she would never have a sexual relationship with one of her clients.

She frowned, dropping his file in front of her and flipping it open to read again. Before she'd freaked out, he'd said something that had confused her. Something about not getting drunk or high since his sophomore year of college. But according to his file, he had just turned thirty. If he'd started college at eighteen, it had been about eleven years since he'd been drunk. Eight of those years had been spent behind bars...which meant that he couldn't have been drunk the night of the accident, at least according to what he'd said.

It wasn't unusual. Most of her parolees continued to maintain their innocence no matter how much evidence there had been against them or how much time had passed. But it wasn't what he'd said, so much as how he'd said it. He'd just thrown it out there, as if it wasn't significant. Maybe he'd lied so many times, it had become second nature to him, but she got the sense he'd been telling the truth.

She shouldn't have cared. He'd already paid the price for his crime. Guilt and innocence were irrelevant at this point. She was exhausted after the long day and she needed to go home to soak her sore muscles. But Cash's words had made her curious.

So for the next fifteen minutes, she buried herself in the past of Cash Turner, first rereading his file and then perusing some local news articles online.

The night of the accident, witnesses had seen Cash's car veer left into the concrete wall of the highway, flip over twice, and eventually land upright. The vehicle had been so crumpled, the fire department had needed to use the jaws of life to rescue him.

Unconscious and bloody at the wheel when EMS had arrived, he'd awoken minutes later having no memory of the moments leading up to the accident. Cash had passed out once again upon learning that his pregnant wife and unborn baby had died at the scene. Before being wheeled into the ambulance, a policeman was able to rouse Cash just long enough to give him a Breathalyzer test.

He had pled guilty to involuntary manslaughter, forgoing a trial. The judge had sentenced him to ten years and Cash had served eight.

Dreama thought back to the man she'd met that morning.

He'd had a wife.

They were having a child.

At thirty, he'd gone through more than most went through in a lifetime.

Dreama shuffled the papers in his file, searching for the results of the breath test from the scene of the accident. She found it in the arresting officer's notes.

She frowned, reading the information over twice just in case she'd misinterpreted it. Cash's blood alcohol level was well below the legal limit. In fact, his results seemed to indicate he hadn't been drinking at all.

Weird.

She thumbed through the rest of the paperwork, looking for a toxicology report that would have come from the standard blood test, a test that was protocol in cases like Cash's.

If there had been one performed that night, it wasn't in his file.

She read through the court transcript of him accepting the plea bargain of involuntary manslaughter and the sentencing for it, and neither mentioned any specific test, just that there was evidence Cash had driven while intoxicated.

What evidence were they referring to?

Within the transcripts were the names of the prosecutor and Cash's court-appointed attorney, Stephen Browner. His name wasn't familiar, but there were dozens of public defenders and the office had a high turnover. Plus, it had been eight years. Even if he was still working there, it was doubtful the guy would remember the case, but maybe he could locate some additional records for her and fax them over.

Using the online attorney database, she looked him up.

Sure enough, there was a Stephen Browner now working for the law firm of Williams, Beck, and Browner in its private equity division.

Huh. She didn't even know what *private equity* meant, but she did know the average attorney at that firm earned about five hundred dollars an hour. Unless there was another Browner at the firm, Stephen Browner was a partner, which meant he earned even more.

Browner had come a long way from a paltry salary of the public defender's office.

Although it was late, she picked up the phone and dialed his number, figuring a guy at that firm would probably be working for another couple of hours.

After going through the phone tree, she waited for either Browner or his voice mail to answer.

A voice came through the line. "Stephen Browner."

"Yes, good evening, my name is Dreama Agosto, and I'm calling from the Michigan Corrections office. I have a parolee by the name of Cash Turner. He was your client about eight years ago, and I have some questions about his case."

Silence.

Did they get disconnected?

"I'm sorry, Ms. Agosto. I had a lot of clients while I worked there. I'm afraid I don't remember him."

"Oh, I definitely understand. After all, it was a long time ago, but if I could just take a couple minutes of your time, I'm sure I can help jog your memory."

"I'm in the middle of something. Perhaps—"

"One minute of your time, then," she said. "And then I can tell my good friend Ryder McKay how much you assisted me in this matter. Maybe recommend he use your services in the future." She had no idea what private equity attorneys did, but she figured mentioning her best friend Jane's billionaire husband would be just the right bait for a shark like Stephen Browner.

There was another beat of silence before he spoke. "Of course. Whatever I can do to help."

"As I said, it was eight years ago. Cash Turner was a college student when he'd gotten into a car accident after leaving an event at the Detroit Zoo. The state charged him with involuntary manslaughter in the death of his wife because he'd allegedly been intoxicated. You negotiated a deal for him to plead guilty to involuntary manslaughter. The problem is I can't find any evidence proving he was intoxicated at the time of the accident in his file, and he claims he wasn't drinking that night," she said, embellishing that last part. "Does any of this ring a bell?"

"You're a parole officer. You know as well as I do that they all say they're innocent."

"Yes, but his Breathalyzer was—"

"I arranged hundreds of plea deals during my time as

public defender. I probably spent no more than a total of two hours working on the case. I don't remember anything about Cash Turner or the evidence involved. Maddie Turner was just one more victim in a long line of them while I worked for the state. I'm sorry I can't be more help."

She froze in her chair. He was lying to her. "If you don't remember the case, how do you remember Cash's wife's name?"

"You just mentioned it a few moments ago," he said smoothly.

She wasn't the type to let a man gaslight her. She hadn't mentioned Maddie by name. He had to know more than he was saying. "I think you and I should meet in person. Perhaps we could—"

"I'm a very busy man, Ms. Agosto. I don't have time to waste on an eight-year-old case I don't remember. If you have any more questions, I'm sure someone at the public defender's office would be happy to assist you. Goodbye, Ms. Agosto. And do remember to mention me to Mr. McKay."

He hung up before she could get another word in.

Dick.

Yeah, she'd be mentioning his name to Ryder. She'd tell him to avoid Stephen Browner at all costs.

It was clear to her that Browner remembered more about the case than he claimed and that he didn't want to talk about it. The question was why. Was it because he was too busy and pompous to give her more than sixty seconds of his time or was he hiding something?

She stood from her desk, the fatigue in her body making her stiff and unsteady on her feet. Her doctor had insisted she use a cane, but she'd discovered early on that it only led to additional pain in her arm and back. Not to mention, she felt as if she was advertising her disability with it and the last thing she wanted to do was give the impression that she was an easy target.

She could just imagine what Meg would do if Dreama came into work with a cane in her hand. No doubt she'd pull her entire caseload.

Without her parole officer salary, Dreama couldn't afford her apartment.

She'd have to go back to living with her parents and deal with her mother hovering over her as if she were a toddler.

Therefore, there were no canes in Dreama's future other than the candy ones.

Dreama put her coat on and closed her office door behind her. Thankfully, she wasn't the last one to leave and was able to walk out to her car with a couple other employees. An inch of snow had fallen since she'd parked that morning and temperatures had already dropped below freezing.

Neither did her mended bones any favors. Twenty-seven years old and she felt like an old arthritic woman with a dull nagging ache all over her body. Plus, the walk from her office had knackered her out. She couldn't wait to get home and get under the blankets with a steaming hot mug of cocoa. Driving like this was uncomfortable, but at least her injuries and the associated pain no longer prevented her from being behind the wheel. Before her doctor had cleared her to drive last month, she'd had to rely on her parents to get around.

A half hour later, she walked inside the lobby of her apartment building. It was a far cry from the one she used to share with her best friend, Jane, with its minimal security and rickety stairs. This one came with extra security, including an armed guard in the lobby and an elevator. It was considered a "luxury" property, which wasn't a term she would've thought she'd ever apply to herself. Luxury to her was taking a bath rather than a shower.

But there was no way she could live on her own anywhere without security. Not since the attack. Hell, she still hadn't managed to sleep in her bed.

Ironically, it was because of her attack she was able to afford her apartment. At first, she hadn't wanted the settlement money, but Jane, who now controlled the entirety of her family's vast fortune, had insisted. After all, it had been Jane's grandfather who'd sent the attacker to their apartment. Now that he was in prison for all his crimes, including the murder of Dreama's attacker, she was supposed to be able to put the past behind her. She kept waiting for the day that would happen.

At her apartment, she used her key to open the door and noticed immediately that her lights were on.

Her heart shot to her throat. She always turned off the lights when she left for the day.

Someone had been inside her apartment. Maybe they were still there, but she wasn't going to stay to find out. She backed up a step and pivoted to leave when a familiar voice called out to her from inside her apartment.

"Welcome home. I made dinner for you."

She should have guessed. Dreama might have moved out, but she couldn't escape her mother.

Dreama took a deep breath and stormed inside, dropping her coat and purse on the couch. "You scared the crap out of me, Mom. I thought someone had broken in." Now that Dreama was inside, she smelled the oregano and basil.

Wearing an apron stained with tomato sauce, her mother came out from the kitchen. She picked up Dreama's coat and took it to the closet by the front door.

Dreama had only lived there two weeks, but one of the allures of living alone was the ability to come home, strip out of her clothes, and not be accountable to anyone for her mess. She was tired and cranky, and had been looking forward to eating a Hot Pocket and drinking a glass of wine while she took her bath. But in typical form, her mother had thrown a monkey wrench in her plans.

"I left a message on your cell and you didn't call me back. I was worried. Then I remembered you were starting back at work today and I thought you'd be too tired to make yourself dinner, so I decided to come here and make you a home-cooked meal."

Her mother was always worried about her. She worried about what she ate and how often, and how much she slept. Nothing was off-limits to her mother.

God, if her mother knew the kinds of kinky shit Dreama

used to do, she'd probably lock Dreama in the house and throw away the key.

"Mom, you can't just come over here whenever you want. I told you when I gave you your key and added you to the approved guest list that you had to ask first."

Her mother sighed. "I know what you said, but you need to eat healthy. I looked in your refrigerator and it's all processed food. You should let me do your grocery shopping for you. I know it's hard for you to stay organized with your ADHD."

Dreama flopped onto her couch and put her head in her hands. Her mother was going to drive her insane. "I'm plenty organized and I have no problem doing my own grocery shopping. I just so happen to like processed foods."

Her ADHD diagnosis gave her mother yet one more reason to worry about her. Dreama had never suffered from the hyperactivity component of the disorder, which was why she hadn't been diagnosed until she was a teenager. Before that, she'd struggled in school, especially with reading, and had suffered low grades because of it. Eventually, it became easier to stop trying. It hadn't helped that her mother babied her and treated her as if she wasn't capable of making decisions for herself. In rebellion, Dreama fell into a bad crowd, skipping school, drinking alcohol, and smoking cigarettes, all by eighth grade.

It wasn't until her high school social worker had ordered Dreama be tested for ADHD that she'd gotten her diagnosis. Between medication and some behavioral modification, she'd gone on to graduate in the top 10 percent of her class. But her mother had never accepted that ADHD no longer ruled Dreama's life and still treated her as if she were a helpless child.

"Fine, fine," her mother said, waving her hands in the air. "Eat what you want. But since I've already cooked, why don't we sit down and talk while you have dinner."

Dreama groaned. That was the last thing she wanted to do. "Mom, I'm tired. It's been a long day and all I want to do is take a bath and go to sleep. Thank you for making me dinner and for checking in with me, but I'm a grown woman. I can take care of myself." She felt as if she'd spoken these same words to her mother more than a hundred times. When would the woman finally believe her?

Her mom removed her apron. "You don't want me here? Fine, I'll go. Just promise you'll call me back when I call you."

"I always do...eventually," Dreama mumbled, getting up from the couch. "But you can't expect me to call you back while I'm at work, and no more dropping in unannounced."

Coat now on, her mother opened her arms wide and crossed the room to take Dreama into her warm embrace. "I can't help worrying about you, not after I almost lost you."

Dreama gave in, hugging her back. "I know, Mom."

"Jane told me she hasn't heard from you in two weeks. Maddox misses his auntie. You should go over and see them."

Dreama's chest tightened at the thought of the toddler

who'd once been a huge part of her daily life. She'd been Jane's birthing coach and had been there when Maddox was born. She'd lived with Jane and Maddox for those first few months, essentially co-parenting Maddox with Jane. But things were different now. Maddox and Jane now lived with Ryder.

And Dreama was all alone.

She pressed a hand to her lower abdomen. In addition to several surgeries to repair all her broken bones, she'd also required a hysterectomy as a result of her attack. Someday she'd see a child and not feel the loss. "I'm not ready. But I'll call her, okay?"

"I love you, Dreama. Don't forget that." Her mother kissed her cheek.

Dreama swallowed down the onslaught of emotions her mom's words brought. "I know. Love you too."

After her mother left, Dreama stripped out of her clothes and warmed up the lasagna her mother had cooked for her. She had to admit her dinner was much tastier than the frozen meal she'd planned on eating. One bubble bath and two glasses of wine later, she sat on the couch in her pajamas and turned on the television.

On the coffee table in front of her, her cell phone seemed to glow as if taunting her to pick it up and call her friend. She reached for it, but immediately drew her hand back. Things between her and Jane had been so strained since the attack at their shared apartment. Even though her attacker had broken in to search for an item in Jane's possession, she'd never blamed Jane. It was just that every time Dreama spoke to her or saw her, she was reminded of the woman she'd been a year ago.

Fearless.

There hadn't been a thing she wasn't willing to try. Life was one big opportunity and she'd wanted to sample it all.

Now she couldn't even pick up the goddamned phone and make a simple call.

Hours and another half a bottle of wine later, the light of the television flickered in the darkened living room as she rewatched last season's episodes of *Game of Thrones*. She kept thinking about Cash and her bizarre conversation with Stephen Browner. Was it possible Cash hadn't been intoxicated the night of the accident? It was true that people took plea bargains all the time for things they didn't do, but usually there was evidence to suggest their guilt. Why wasn't the evidence in Cash's file? And why had Browner lied to her when he said he didn't remember the case? She needed to talk to Cash again and it couldn't wait until his next appointment. Perhaps tomorrow she'd check in on him at his place of employment. Kill two birds with one stone. Cross off the required employment check for his parole and get some questions answered at the same time.

It was late—coming up on one in the morning—but she couldn't seem to take herself to bed even though she was so tired, she could barely keep her eyelids open.

Her bedroom should have been a place of sanctuary and peace for her, rather than the source of all her nightmares. Every time she slid under the covers and closed her eyes, all she saw was the man in the mask who'd broken into her old apartment and beaten her within inches of her life with her own baseball bat.

He was dead now.

But the memory of him lived on.

She shivered as a creepy sensation slithered down her neck.

She felt as if someone was watching her.

As if she'd summoned a ghost with her thoughts.

Okay, she'd better turn off the show because, obviously, all the violence and bloodshed were getting to her tonight.

There was no such thing as ghosts.

She was alone, safe and sound, in her apartment.

Still, maybe it was better that she slept on the couch.

After all, nothing good ever came from sleeping in her bedroom.

FIVE

On his way to his first day of work at the animal shelter, Cash stared out the side window of Rebecca's car. He'd gotten his driver's license reinstated the previous afternoon, but he'd decided it was more convenient to hitch a ride with Rebecca this morning rather than taking two cars to the same location.

The world was much brighter this morning. It was as if he'd been living in darkness for eight years and he was suddenly in the light. While he was inside most of the days in prison, he did get outside for fresh air and exercise. But with the sun's rays bouncing off the snow, there was a glow to the early winter morning that he hadn't experienced in a long time.

A glance at the clock reminded him that this time yesterday, he'd been in the security line at the parole office with Dreama. It wasn't the first time he'd thought of Dreama in the past twenty-four hours or even his fifth.

Most of his thoughts had been innocent. He worried

about her leg and whether the security guard had made the alternative arrangements for her screening to get into the building. He recalled the way her face had lit up when they'd discussed the PAWS program. He wondered what had triggered her panic attack in the lobby.

And then there were those thoughts that hadn't been so innocent. Last night in bed, he'd wrapped his hand around his dick, thrilled he could finally jack off without some guy lying in the bunk underneath him doing the same damned thing. And all he could see was Dreama and those big sultry lips of hers. Normally, the women in his fantasies were faceless, but Dreama's beautifully troubled one kept popping up in his head no matter how hard he'd tried to get her out of it. Finally, he gave up and gave in. Imagining himself forcing her to take his full length into her mouth and down her throat, he'd come harder than he could remember.

He had it bad for his parole officer and that could only mean trouble for him.

Rebecca parked the car in front of the animal shelter and turned to him. "You don't have to be nervous."

"I'm not nervous," he said, looking down at his lap and realizing he was drumming his fingers on his thigh. He'd been thinking about Dreama, but he wasn't about to admit that to his sister.

She snorted, a habit of hers that he'd missed. "You forget I know you. Aside from that tapping thing you do on your leg whenever you get nervous," she said, pressing her fingertip to the spot between her eyebrows, "you get this divot right above your nose as if you're thinking too hard."

He did?

He flipped down the visor and looked in the mirror. Sure enough, there was a divot, just as she'd said. "You never told me that before."

She giggled as she released her seat belt. "That's because I liked being able to use it to my advantage. Made teasing you much easier."

"Okay, besides the obvious"—like his wedding or his prison sentencing—"name one time I was nervous."

She pressed her lips together as if holding back laughter. "When you asked a girl to junior prom at the last minute. You walked around all day with that divot. It was so deep, I could've stored a quarter in it. Meanwhile, you were trying to play it so cool."

Shit, he remembered that. And she was right. He *had* been nervous. "I wasn't trying. I *was* cool. That's why I waited."

Things had been so easy that year. His football team had won the championship. He'd been making good grades. His mom had been alive and well. He'd been on top of the world. All the girls in school had been throwing themselves at him. Which was why he'd waited until the last minute to choose his date, a girl he'd really liked. But when he'd finally asked her, she'd responded with a "maybe." Made him sweat up until the day before the dance before telling him she'd go.

Rebecca smirked. "You were kind of a jerk back then."

"I'm still a jerk." He unfastened his seat belt and shifted in his seat to face her. "I'm living with and working for my younger sister."

"That doesn't make you a jerk."

"What does it make me?"

"My brother," she said, reaching out and bumping his shoulder with her fist. "You'd do the same for me, wouldn't you?"

He shrugged. Of course he would. She was his only family. There was nothing he wouldn't do for her.

"It doesn't make you a jerk," she repeated softly. "You haven't been that guy since..." Her voice trailed off, but he knew what she couldn't say.

He hadn't been that guy since sophomore year of college, when he'd gotten Maddie pregnant and married her.

"You're right. I am nervous," he told her. Her driving him to work wasn't just convenient; he didn't want to walk into the shelter on his first day without her. He felt as if he were starting kindergarten and needed her to hold his hand. "I don't want to fuck it up for you." He pointed at the one-story building in front of them. "People in there are gonna know you've got an ex-con as a brother."

Rebecca's expression turned fierce. "When have I ever given a shit what other people think?"

"Never, but you shouldn't have to deal with my baggage," he said.

While Cash had been the high school jock concerned about image and popularity, his sister had been more of the artsy loner. He couldn't imagine what she'd gone through when he'd gone to prison, but knowing her, she'd done it with grace.

"Name a person who doesn't have baggage," she said,

getting out of the car. Hands in the pockets of his coat, he walked with her to the shelter's front door. "You made a mistake. Who hasn't? Besides, you're not the only parolee working at the shelter."

Ever since Cash could remember, he'd wanted to become a veterinarian. His first memory was of his father bringing home a dog from the local shelter as a birthday gift for his mother. Looking back, Cash realized Maisie the shih tzu had been ugly at first, underweight and furless. But that hadn't mattered to him. All he saw was this little dog with an overeager tongue and a constantly wagging tail who desperately wanted to love and be loved.

Rebecca loved animals as well, but she'd loved art more. She'd been so gifted, everyone was certain she'd move to New York after graduation to pursue it. But with their father dead, Cash in prison, and their mother dying of cancer, she'd chosen to stay in the state and pursue Cash's dream instead of her own.

Just one more thing for Cash to feel guilty over.

The door jingled as Rebecca opened it. Cash followed her inside and was greeted by warmth and the distinctive scent of animals. A young woman, probably close to Rebecca's age, hauled a large bag of dog food over her shoulder.

Rebecca took off her coat and went over to her. "Morning, Nancy. How's everyone doing?"

"Fed and happy." Nancy put the bag on the ground. "You must be Cash. Rebecca said you'd be starting today."

He nodded to her, jamming his hands into his pockets. "Nice to meet you."

"Nancy's in charge of the kennels, which makes her your boss," Rebecca said. "You're not working directly for me."

He and Rebecca had already discussed that while technically Rebecca had hiring and firing power over him, he would have a separate supervisor who would also have that capability. That way she wouldn't be in the middle if things didn't work out. Even he knew that Rebecca would never fire him. She was too loyal of a sister.

"Come on," Nancy said to him as she grabbed the dog food bag again. "I'll show you where you can hang up your coat and then I'll give you a tour and introduce you to everyone."

After saying goodbye to his sister, he followed Nancy around the facility, first stopping in the employee break room. It was comprised of a kitchenette, which contained a refrigerator, a microwave, and a coffee maker on one side of the room; a row of lockers on the other; and tables set up in the middle. "You can store your coat in here," she told him, opening a locker. "Best bring a lock with you tomorrow. We've had some thefts in the past. Better safe than sorry."

Nancy gave him a rundown of his duties as she brought him back to the kennels.

Dozens of dogs barked from within their cages, jumping against and clawing the wire as if begging to be let out. It took him back to only days before, when he'd been in a similar cage, aching to return to the real world. Now he stood on the outside, looking in. But at the same time, he was still caged, branded a criminal by those around him and subjected to an extra set of rules that if broken, would return him to prison.

Dogs he could relate to.

People were another matter.

Cash got to work, the menial task of sweeping and mopping the floors keeping him busy. He familiarized himself with all the dogs, memorizing their names and attempting to figure out what breed each was. Most were mutts, the majority a mix of pit bull and Labrador. Like ex-cons, these types of dogs were often considered dangerous.

They weren't.

He stopped his mopping and crouched, reaching his fingers through the fencing and petting the nose of one of them. The dog preened under Cash's touch, nudging his wet nose into Cash's hand.

One day when Cash was moved into his own place, he'd adopt a few of the dogs from here. Give them a real home with a yard where they'd be free to run and play.

Just as his parents had done for him.

When he stood, he bumped into an older man standing right behind him. "Sorry. Didn't see you there."

"Nah. It's my fault. Should've known better than to come up on you like that." He extended his hand. "Buddy. Just got out, huh?"

"Yeah," Cash said, accepting it. "Couple days ago."

"Takes some getting used to."

Buddy must be the other ex-con that Rebecca had mentioned worked there.

"What does?" Cash asked.

He tried to picture what would have put the man behind bars. Buddy didn't appear as if he could harm a fly. He was short, probably only around five and a half feet, and on the slim side.

"Being on the outside," Buddy said, lowering his voice. "Word of warning for you. The others who work here will tell you they're happy to have you while keeping their hands on their wallets. With the exception of me and your sister, it's best to keep to yourself and not give anyone ammunition to use against you."

Cash thought back to Nancy's comment about the lock. He hadn't taken it as a personal dig at the time, but he could understand that if anything went missing, as an ex-con, he'd be one of the first they'd accuse. It was good to have Buddy here, someone who knew what it was like for him. In prison, Cash had been part of a small group that watched each other's backs. He wouldn't exactly call them friends, but more of a necessity. Seemed the same applied once they got out.

Cash nodded and picked up his broom to get back to work. "Thanks. I'll keep that in mind."

The next few hours passed by quickly as he fell into a routine. Each dog would be let outside for some fresh air while Cash cleaned out their cage. Buddy worked on the other side of the room, doing the same. Occasionally, another employee or a volunteer would come in and take the dogs on a longer walk. Then there were those few people who came in looking to adopt. They'd walk up and down the aisles, *oohing* and *aahing*, but as far as he knew, none of them filled out an application in the end.

At noon, Rebecca came by and took him to the lunchroom, personally making sure he ate what she'd packed for him. The other employees gave them a wide berth, and he wondered if that was the norm for her, because she gave no indication that she noticed.

His afternoon was filled with much of the same as his morning, feeding the dogs and cleaning the kennels. Running out of garbage bags, he went into the storage closet and turned on the light, then scanned the shelves for them.

He whipped his head around as he heard the click of the door shutting behind him. A stunning blonde stood there, with a huge smile on her face. He didn't recognize her from any of the employees Nancy had introduced him to, and there was no way he would've missed her, not in that tight black tank top and those tight jeans.

Resting her back against the closed door, she folded her arms under her chest, drawing attention to her cleavage. "Hi. You're new here."

He turned around but kept his distance. "Yep."

"I'm Laci. I'm a volunteer here."

"Cash."

"You're Rebecca's brother, right?"

"I am."

She took a step toward him. "Are you looking for something?"

The room suddenly got a lot smaller and a whole lot hotter. He tugged the collar of his shirt and tore his gaze off the girl's chest, looking at the stocked shelves instead. "Garbage bags."

Something about being in there with the girl felt . . . off. *Wrong.*

Laci moved closer.

Too close.

She reached around him, her breasts brushing his abdomen. He froze, not moving. Hell, not even breathing.

What was this woman playing at?

Was she...coming on to him?

She pulled back and held out a box of garbage bags. "Here you go. If there's anything you need, anything at all, don't hesitate to ask me." She licked her lips. "I imagine it's been a while for you."

He took the box from her. "Sorry?" he asked, knowing full well what she was insinuating but clarifying just to make sure.

She smelled decisively female, like powder and flowers. The scent of it should have gotten him hard. Made him want. She was right. It had been a while since he'd gotten laid. More than eight years. Heck, at this point, a light breeze was enough to make his dick twitch.

But she didn't do it for him.

She invaded his space once again, scoring her long nails down his chest. "I can make you feel *real* good."

His eyelids temporarily closed as he ate up the sensation of Laci's touch. In the darkness, he could almost pretend he wanted her.

She was a beautiful girl offering herself up to him on a silver platter.

Therein lay the problem.

His eyes flew open as Laci dropped to her knees and began to unbuckle his belt.

It would be so easy to allow her to pleasure him.

Too easy.

He placed his hand over hers, trying to be gentle. "I don't think it's a good idea."

She smiled up at him and continued to work at unbuckling his belt, ignoring his polite refusal. "I promise I won't tell anyone. Your sister will never know."

"No!" In an effort to get away, he slammed himself backward into the shelves. Rolls of toilet paper fell to the floor.

Laci shot to her feet. "What the hell is wrong with you? What kind of guy turns down a blow job?" Her jaw dropped. "Oh. Are you—"

No, he wasn't, but she didn't need to know that. Frankly, either way, it was none of her business.

"I've got to get back to work." He awkwardly lifted the box he was still holding in the air. "Thanks for helping me find the garbage bags."

She nodded, seemingly unperturbed by their little tête-à-tête, and put a finger against her lips as if she was privy to a secret. He blasted past her out the door, eager to get away.

A glance at the clock indicated he only had a few minutes before he was supposed to meet Rebecca in the lunchroom. He finished emptying the trash cans and put new bags in each one.

As Cash was preparing to leave the kennel area, Buddy joined him by the door. "I saw you met Laci, our resident welcome wagon. She's quite friendly, isn't she?" he asked with a knowing smile.

Cash shrugged, not really wanting to discuss it. "Little too friendly for my taste."

Too aggressive. Girls like Laci had thrown themselves at Cash all through high school and then at college. He didn't judge them for it. Not then and not now. A few he'd fooled around with. But there was always something missing for him.

Since he could remember, all his sexual fantasies had involved some aspect of BDSM. When he was barely in his teens, he'd begun jacking off to thoughts of tying up pretty young girls and them crying for him to stop as he pushed his cock inside them. Later, his fantasies became more elaborate, filled with images he'd discovered online and through porn.

In his freshman year of college, he'd met a girl who'd been game to fulfill his fantasies. Just like with Dreama, he'd been drawn to her from the start, as if something inside of him recognized something inside of her. Without having a name for it, they fell into a kind of Dom/sub relationship. It began when he'd ordered her to wear a skirt and no panties so that he could finger her under the table at dinner. From there it escalated into bondage, spanking, and some serious hardcore toys. But while they were in tune when it came to sex, they'd had nothing else in common, which led to the inevitable breakup. It wasn't long after that he'd met Maddie. Too bad he hadn't had the experience in the lifestyle to recognize he'd confused psychologically unbalanced for submissive.

"Some girls like the thrill of being with a bad boy, you know?" Buddy said. "She's like a 7-Eleven. Always open."

Cash snorted at the analogy. "Not my type."

"What is?"

"Submissive," Cash said automatically.

Shit, the word had just slipped out. "I mean—"

Buddy took a step closer. "I know a place. Owners run a tight ship. Won't fuck with any terms of parole. No alcohol, no drugs. Caters to our kind of sex."

The whole world seemed to stop and Cash's pulse kicked up. It was as if Buddy was a drug dealer tempting Cash with a drug he'd sworn never to do again. What if he made the same mistake he'd made with Maddie?

"You talking 'bout a BDSM club?" Cash asked quietly.

Buddy nodded. "That more your type?"

There was a loaded question if he'd ever heard one.

"Maybe." Cash swallowed thickly. "I've never been to one."

Buddy dug into his wallet and pulled out a card. He held it out to Cash.

Club X.

Cash eyed it for a moment, his fingers twitching in his pockets. He couldn't say he wasn't curious about what went on in a club like that.

Figuring it wouldn't hurt to check it out, he snatched the card from Buddy's hand. Just as he slid it into his pocket, there was a tap on his shoulder.

Nancy stood behind him wearing a frown.

Shit, how long had she been standing there? Had she overheard their conversation? Not that his sex life was anyone's business, but it wasn't exactly professional for him to be talking about it at work. Or had she seen him in the closet with Laci?

First day at work and he'd already fucked up. Rebecca would be so disappointed in him.

"Cash," Nancy said solemnly, "you need to come with me."

SIX

For Dreama, employment checks were always a bit weird.

It was a required part of her job, but it made her feel as if she were a parent checking up on her kid. Back when she had been a teenager, her own mother had done it to her a time or two and it had embarrassed the heck out of her. No one wanted to draw attention to herself at work by having a parent—or in this case, their parole officer—show up.

But she had to do it at some point, and after staying up half the night thinking about Cash's comments and Browner's strange behavior on the phone yesterday, she decided to skip lunch today and use the hour to visit the county's animal shelter.

Of all the places she'd gone for employment checks, she could say this location was her favorite. Five minutes inside the lobby, and she'd already gotten to pet two puppies and one kitten.

She'd spoken to Cash's supervisor, Nancy, who'd reported that Cash had only been working there a few hours, but so far, there were no problems. Obviously, Nancy didn't have much to say before she'd gone to get Cash, but she'd left Dreama with the impression that she'd thought it was a bad sign his parole officer was already checking up on him.

Dreama's attention was pulled to the door on the right side of the lobby as all six-feet-something of Cash lumbered into the room. Maybe it was because they were outside of the parole office or maybe it was because he was wearing jeans that hugged his thighs just right and a solid black T-shirt that showcased the sculpted muscles of his arms, but all at once Dreama's mind went blank and other parts lower south lit up like accelerant on a bonfire.

"Hey," he said, coming to stand in front of her. "Nancy said you're here on an employment check?"

Now she was mesmerized by his chest. He hadn't seemed this ripped yesterday. "No."

"No?"

Shit. What had he asked? She looked up from his chest and noticed a deep divot between his brows. "Yes, of course I'm here on an employment check." She could have left it at that, but Nancy was staring at them with her lips pressed together, and Dreama hated that the woman could possibly be unfairly judging Cash for Dreama's visit. "I know it's unusual to do an employment check on the first day of work, but I have an ulterior motive. I'd also like to look at the dogs. I thought you could take me back to the kennels and we could talk there."

From the corner of her eye, she saw Nancy's expression smooth out. Nancy turned away from them and went behind the reception desk.

Cash shoved his hands in his pockets and nodded. "Sure. Follow me."

She did follow him. Problem was, it gave her a great view of his ass in those jeans. Her poor neglected pussy was clenching in a reminder of how long she'd gone without sex. She bit down on the inside of her cheek. *Get it together, girl.* She could not be lusting after her client. Then again, with her damn phobia, she couldn't do anything about it even if she wanted to.

He brought her into a large room with rows of cages. Yeah, she knew they called them *kennels* to sound better, but the reality was the dogs were in cages, the bigger ones with barely enough space to move. It broke her heart to see it.

She went over to the closest kennel and knelt down to read the information about the pup. The dog stuck his nose through the chain-link fencing and she rubbed her knuckles against him.

"I take it you're a dog lover?" Cash asked, crouching beside her.

A warmth settled in her belly at his nearness. "Yeah. Um, I know I made it sound like I came here to adopt a dog, but I really am only here to look. I always wanted one when I was a kid. But..."

"But?"

How to explain it without sounding as if she was complaining? After all, she was lucky to have two parents who loved her so much. All she knew about Cash's parents was that they were now both deceased. "My parents were— are—overprotective. Well, my mom anyway. My father just kind of goes along with it."

"A dog should've been right up their alley. What's more protective than a loyal dog?"

"You'd think so, wouldn't you?" She stood, her legs aching from being in the kneeling position. "But dogs have germs. My mom's words, not mine. What if the dog licked a paper cut on my finger and it got infected? And of course, dogs bite. Did I want to have my lovely face destroyed by a rabid animal?"

He winced. "Sounds a bit extreme."

Surprisingly comfortable around him, she kept going as they moseyed down the aisle. Some of the dogs were sleeping, but others perked up when they noticed her approaching. "That was nothing. My parents held my hand when we crossed the street until I was ten. I couldn't go outside without wearing sunblock because she worried that I'd get skin cancer from too much sun. Oh, she worried I'd catch something from using a public toilet. She gave a whole new meaning to the phrase 'helicopter parent.' Frankly, it was exhausting just being her daughter, but it was even worse if I tried to reason with her."

"What about now that you're older?"

Dreama paused, thinking about her mother's impromptu visit last night. "She still worries, but I've gotten better at dealing with it."

"So, what's keeping you from getting a dog now?" he asked.

She considered it. "I work a lot of hours. I live in an apartment."

"Excuses."

She shrugged. The truth was she could barely take care of herself these days much less a dog. Even the small task of walking the dog would be hard on her right now. "Yeah. Maybe. What about you?"

"We've got cats," he mumbled.

Pretending she didn't hear, she cupped her ear. "What? I can't hear you."

He groaned. "Cats. They're my sister's."

"Excuses," she mimicked. The annoyance in his admission made her smile. "I take it you're more of a dog person."

"I like cats, but yeah, if I had my choice, I'd have a couple dogs. I've been home a few days, and I've only seen the cats once when they attacked my ankles before hiding underneath my sister's bed."

"What kind of dog would you get?" She stopped in front of one kennel, captivated by one of the ugliest dogs she'd ever seen. The card attached to the cage stated his name was Butch and he was a mix of mastiff and wolfhound.

She leaned in to get a better look. He was a mix of brown and gray, and although the lighting wasn't great in the room, she thought she saw some patches of black in his wiry fur too. His snout was unusually shaped, sort of rectangular. But it was his brown eyes edged by bushy gray brows that drew her in. It was like she was peering into the eyes of an old soul, one that had seen the darkest side of life. If circumstances were different, she'd take him home in a heartbeat.

"Doesn't really matter to me. But if I had to choose, it would be the forgotten ones, the ones everyone else has given up on. Because all dogs, even the broken ones, deserve to be loved." He paused for a beat. "Rebecca and I were both adopted. I guess that's part of why I've always felt a kinship with the shelter dogs. When I was a kid, I wondered why my biological parents put me up for adoption and what would have happened if my mom and dad hadn't adopted me. Would I have ended up broken and unloved like some of the dogs in here?"

She pulled her gaze away from the dog to look over her shoulder at Cash. Although his eyes were gray, not brown, they held the same wounded wisdom in them. And just like with Butch, she wished circumstances were different. Because in that moment, she wanted nothing more than to wrap her arms around him and press her lips to his. Afraid he'd see her feelings on her face, she flipped back around to Butch and rested on her haunches.

"Have you ever looked into finding your birth parents?" she asked, hoping she wasn't overstepping.

"Actually, yeah. I started the process when Maddie got pregnant because she was worried about unknown genetic or medical conditions that might affect the baby. But after she died and I went to prison, I canceled the paperwork."

"Are you still interested? Because it's actually a lot easier to do than it was eight years ago. There are reunion registries on websites where you can add your information and search for a match. My friend Ryder is using the registries to help find a brother he hadn't known about until recently. They're even using DNA now."

He lowered himself to his knees, directly beside her, and reached two fingers of his sexy hand through Butch's cage to rub the top of his snout. "Maybe. I have to admit, Maddie hadn't been the only reason I started looking for my birth parents. I loved my mom and dad. They were always enough. But my whole life, I've felt as if there were unanswered questions hanging over my head, and they won't go away until I get all the answers."

She understood that feeling. Those hours of not knowing why a stranger had broken into her apartment and attacked her had nearly driven her insane. She'd worried he'd come back to finish the job, and she hadn't calmed until Jane had visited her in the hospital with the full explanation. The man had been looking for a flash drive in Jane's possession and he wasn't coming back for Dreama...because he was dead.

Unanswered questions reminded her of why she was really there at the shelter.

Dreama hooked a finger around the metal of Butch's cage. "Yesterday you mentioned you haven't gotten drunk or been high in over a decade."

"Yeah. That's right."

She didn't understand. "But you took a plea deal. If you were innocent, why plead guilty?"

"If I went to trial, I was looking at fifteen years behind bars. My defense attorney said the labs from the hospital came back showing an elevated blood alcohol level and there were multiple witnesses that said I'd been drinking champagne."

When Butch moved his nose away from Cash and toward her, she took it as a signal he wanted her to pet him. "How much champagne do you remember drinking?"

"That's the problem." He turned his face to look at her. "I don't remember drinking any of it. I don't remember anything from the party I attended that night or the accident. One minute Maddie and I were in our car on our way to the party at the zoo and the next I was in the hospital learning from my sister that Maddie had died. The doctors in the hospital said I either suffered from a brain injury in the accident that caused some form of amnesia or that my brain"—he angled his face away from hers and dropped his chin toward his chest—"chose to forget because it was too hard for me to remember."

The way he turned from her as he spoke those last words gave her the impression he believed them. He felt guilty because he believed he *was* guilty. But if he'd gotten drunk at the party, it would have taken a big guy like him several glasses of champagne to get drunk. How much champagne could he have drunk from the time he arrived to the time he left?

"What did your attorney say when you told him that you don't remember drinking and that you hadn't been drunk in years?" she asked.

He frowned. "I spent maybe ten, fifteen minutes with the guy. He told me he'd go to trial if I wanted, but with the evidence against me, it was risky."

That wasn't unusual. Public defenders were notoriously overworked and underpaid. "Why did you choose to use a public defender rather than hiring an attorney?"

"I considered it. My sister and my boss, Thomas, both argued with me over it. Thomas even offered to pay. But I didn't want to put my mother or sister through a trial, especially if it was unlikely that a jury would find me innocent." He exhaled a shaky breath, and when he spoke again, his tone was choked with guilt and regret. "Fact was, I caused the crash that killed Maddie. I lost her and our son that night. I deserved to go to prison."

She didn't agree. In her eyes and, more importantly, the eyes of the law, there was a huge difference between an accident and manslaughter. "Your hospital labs weren't in your file and your Breathalyzer was under the legal limit. Did your attorney ever show you the results from either?"

"No." Confusion swirled in his gray eyes. "My Breathalyzer was under? I could have sworn..." He shook his head.

"What?"

He let out a short, bitter chuckle. "I never thought to ask. I'd just assumed it had been above the limit. My defense attorney never mentioned it."

"Stephen Browner?" she clarified.

"Yeah. That was his name."

Overworked and underpaid was no excuse for malpractice. Public defenders still had the responsibility of giving their clients a competent defense.

"I called him," she said. "He claimed he didn't remember your case."

Cash's brows dipped as if he had no idea why that fact was significant. "Okay. It was a long time ago."

She lifted her butt off her haunches and went to her knees. "He was lying, Cash. He slipped up and mentioned Maddie by name."

"That doesn't mean—"

"And he was really evasive. I got the impression he was hiding something."

There was something about Cash that called to the warrior inside of her, the same part that had led her to get her social work degree. She'd always gone above and beyond for her clients, whether it was helping them to regain visitation of their kids or finding them an Alcoholics Anonymous sponsor. Making a phone call on Cash's behalf wasn't anything she wouldn't do for any of her other clients.

Yet, if she was being honest with herself, it was different because while she always championed her clients, this particular one felt a lot more personal. She wanted to believe he was innocent. Maybe it was because of the kindness he'd shown her in the lobby during her meltdown, or maybe it was because as hard as he'd tried to pretend he wasn't a good man, she couldn't help but like him, but she needed to prove to herself that her instinct was right.

It gave her a sense of purpose. She might not be able to help herself right now, but she could help Cash.

She should go back and look at Browner's history at the public defender's office. Maybe he'd encouraged all his clients to take a plea deal out of sheer laziness. If she could find proof that Browner had intentionally withheld the results of the Breathalyzer from Cash, the court might not find it was enough to overturn Cash's conviction. But if she found evidence that it was a common practice of Browner so that he could get his clients to take a plea deal, Cash might have a shot at getting the court to consider it.

Excited by the idea, Dreama temporarily forgot that her legs didn't work the way they used to and tried to get to her feet too quickly. Sharp pain, like a dozen knives slicing into her skin all at once, wrapped around her thighs. Her muscles resisted the move and refused to support her weight. Toppling sideways, she prepared herself to feel the slam of cold concrete against her shoulder, but instead, she felt only cradling warmth.

There were a few brief moments where her mind allowed herself to indulge in the sensation of Cash's strong arms around her waist and the solidness of his chest against her back. But then, like a nightmare creeping in to steal the bliss of a dream, ice-cold fear consumed her.

Cash and the animal shelter disappeared. All she knew was pain and despair. There was a heavy weight on her chest, pressing her into the carpet, and hands at the waistband of her sweatpants. She wanted to fight him, but she was a prisoner inside her broken body.

She'd rather die than deal with what was coming next.

A faraway voice broke through the darkness. "*Shh*. You're safe, Dreama. No one is touching you."

Her eyes opened.

She was lying on the floor. Dogs were barking and one was whining. Her thighs still ached, but all the other pain had gone. She turned her head to the right. Cash was kneeling over her, his hands in his lap. Behind him, a whining Butch was butting his head up against the front of his kennel as if trying to get to her.

Mortified that she'd melted down again in front of Cash, she slowly got up off the ground, using Butch's cage to help her. As soon as she got to her feet, Butch stopped whining.

Cash stood. "Dreama, there's nothing to be embarrassed about."

There was a divot between his brows and concern in his eyes.

She hated being weak. This wasn't her. And she hated that Cash had been a witness to it—twice.

"I need to get back to work," she said, refusing to look at him before limping away.

He didn't stop her.

Twenty minutes later, she'd returned to her desk and was about to call her first afternoon client back when Meg called her down to her office.

Forgoing any fake pleasantries, Meg began her interrogation the second Dreama stepped into the room. "Where have you been?"

Dreama was not in the mood for Meg's passive-aggressive bullying. "I was doing an employment check."

"On who?"

Why did Meg care? Dreama folded her arms across her chest and stayed standing by the door. "Cash Turner."

Meg played with her glasses. "Interesting. I received a call from an attorney who said you'd phoned him last night to ask him questions about that very same case."

Stephen Browner had called Meg? *What an asshole.*

"I did," she admitted, not seeing the problem.

"He claimed that after informing you he was unable to answer questions because he was bound by attorney-client privilege, you proceeded to threaten and harass him."

She strode toward Meg's desk. "I did no such thing! He's lying."

Meg reclined in her chair with a smug grin on her face. "He had no reason to lie. You, on the other hand..."

Dreama's leg was throbbing, but she remained standing. "I'm telling the truth. There were inconsistencies in his file and I had some questions about them."

"Inconsistencies?"

"Yes. Cash Turner might have been innocent."

Meg looked at Dreama as if she were a cockroach. "Who cares? That has nothing to do with you or your job as his parole officer. Did you tell this Turner about the inconsistencies? Is that why you visited him today?"

Dreama had a feeling the truth would only hurt her in this case. Meg only believed about doing the bare minimum for the parolees. She treated them as if they were a number rather than an individual. She'd never understood, and never would understand, why Dreama did more for her clients than was required.

"No. I didn't mention anything to Mr. Turner." Dreama hissed as a cramp seized her thigh. Her leg buckled beneath her, but she caught herself before she fell. "I only went to see him in order to complete his employment check. Nothing more."

Meg gazed dropped to Dreama's leg. "Maybe this job is too difficult for you to handle."

"No, ma'am," she said, hating that she had to show this witch any sign of respect and that Meg had seen her moment of weakness. "I can handle it."

Meg's eyes narrowed into slits. "Consider this a warning, Dreama. Do your job and your job only. If I hear you're sticking your nose where it doesn't belong again, you'll find yourself without employment."

There was no way she would ever let Meg have the satisfaction of firing her. Besides, this job was important to Dreama. When she'd been lying in her hospital bed, unable to walk, she'd sworn to herself she wouldn't let the attack change her. But it had. The phobia caused by the attack had stolen a huge part of her identity. She couldn't bear to lose another. If she wasn't a sexual submissive or a parole officer, who was she?

Yet, she couldn't stop her search for the truth. Browner's phone call to Meg only reinforced her suspicions about Cash's case. The old Dreama had been fearless. She would have never allowed anyone, especially Meg, to prevent her from doing what she believed was right, and she wasn't going to start now.

It was time to reclaim the old Dreama... in more ways than one.

"Don't worry," she assured Meg, not feeling an ounce of remorse for her lies. She smiled. "I won't."

SEVEN

Friday night, Cash leaned forward and nabbed another piece of pizza from the square cardboard box on the coffee table. What a difference a week made. Last Friday at this time, he'd been in his prison cell, lying on his lumpy cot and reading the latest Stephen King novel. Now he was free, lying on a plush couch and watching television.

He bit into his slice of pizza, not caring that he'd already devoured five slices. This was the first time since getting out that he'd eaten it and he'd forgotten how delicious it was. Pizza in prison just hadn't been the same.

It amazed him that with three hundred television channels, he couldn't find one thing he wanted to watch. After spending ten minutes scrolling through the guide, he settled on a re-airing of last week's football game. It was either that or a show on lake fishing.

Didn't matter. Nothing kept his attention riveted enough to prevent his thoughts from returning to Dreama.

He hadn't stopped thinking about her or what she'd told him about the Breathalyzer all week.

She was like a giant puzzle that he couldn't put together because he was missing pieces. But that didn't stop him from trying anyway.

Since the other day, he'd spent hours on the Internet, reading about panic attacks.

In prison, one of his cellmates had suffered from them. He would shake and sweat. Hyperventilate until he almost passed out. It had taken Cash a while before he'd figured out how to talk him down from them.

That was why he'd known what to do for Dreama.

But it wasn't until today that he'd identified what had triggered it.

Haphephobia.

The fear of touch.

The question running through his head was *why*?

And why did it bother him so damned much?

It wasn't his responsibility to fix her. He'd already been down that road with Maddie. When he'd met her on campus, she was like a meek little lamb living in a world of wolves. Coming off his first Dom/sub relationship, he'd confused Maddie for a submissive and trained her both in and out of the bedroom. She'd not only allowed him to take care of her, but she also came to expect it.

A few months later, doubt began to creep in. Maddie had become so possessive of him, she'd threatened to kill herself when he'd told her of his plans to go to a football game without her. That's when he'd discovered she had a long history of mental illness. Still, he'd thought he could save her. By the time he realized he'd been wrong, it was too late.

But his past experience with Maddie didn't change his desire to help Dreama...or his desire *for* her. Dreama was nothing like Maddie. She was a strong-willed and passionate advocate for her parolees. She liked dogs. She hated that her mother was overprotective. And after she suffered a panic attack, she picked herself up and kept on moving.

The research on haphephobia was staggering. It could be caused by anything from trauma to the fear of germs.

Fiddling with her dangling earring and all decked out for clubbing, Rebecca strolled into the room. "I think you've left a permanent impression in the couch cushion with your ass. It's Friday night."

In less than an hour, she'd switched from her work clothes to a clingy black dress and high-heeled boots. He eyed her, wondering if he could play the big brother card and make her change into something less revealing. "I'm aware of that fact since yesterday was Thursday and it's currently dark outside."

She sighed and put a hand on her hip. "I meant you should go out somewhere."

"I know exactly what you meant." He sat up and rested his feet on the coffee table next to the pizza box.

"Do you want to come out with me and my friends?"

Somehow, he doubted her friends wanted her ex-con brother hanging around. Besides, he couldn't go anywhere that served alcohol and he wouldn't be the reason she changed her plans.

"Rather not," he said, resting his feet on the edge of the coffee table. "I'm good, Becs. You go out and have some fun." He waved a finger at her and added, "But not too much fun."

No matter what, she was still his little sister.

"You don't have to go out with us. There's plenty of other stuff to do. See a movie. Go bowling. Go to the gym. Hell, go to Walmart. Just get off the damn couch and stop sulking."

"Sulking," he repeated.

"Yes, sulking." She sat on the couch beside him and shut off the television with the remote. "I know it's been an adjustment and everything is different from before you went in. But Maddie wouldn't want you to live your life this way."

No longer having an appetite, he threw the rest of his pizza into the box in front of him. "What way?"

"Not living at all." Rebecca softened her voice. "She would want you to move on. To fall in love again."

His sister didn't know the first thing about what Maddie would want.

No one did.

And it would stay that way. He didn't need to tarnish her memory with the truth.

"Well, she doesn't get a say in the matter, does she?" he said, much too bitterly.

He immediately regretted his tone. His sister didn't deserve it. She was only trying to help.

"If you won't talk to me," she said, "you should find someone else to talk to."

He immediately thought of Dreama. He'd already found

himself opening up to her. She was easy to talk to, and if she wasn't his parole officer, things might be different, but Dreama was a dangerous temptation he couldn't afford. "Like a shrink?" he asked.

Rebecca pat his knee. "Or a friend."

Friends.

He wasn't sure he ever had real friends. In high school, he'd always had a group of guys surrounding him and wanting to be his friend. Wanting to *be* him. Football players. The jocks. The kids who ruled the school as if they owned it. He'd been their king. But did they ever give a shit about him other than what he could do for their status? It had been much of the same in college. At least up until his life had gone to shit.

"That's the thing about going to prison," he said. "All your so-called friends tend to disappear on you."

Rebecca was quiet for a moment. She played with the bracelet on her wrist. "Have you started filling out the vet school applications yet?"

He chuffed out a laugh. "Why bother? They're never going to accept me."

"You don't know that. You made straight As in your junior and senior years."

Easy when there was nothing better to do with your time than study. "While I was in prison."

"You started the PAWS program."

"Again, *in prison.*"

"You used to work for one of the leading veterinary pharmaceutical companies," she reminded him.

Lundquist Animal Health had been small peanuts in the veterinary pharmaceutical industry when Cash had worked there. All of its financial success had happened while Cash was in prison.

Thomas Lundquist, the sole owner of the company, had been an old friend and childhood neighbor of his father's. Thomas had never married or had kids of his own, so when Cash's father died of a brain aneurysm when Cash was twelve years old, Thomas stepped into the role of father figure. He'd come to all of Cash's football games, gave him advice on girls, and as an animal lover himself, had encouraged Cash's dream of becoming a veterinarian.

Cash had begun working for Thomas back in high school and continued in college. There'd been discussion that Thomas would pay for Cash to go to vet school in exchange for him working for the company for five years after graduation. The night of the accident, Cash and Maddie had been celebrating Thomas's success in achieving FDA approval for a revolutionary drug that would reduce the mortality rate of animals during surgery.

Despite all the national attention he'd been getting at the time, Thomas swore he'd stand behind Cash and even offered to pay for a defense attorney. But between feeling as if he'd disappointed Thomas and knowing that he didn't need a criminal associated with his company, Cash had refused his help.

Rebecca smiled, looking triumphant. "No comeback?" she asked, not realizing Cash had been deep in thought.

"It was a long time ago."

"Have you called Thomas?"

"No," he admitted. He hadn't spoken to him in eight years.

"Thomas and I have kept in touch. He was hurt that you cut him out of your life after Maddie died. You should call him."

"And say what?" His feet slid off the coffee table as he stood. "I'm out of prison. Want to give me a job and help me get into vet school?"

"How about you start with 'hello' and go from there?" Rebecca shook her head. "God, you've turned into a whiny bitch."

"A whiny bitch?"

Her lips tilted up even as the rest of her radiated anger. "A whiny bitch."

Those are fighting words.

"Take that back," he demanded.

She shrugged. "If the shoe fits..."

He attacked, zeroing in on her tickle spot on the right side of her lower rib cage. She shrieked and tried to get away, but with years of tickle torture experience under his belt, he hit the exact location that made her explode into laughter.

"Stop! Stop!" She slapped at his chest. "Okay, you're not a bitch." As he pulled his hands away to let her catch her breath, she added, "Only whiny."

God, he'd missed this. It brought him back to a time when life had been so simple. When he'd had nothing more to worry about than grades and catching a football. If only his mother was still alive, he could almost pretend nothing in the last eight years had happened.

Cash hated that Rebecca was worried about him. Maybe she was right. He should get out of the house. It wasn't as if there was a prison warden to stop him. He could go see a movie. Or he could do what he really wanted to do. Since Tuesday, the card for Club X had been burning a hole in his wallet.

He'd never gone to a BDSM club before. Not comfortable dominating a stranger, he could just go and observe. Maybe even find someone to train him in domination.

"You win," he said to Rebecca. "I'll go out."

He looked down at his black Henley and worn-out jeans.

What exactly did one wear to a sex club?

EIGHT

Dreama parked in the lot across the street from Club X and turned off her car. Because she generally preferred intimate play parties held at people's homes over the anonymous feel of a BDSM club, she hadn't been to one in years. But things had changed. She didn't want to witness the pity in her friends' eyes when they saw her scars or hear them console her when she couldn't participate. Chances were she'd run into people she knew at Club X, but not her immediate circle of friends in the lifestyle, which included Jane, and Dreama's cousin Isabella.

She couldn't make herself get out of the car. It was complete darkness outside. The only light came from the lamp in front of the entrance. In the distance, she heard the sound of police sirens.

Here she was at a dungeon yearning to be whipped, caned, cropped, and slapped, and she was afraid *of the dark*. But that was the crux of it, wasn't it? Control. During a scene, she had it. Sure, the Dominant was the person in charge, but it was the submissive who held the power. One word from her and the action stopped. There were limits, soft and hard, and negotiations between the Dom and sub prior to the scene. And most importantly, there was *consent*.

But the dark had a power all its own. She couldn't stop it. No matter what, night followed day.

Gripping the steering wheel with both hands, she took a deep breath and slowly let it out. She had to get her butt out of the car and take the first step toward reclaiming her sexuality.

I can do this.

Sex had been a pivotal part of her identity for more than a decade. Once she had identified herself as a sexual submissive and masochist, a piece of her had clicked into place. Sex was more than a pleasurable act for her. Being dominated gave her the chance to release all the things she couldn't say out loud and cry without feeling weak. Since her attack, those things had been bottled up inside her with no means of escape.

Masturbation used to be a daily occurrence in her schedule. She hadn't once, in all these months, felt the desire to touch herself or use anything from her huge collection of sexual aids. In fact, she hadn't experienced a glimmer of attraction to a man...until Cash. And he was off-limits.

She'd moved out of her parents' house and had returned to work. Both were huge steps in reclaiming her old life. Her body's reaction to Cash gave her hope that the sexual woman inside of her hadn't been extinguished with the attack. She was afraid the longer she repressed that vital part of herself, the greater the chance she would never get it back. That was why she'd made the decision to come here tonight.

Now it was time to put on her big-girl panties and show them off in a BDSM club. She wanted to immerse herself in the experience again in the hopes that maybe it would help her overcome her phobia of touch.

Her toes curled in her boots as she squeezed her fingers around the smooth metal handle and pushed open the car door. An icy blast of air whipped around her, stinging the inside of her nose. Purse in hand, she gritted her teeth and hoisted herself out of the seat. The wind's force slammed the car door shut before she could chicken out and get back in the car.

She crossed the empty main road to the entrance of the club. Now that the sirens had disappeared, it was eerily silent. Even the wind didn't make a sound.

Once inside Club X, her eyes adjusted to the dim lighting. She paid twenty dollars to the bouncer and handed over her personal items to the attendant. Phones and cameras were not permitted in the dungeon, and since alcohol wasn't served there, the entrance fee included soft drinks and water.

In front of the attendant station, she adjusted her corset so that her boobs weren't falling out and her skirt covered her butt. She'd designed and sewed almost all of her fetish wear herself, even the outfit she wore tonight. Since her attack, she hadn't touched her sewing machine.

Tonight's outfit had been inspired by her love of steampunk. The buttery brown leather was fastened by four timepiece clips and had garters that connected to cream sheer stockings. In the front, her skirt came only to the top of her thighs and was made from the same leather as the corset, but in back, she'd sewn a long train of lace to the leather's edge, the bunched fabric reminding her of a peacock's tail.

For a brief time, she'd considered a career as a fashion designer, but her school social worker had been so pivotal in changing her life for the better when she'd helped Dreama get her ADHD diagnosis, she decided to follow in her footsteps and get her degree in social work. She'd chosen to become a parole officer because she believed everyone deserved a second chance.

She stepped out from the entrance area and moved inside the club, surprised to discover it was more spacious than it had seemed from the outside. The club was actually an old converted warehouse with concrete floors and high ceilings. Lit by flickering sconces and surrounded by the echoes of chains and whips, she felt as if she'd entered a real dungeon.

For someone like her, it was sensual as hell. A haze of sweat and sex hung heavy in the air. It was so pungent, she could almost taste the saltiness of it when she licked her lips. Low industrial music played backup to the moans and cries of the people in scenes. Unlike the play parties she used to go to, this club permitted public sex and hardcore play.

She was immediately seduced by the various scenes

around her, each one roped off by red velvet barriers. At first glance, most of the bottoms appeared to be men, while the tops were a mix of genders.

Spying a small crowd gathering in front of one particular scene, she wandered over to watch. A middle-aged man wore a chastity cage over his cock as a woman fucked him from behind with a strap-on dildo. Dreama shivered at the knowledge that the cage prevented the bottom from achieving climax. The man had a heavy-lidded expression she recognized as subspace. She desperately missed the floaty high that came from submission. Envy squeezed her tight, but disappointedly, the scene did nothing to arouse her.

Dreama's attention was caught by the sound of a man's deep growl coming from the next scene over. The rough voice sent shivers through her body, hardening her nipples.

Hope filled her chest. Lord, she hadn't even seen the man yet and her body was responding. She sent up a silent plea that the voice belonged to an available Dominant.

With an intentional sway of her hips, she left her spot within the crowd and strolled toward the next scene.

A female top was whipping her male bottom. The man stood with his back to her with his arms overhead and his wrists shackled by chains that dangled from the metal frame above him. A spreader bar between his muscular thighs forced his legs apart and cuffs connected to metal posts in the floor restrained his ankles.

She felt a pang of disappointment that the man wasn't a Dominant. *Oh well.* With her stupid phobia of a man's touch, it wasn't as if she could do anything about it anyway.

That didn't mean she couldn't watch and enjoy the simmering in her pussy and the tingling of her clit. Maybe she'd leave here horny enough to break out her box of toys tonight and reacquaint herself with her favorite vibrator.

The man's body was perfection. Wide shoulders made way to a narrow waist and thick thighs. Sweat glistened on his honey-colored skin and his perfectly contoured ass clenched with each lash of the whip.

Dueling emotions warred within her. Part of her wanted to push the man out of the way and take his place beneath the whip. She could almost feel the fiery sting of the tail flicking her skin. But the other part wanted to drag her tongue along the outline of his shoulder blades and press her naked self against his back as she did it.

She literally ached to see the front of him, and thankfully, there was nothing to stop her from doing it. She repositioned herself on the other side of the scene to get a better view.

Her pulse quickened to double time. For the briefest of moments, she thought she was hallucinating. The man looked exactly like Cash, but her mind had to be playing tricks on her. Cash would never be at a BDSM club, and even if he was, she couldn't imagine him being on the receiving end of a whip.

She blinked a few times and took a step closer.

She wasn't hallucinating.

It was Cash. He was there, as if she'd summoned him with her thoughts.

But what the hell was he doing on that side of the whip?

She supposed it was possible he was a switch or a masochist like herself, but she'd never been attracted to a submissive man. And there was no question, she was attracted to him.

His front was even better than his back. He wasn't ripped, but the muscles of his arms and chest were impressive just the same. If she had to describe his body in one word, she'd describe him as . . . *solid*. She could only imagine the power it could harness. In her mind's eye, she saw herself flipped over his lap, him fisting her hair in one hand while smacking her ass red with his other.

Growing damp between her thighs, she sucked her lower lip into her mouth as she unabashedly took in the rest of him. Her gaze followed the trail of brown hair that started between his nipples and ended between the V line at his hips . . . and then down to the heavier nest of dark curls surrounding his cock.

Although still impressive in size, his cock hung limp against his thigh. It was obvious to her Cash wasn't a masochist or his dick would be as hard as steel right now. So why was he there in a BDSM club getting whipped?

Cash opened his eyes. Only a second passed until his mouth dropped open and his eyes widened at the sight of her standing there.

A voice inside her head whispered that watching him was inappropriate and that she ought to give him his privacy. But her feet were glued to the floor.

His gaze felt like a gentle caress as it slowly raked over her, leaving goose bumps in its wake. A fierce tug of want spiraled in her pelvis. Her pussy clenched relentlessly, aching for Cash's cock to fill her, and her arousal soaked the gusset of her panties.

Her body sparked to life as if she were a candle and Cash the flame.

Damn it. Out of everyone in the world, why did her parolee have to be the one to finally ignite her?

Her hands seemed to have a mind of their own as they drifted down to where the drenched fabric covered her needy pussy. For the first time in thirteen months, she slid two fingertips into her panties and pinched her pulsing clit between them. It felt so amazing, her whole body shuddered and her eyes practically rolled back into her head.

Cash's gray eyes darkened. As he watched her touch herself, his cock lengthened and thickened until fully erect. She didn't go around measuring dicks, but she'd been around a lot of them in her time, and Cash's was one of the longest and thickest she'd ever seen in person. She shifted her hand, using the pad of her thumb to rub her sensitive bud in circles as she plunged two of her fingers inside of her.

A tortured moan spilled from her throat.

She'd barely gotten started and she was already on the precipice of coming.

She wished it was Cash's fingers on her and in her. That it was his thumb caressing her clitoris as two of his thickest fingers penetrated her opening.

Cash looked hungry for her, even as his face contorted in pain from the whip. He caught his bottom lip between his teeth and pearly drops of liquid gathered at the tip of his cock. She ached to take him deep into the cavern of her mouth and taste every bit of him until she sucked him dry. Even in chains, he was Dominating her.

Tension coiled in her belly, her muscles tightening as heat raged inside her core. Her pussy throbbed in time with her pulse as she fucked herself on her fingers, pretending they belonged to Cash. And then, the impossible happened. That tension uncoiled like a spool of thread, pushing her over the edge and into a freefall. A rush of boiling heat poured through her pussy and outward, shooting up to the top of her head and down to the ends of her toes. The strength of the climax nearly knocked her off her feet.

Holy shit. She'd had an orgasm. She didn't know whether to laugh or cry. Maybe she'd do both.

Cash burned a hole straight into her with his stare. His expression had gone from hungry to ravenous. He said something to his top and the whipping stopped. Dreama's heart was playing jump rope as she watched the woman move closer to Cash and reach around his waist.

If the top did what Dreama currently wanted to do to Cash, she couldn't bear to watch. It would crush her to see another woman's hands or mouth on him. But rather than do what Dreama expected, the top released Cash's right wrist from the cuff.

Cash immediately wrapped his beautiful fingers around his cock and began to stroke himself from base to tip. Her gaze zeroed in on it with laser precision focus. She'd never seen a sexier image in her life.

Tossing back his head and shouting her name loud

enough she could hear it over all the noise in the club, he climaxed, milky-white streaks of semen bathing his stomach, cock, and even the floor. It was beautiful. It was a sight she wanted to see again...

But never could.

Oh my God.

Reality sucked the lingering pleasure from her body like a vacuum.

What had she done?

As Cash's parole officer, she'd just crossed a line she never should have. If anyone at the parole office found out about this, she'd lose her job. Meg would relish the opportunity to fire her. In under ten minutes, she'd proven her mother right. Just swap out Cash for the Hot Pocket. She didn't make healthy decisions. She was irresponsible, thinking little of the consequences of her actions.

Cash's top handed him a towel and then began the process of removing his restraints.

The right thing would be to stay and talk with him about what just happened, but she couldn't face him, not now when all her emotions were raw. She took a step backward and mouthed "Sorry" to him right before turning around and fleeing like a coward.

* * *

Desperate to find Dreama, Cash declined his Dominatrix's offer of aftercare and quickly dressed, tugging his T-shirt over his head and shoving his legs into a pair of sweats.

He flinched at the pain coursing through his body from the move. There would be time later to deal with it. Right then, he had more pressing matters at hand. He had to find Dreama.

He'd been shocked to open his eyes and see her standing behind the velvet ropes. He'd initially thought she was a mirage. Only seconds later, he'd processed that she was really there.

That was all it took for a shot of lust to slam into him and the pain from the whip to disappear. It was as if it wasn't happening at all. He only saw Dreama. Thank fuck he'd been in chains, because he'd wanted to claim her, right then and there, and show everyone that she belonged to *him*.

He wouldn't have been nice about it either. If he'd had his wish, he would've pushed her to her knees, shoved his bare cock into her pussy, and fucked her so hard, she'd be both crying for him to stop and for more. He'd squeeze his hands around her neck to show her what it was like to truly submit to him. Her life would literally be in his hands as he exerted pressure on her windpipe. And just as her cunt convulsed with her orgasm, he'd yank himself out of her and come all over her ass. Then to show everyone he and Dreama belonged together, he'd force her to stroll around the club with her skirt hiked up and their mixed cum sliding down her legs.

Even in her boring-as-fuck professional wear, she was fucking sexy, but in leather and lace? She was a goddess, and he wanted to worship at the altar of her pussy. She tempted him like heroin to a junkie. One single hit of her would be his downfall, but it didn't make him want her any less. There was some kind of connection between them. He'd felt it the day he'd met her and at the shelter, and now he knew she felt it too. Tonight, that connection had sizzled between them like a downed live power line twisted up in tree branches.

Fully clothed, he strode toward the entrance of the club. As he approached, he swore he saw a flash of Buddy walking out the front door, but it was hard to tell since he saw the guy from the back. He'd have to remember to ask Buddy if it was him the next time they worked together and thank him for giving him the card to this place.

Cash grabbed his coat at the front, hoping he could catch Dreama before she drove off, but unsure of what he was going to say if he did.

He wanted her to know that the pink scars on her arms and legs did nothing to diminish her beauty and that if their situation was different, he would have loved to take her out to dinner and discover everything there was to learn about her.

But he wasn't sure she'd want to hear any of that. He didn't know what was going through her mind. That's why they needed to talk.

Cold air slapped him in the face as he stepped outside. It wasn't snowing, but the wind was blowing so hard, it made it seem as if it was. After being locked up for years, he wasn't ever going to complain about the weather. His freedom was worth more than that.

He spotted Dreama about twenty feet ahead and stomped

toward her. Her head was down as she began to cross the road.

An engine revved from his right. Without streetlights, he could just barely make out the shape of the car in the middle of the road. Headlights off, it was speeding down the street...and it was aiming straight for Dreama.

NINE

Cash's heart catapulted out of his chest as he took off running. "Dreama, get out of the road!"

Standing in the middle of the street, Dreama glanced over her shoulder in his direction before turning her head toward the speeding car.

Cash harnessed every bit of energy inside of him and raced into the street. The engine's roar grew louder as the car got closer.

Dreama had almost made it to the snowy berm on the other side of the street when the car shifted its course from the middle of the road to the far right. With Dreama's limp slowing her down, she was never going to get out of the way in time.

Like he was back on the football field, he tackled her. The force of it propelled them off their feet and onto the mound of snow just milliseconds before the vehicle rushed by them...and over the exact spot where Dreama had just been. Pain from the whip flared in his back, but it was worth it because Dreama was safe.

Cash watched as the car kept going and turned left onto the next street. The noise of the engine quieted, eventually dying off.

Dreama whimpered, jolting him into awareness. Cash suddenly realized that he was lying on top of her with his groin nestled between her spread thighs. He enjoyed exactly two seconds of it before he heard her crying beneath him.

Oh shit.

Had he injured her?

He catapulted his body off hers and knelt beside her in the snow. "Dreama? Are you okay?"

Her eyes were shut but tears rolled down her cheeks. "It hurts. Make it stop."

Guilt wrapped around his chest and crushed it. He must have pushed her too hard. "Sweetheart, I'm so sorry. Tell me where it hurts." He swept his thumb over her cheek, catching a tear.

She rolled her head from side to side. "Don't touch me! Leave me alone. Your hands are burning me!"

What did she mean his hands were burning her?

He snatched his hand back when it hit him. "Fuck." How could he have forgotten about her phobia? He was such an idiot. He might have saved her from the car, but his actions had thrown her straight into a panic attack. "Dreama. You're safe. No one is going to hurt you."

Her entire body shook and her teeth were shattering. "Oh God! It hurts. It hurts."

He needed to move her from the snow. "Dreama, can you stand? You're freezing, honey."

Not responding to him, she continued to mumble a bunch of senseless words he didn't understand. He didn't have a choice. She needed to get warm.

He carefully scooped her up and carried her toward his car, ignoring how right she felt in his arms. She didn't fight him, but she seemed as if she was lost in a nightmare that she couldn't wake from, sobbing and whimpering.

What had happened to cause her panic attacks? Were they related to her scars?

Judging by the color of the scars, whatever had made them had occurred relatively recently. They were bright pink, as if they'd only begun the healing process, and from what he could tell, they were straight rather than jagged, much like surgical scars. He couldn't help thinking that if Maddie had survived the crash, she would have been left with scars much like Dreama's.

The two women couldn't be more different. Maddie never would have gone to a place like Club X. Although she'd played the part of a sexual submissive, he now understood she hadn't been one. She'd indulged his fetishes because she hadn't wanted to lose him, but the fact was, he wasn't sure Maddie had even enjoyed sex. As soon as he'd married her, she'd given him excuse after excuse to avoid making love.

Dreama, on the other hand, had come to Club X on her own. She overflowed with sexuality and sensuality. Her eyes had radiated so much heat, he practically saw the flames in them. And the steampunk corset dress she wore had to be one of the hottest and most unusual pieces of lingerie he'd ever seen. The way the fabric had accentuated her curves and molded to her breasts had set his blood on fire. Something told him Dreama enjoyed sex...a lot.

As he neared his car, he gazed down at the trembling woman in his arms. He would much rather she be trembling for a reason other than fear. How could such a sexual creature go without touch? She'd been so brave to come to the club tonight. He only wished there was something he could do to help her.

Then again, it hadn't gone well for anyone the last time he'd tried to help a woman. Although Dreama and Maddie had plenty of differences, he had to remind himself they had one huge thing in common—emotional baggage. And they weren't the only ones. He had enough baggage to open his own luggage store. He wasn't qualified to help Dreama.

Once he settled her into the passenger seat of his car, he circled around to the other side and slid into the driver's seat, turning on the engine and cranking up the heat to full blast.

"Dreama?" Speaking softly, he leaned across the center console. "You're safe now. No one is going to hurt you. Do you hear me? I won't let anyone ever hurt you again."

It took a couple minutes before her murmuring stopped and her eyes fluttered. "Cash? What happened?" She looked out the passenger window and then at him. "Where am I?"

"My car." Relieved she was okay, he let out a breath. He ran his hand over his buzz cut. "What do you last remember?"

"Um..." Her brows furrowed. "Crossing the street. You called out to me and I heard a car." Her eyes popped wide. "You pushed me out of the way."

"I'm sorry. I didn't have a choice. That car would have hit you if I hadn't. My touch triggered a panic attack. I couldn't leave you in the snow, so I brought you to my car. I swear, Dreama, I never would have touched you if it wasn't necessary." It was the truth and yet, it was also a lie. Despite all the reasons it would be a bad idea, he feared if she ever asked, he wouldn't have the strength to resist her. "How do you feel? Are you hurt?"

She gave him a little smile and held her hands up to the vents. "Only my pride."

Now that she was safe and sound, he pulled his cell from his coat pocket. "We need to call the police."

Her brows dipped. "And say what? Some kid was speeding? Believe me, the Detroit cops have better things to do with their time."

"Dreama, whoever it was intentionally tried to hit you. The headlights were off and he increased his speed the closer he got to you." Not to mention he'd aimed right for her. There was no mistaking the driver had intended to run her down. Had Dreama been a random victim? Or had the driver waited specifically for *her*?

"I'm sure it was just a prank. They probably would have swerved at the last minute if you hadn't gotten me out of the way."

She might be right, but he had a bad feeling about it.

"Thank you for"—she dropped her hands and her gaze to her lap—"everything." She sucked her lower lip between her teeth and exhaled. "I'm just gonna go."

His protective nature clawed its way out. "You're still

shaking from your panic attack. You're in no condition to drive right now."

She grabbed the door handle. "I'll be fine. It doesn't last long. I'll just wait in my car until it stops."

He began to reach out to stop her, but immediately snatched back his hand and locked the doors. "Someone just tried to run you down with a car, Dreama. I'm not going to let you sit out here all alone."

She turned her head toward him, flames in her eyes again. Only this time it wasn't passion but anger in them. "I don't need a keeper."

"I know you don't. That's not what I'm suggesting." He hadn't meant to imply that she couldn't take care of herself. "It's just part of who I am, I guess."

She released the door handle and smirked. "Bossy?"

Pandora's box had already been opened. Might as well discuss what was inside.

He made sure to look in her eyes as he revealed the truth about himself. "Dominant."

* * *

Any remnant of embarrassment Dreama had over her panic attack quickly faded as she tried to pretend hearing Cash call himself a Dominant hadn't caused her pussy to clench. The word had never sounded better than coming from his lips.

"If you're a Dominant, then why were you being whipped?"

"I hired a Dominatrix, Mistress Naomi, to train me to be

a Dominant. I met her tonight. She's been in the lifestyle for thirty years, and like me, she's not only a Dominant, but a sadist."

She shuddered, but not from revulsion. The only thing better than a Dominant was a sadistic Dominant. Her tongue felt thick in her mouth. "Have you always known what you were?"

"Since college." He tapped his fingers on his thigh and the divot between his brows made a reappearance. "Maddie wasn't only my wife. She was my submissive. But we were young. I didn't have a lot of experience with it and when she got pregnant..." He sighed. "Anyway, someone gave me the card for Club X. I wasn't going to come, but then I thought I'd at least see what it was like."

Dreama wanted desperately to ask him to finish telling her about what happened when Maddie got pregnant, but judging by the change of subject, he obviously didn't feel like sharing. She didn't blame him. It had to be painful to talk about everything he'd lost.

Regardless, it was clear Cash was a relative newbie to BDSM. Dreama had more than a decade of experience, and he was a Baby Dom about to embark on his journey of exploration. Some lucky sub was going to reap the benefits from it, but it wouldn't be her.

She rubbed her fist over the burn in her chest. "You've never been to a club before?"

"No. You?"

"A few, but not Club X." She decided to leave out that she'd been in a couple collared relationships and had played with dozens of partners. This conversation wasn't about her. "So, what did you think?"

He tilted his head. "It was definitely...eye-opening."

That was one way of putting it. Even with all her experience, she'd witnessed things at Club X she'd never seen before. *Like Cash. Naked.* "You didn't look as if you were enjoying the whip."

"Not even a little." He laughed. "But now that I know how it feels, the sadist in me is looking forward to being on the other side of it. Naomi has agreed to train me on how to use the whip and other impact toys."

He gave her a wicked smile that sent shivers running through her now-warmed-up body. It promised long, sweaty nights filled with sweet agony at his large, capable hands. She missed that kind of pain. Unlike her scars, it was a pain that led to escape and release.

"Cold still?" he asked, mistaking the origin of her shiver for a temperature-related one.

"No." She needed to get out of that car, go home, and spend some time with her vibrator before she did something crazy like masturbate in front of him. *Again.* "Cash, I want you to know that my problem with touch and my panic attacks won't affect my ability to fulfill my duties as your parole officer."

He reared back, deep lines etched on his forehead. "I never thought it would. Nothing about tonight changes how I see you. I won't tell anyone about what happened in or out of the club." He paused briefly as if considering what to say next, then began tapping his fingers on his thigh. His eyes softened and his forehead smoothed. "But you should know—"

"Stop." She shifted in her seat, holding up her hands. As much as she wanted to hear he felt the same way, it would make it much harder to resist him. "Please, don't finish what you're about to say. Once it's out there, we can't take it back, and I don't want to lose my job."

Nodding, he didn't speak for a long time. He swallowed, his Adam's apple bobbing in his sexy corded throat. "Couldn't you pass my file to another person in your office?"

For a moment, she considered it. Just because she wasn't his parole officer didn't mean she couldn't help him. But to reassign his case, she'd have to go through Meg, who would undoubtedly want to know why. That was a can of worms she didn't want to open.

Even if he wasn't her parolee, any relationship between them would still be frowned upon by the parole office. And if she was honest with herself, she didn't want to give up his file. "Possibly, but I don't want to. When I returned to work after visiting you at the shelter, my boss, Meg, reprimanded me because of the call I made to Stephen Browner."

"Dreama, I'm sorry. I never—"

"Don't apologize. You didn't ask me to call him. That was all on me." If she had the chance to do it over again, this time knowing the trouble she'd get into with Meg...she'd still do it. "Meg doesn't like me. She never has. She's just looking for a reason to fire me. I know I should play it safe and not stir up trouble, but Browner wouldn't have tattled on me if he didn't have something to hide. If there's a chance that you were railroaded into taking a guilty plea for any other reason than it was the best option for you to take, you should know about it."

He squinted and pinched the bridge of his nose. "I don't want you getting into trouble with your boss over some slim hope."

What else did she have but hope?

She had an idea of how to keep Meg from knowing she was still looking into Cash's case and at the same time, mend old wounds. "Give me time to do a little more digging. I won't mention your name, but I'm going to talk to a friend of mine who might be able to help check Browner out for us. In the meantime, I need you to order your medical records from the hospital and talk to witnesses who saw you drinking that night."

"You're risking your career for me," he said softly. "Why?"

She made him a promise. "Because guilty or innocent, you deserve to know the truth about what happened that night. And we're not going to stop until you do."

TEN

Dreama walked up Jane's driveway with a wrapped gift under her arm. It was the least she could do for her godson, considering she hadn't seen him in more than a year. Before that, she'd been a constant presence in his life from the time he was born. She'd been there when Jane delivered him, given him bottles at midnight, changed his diaper hundreds of times, and had rocked him to sleep against her chest.

She hadn't seen him since he was four months old. What would he look like now? Was he talking yet? What was his favorite food? She should know these things, but she'd been a coward, avoiding Jane, Ryder, and Maddox since going to the physical rehabilitation center after her long hospital stay. She'd talked on the phone with Jane, but it wasn't the same. She'd been a bad godmother and a terrible friend. That was why she'd been shocked when Jane had not only agreed to Dreama's request to come over to their home tonight, but also had invited her to stay for dinner.

Guilt choking her, Dreama knocked on their front door. Their pug, Otis, started barking to announce to his owners they had a visitor.

She had an ulterior motive for coming here. She needed a favor from Ryder, Jane's husband, but to be fair, it had only served as a gentle push to get Dreama to do what she'd been too chicken to do. She missed Jane and Maddox. It was time to apologize and beg for forgiveness.

The door swung open to a pissed-off-looking Ryder McKay.

Apparently, she'd have to get past Jane's gatekeeper first.

She'd actually known Ryder before Jane. He was best friends with Tristan, Dreama's cousin Isabella's fiancé. Both Tristan and Ryder had been regulars at the play parties Dreama had attended, although thank goodness she'd never played with either of them. In fact, Ryder had thrown several of those play parties here at his house before Jane and Maddox had moved in. Tristan and Isabella had met there. Dreama wondered if the basement was still outfitted as a dungeon.

Ryder was a good guy and had proven himself to Dreama more than once. He'd not only saved Jane and Maddox from Jane's lunatic grandfather, but he'd also been the one who'd found Dreama right after the attack. He'd started CPR on her when he couldn't find her pulse. He'd saved her life.

Looking at Ryder's gray eyes, she was thrown by an overwhelming sense of familiarity. There was a whisper in the back of her mind, telling her there was a reason for that déjà vu, but she couldn't put a name to it.

He peered over his shoulder and moved in front of the door, closing it a bit. "Before I let you in, I need to say something."

She nodded. "Okay."

"I know she hasn't said anything to you, but you hurt Jane. For a long time, she felt responsible for your attack. It didn't matter that you told her she wasn't. Other than a few phone calls here and there, you ghosted her. She blamed herself and it took a long time to convince her that your disappearance had nothing to do with her. She was so excited when you called her today and told her you wanted to see her, but I won't allow you to come in here and get her hopes up only to crush her again."

Her throat ached with regret. She hated that she'd hurt her best friend. "We all make mistakes, Ryder. I'm sorry I hurt her, but I'm here to apologize and see if we can repair our friendship. I promise I won't hurt her again."

He shrugged and smiled. "That's good enough for me. Come on in. It's good to see you, Dreama."

She stepped into the house, seeing at once how much had changed inside. There were toys scattered in the entryway and framed photos of Maddox on the wall. She crouched to pet Otis between his ears. "It's really good to see you, too, Ryder."

Jane came out from the kitchen and stopped as her gaze fell on Dreama. Tears shimmered in her eyes.

"Hi, Chickie," Dreama said, using the nickname she'd always used for Jane. Her gaze fell on Jane's stomach. Jane's *humongous* stomach. Okay, now Dreama was getting teary.

"Oh. Wow. I've missed a lot. Why didn't you tell me during one of our phone calls?"

"I wanted to tell you in person and I didn't think we'd go that long without seeing one another." Jane put both her hands over the basketball-shaped bulge. "I'm eight months."

Because of the hysterectomy, Dreama would never have the chance to carry a child inside of her, but that didn't mean she didn't have the capacity to love other people's children.

She'd been terribly selfish in staying away from Jane and Maddox.

That behavior ended now.

Dreama was going to be an aunt again. She smiled as she pulled Jane into some semblance of a hug, both laughing when Jane's huge belly prevented them from getting close.

Jane had a glow to her that had been missing during her previous pregnancy, and Dreama bet it had everything to do with the fact that she had Ryder with her this time.

"You look beautiful," Dreama said. "Any morning sickness?"

Jane led Dreama to a couch and they both sat. "Oh yeah. It's just like it was with Maddox. I keep saltines and lemon candy on my nightstand. But my cravings are completely different."

Dreama put the gift on the coffee table in front of the couch. "You mean you don't make Ryder run out to Taco Bell at eleven at night like you did to me?"

"Ugh." Jane made a sour face and stuck out her tongue.

"Meat makes me want to hurl. I'm on a complete dairy kick this time. If I could live in a cheese shop, I would. Did you know they make chocolate cheese?"

Dreama loved chocolate and cheese, but somehow, the idea of chocolate cheese didn't sound at all appealing. She took Jane's hand and squeezed it, tears blurring her vision. "I missed you. I'm so sorry I haven't been here for you."

"I won't lie," Jane said, squeezing it back. "You really hurt my feelings."

"I never, not once, blamed you for my attack. That's not why I've been avoiding you."

"Why, then?" Jane asked. "Is it because Maddox reminds you of what you lost?"

Dreama glanced down at the floor. The loss of her uterus and her ability to carry children didn't make her feel any less of a woman. "No, I've made peace with that. It has more to do with something else I lost." She looked Jane in the eyes. "My bravery."

Jane frowned. "Dreama, you're the bravest person I know."

"But that's just it. After the attack, I wasn't brave at all." She blew out a breath. "I developed a phobia. If a man touches me or if I even think he's going to, I have a panic attack. I can't even hug my own father."

"Dreama, I'm so sorry. I can't imagine what that must be like. If you had let me, I would've been there for you. I'm still here for you."

She leaned over and laid her head on Jane's shoulder. "I've missed you so much."

Jane sniffed. If it was anything like the last time she was pregnant, Jane would cry over the smallest of things. "I've missed you too."

Just then, Dreama heard the sweetest voice in the world. "Mommy?"

She turned her head to the left of the couch and there was the little boy she used to rock to sleep at night. He had his mother's dark hair, but the rest of him was all Ryder.

"Hey, baby," Jane said, opening her arms wide as Maddox toddled into her. She angled Maddox to face Dreama. "This is your auntie Dreama. Remember all those pictures of her I showed you?"

He shyly peered up at her. Dreama wanted to grab him and hold him tight but realized that might scare him. Thankfully, the idea of it didn't scare *her*. She was happy to learn her phobia didn't extend to male children. She snatched his present off the table and handed it to him. "Hi, Maddox. I brought you a gift."

He immediately let go of Jane and with her help, unwrapped his present. It didn't take long before he saw what the paper concealed. His gray eyes lit up with excitement and he started clapping. "A fuck. Mommy! A fuck!"

The doorbell rang and Ryder strode past them to answer the door.

"Yeah, baby. A truck." Jane's cheeks reddened. "No matter how many times we tell him it's 'truck,' he refuses to call it that. Can you believe *fuck* was his first word?"

Dreama giggled. "With Ryder as his father? Yes. I absolutely believe it."

Ryder returned with another man by his side. "Dreama, have you ever met my brother, Finn?"

"No."

Except for their gray eyes, the two men looked nothing alike. From what Jane had said, Ryder and Finn shared a father but had different mothers. Ryder was tall with dark hair and olive skin while Finn was shorter with reddish-blond hair and paler skin. Both were handsome, but in her opinion, neither came close to Cash's rugged good looks.

Huh. Why she'd compared the three men, she had no idea. Guess she just had Cash on the brain.

Finn approached the couch and thrust out his hand to her. Dreama's heart shot off like a rocket going to outer space.

Jane immediately jumped in to protect her, swatting Finn's hand out of Dreama's way. "Dreama doesn't touch men."

"Yeah, I don't want to catch any cooties," Dreama quipped, trying to remove some of the awkwardness from the situation. She shook her head. "No, seriously, I have a thing. I developed a phobia of a man's touch. Don't take it personally."

Finn didn't hesitate. "I don't." He also didn't ask for details.

Dreama wasn't the only one wounded in the evil plot of Jane's grandfather, Ian Sinclair, to steal Ryder's kitchen automation software. Sinclair had killed Finn's wife, Jane's mother.

"Weren't you out of town for a while?" she asked Finn as Ryder dragged two chairs from the dining room and placed them across from the couch. Jane had mentioned in one of their few conversations that Finn had taken off the night his wife died.

Finn shifted in his seat, his shoulders raised. "Last week."

"Are you just visiting or—"

"Finn bought a house not too far from here," Ryder said, grinning.

There was a temporary lull in the conversation where she'd expected Finn to elaborate. When he didn't, she chimed in. "That's great. I'm sure Maddox is happy to have his uncle home."

"His uncle *and* his aunt," Jane said, rubbing Dreama's shoulder. "Maybe soon he'll have one more uncle home with him."

"You found your brother?" Dreama asked.

"No," Ryder said. "We had a lead but the track grew cold. All we have is a birthdate."

As the four of them made small talk about the weather and the latest political news, Dreama wondered what would be the best way to bring up Cash's case. She couldn't help feeling he should be here, sitting among them. He'd like Ryder and Finn. Considering they were raised by a ruthless and somewhat heartless father, they'd turned out surprisingly normal. With their father now dead, the multi-billion-dollar empire he'd left behind was theirs, but Ryder still lived in the same two-thousand-square-foot home and Finn was dressed in a pair of well-worn Levi's and a plain black T-shirt. They might be obscenely rich, but they didn't live like it.

A few minutes later, Jane called them all to the dining room for dinner. Dreama hadn't had a home-cooked meal since her mother's unannounced visit. She patted her stomach. She was practically salivating over the sight of the homemade roast beef and baked potatoes. Hot Pockets were delicious, but after eating them almost every night, she was ready for something else.

Maddox sat in his high chair with an eager Otis beneath him. Using his fingers, Maddox attempted to shove bits of beef and mashed potato into his mouth. It wasn't long before his face was smeared with food. He was probably getting more on him than in him, but he seemed to be enjoying himself, and Otis was thrilled that some of it landed on the floor. It blew her mind that the last time she'd seen Maddox, he hadn't even had teeth.

All she wanted to do was hold that messy child in her arms and rock him to sleep like she used to. He might be Jane and Ryder's son, but there was a part of that sweet boy that would always belong to Dreama too.

After eating her own fair share of meat and potatoes, she figured now was as good a time as any to bring up Cash's case. "Finn, you're a lawyer. Have you ever heard of Stephen Browner?" Finn had been the senior counsel for his father's company for a short time.

He put down his fork. "Yeah. He's called McKay a few times in the past, offering his firm's services to diversify our assets."

"What's his reputation? Is he a good guy?"

"I have no idea." Finn raised a brow. "Why? Are you dating him?"

She snorted. "God no. Based on the one phone call I had with him, he's an asshole. This has nothing to do with my personal life. It's about one of my parolees. Browner represented him back when he was a public defender. I had some questions about the evidence, but Browner wasn't very forthcoming."

"Not surprising," Finn said. "Even though he's no longer his attorney, he's still bound to the attorney-client privilege."

"I know. It wasn't so much what he said as how he said it. He claimed not to have remembered the case, but he was clearly lying to me. And not only that, but he had the audacity to call and tattle to my boss about the call. Why would he do that if he didn't have something to hide?"

Finn reached for his glass of water. "A bit overkill, sure, but that doesn't necessarily mean anything."

She disagreed. Browner's call to Meg had been his way of warning Dreama not to continue looking into Cash's case. And she wouldn't. She'd have her friends do it for her. "I need to know more about his time at the public defender's office. His record especially and whether he had a habit of encouraging his clients to take plea deals over going to trial. The problem is my boss is just looking for a reason to fire me. I can't be the one digging around into Stephen Browner."

"I'll look into it," Finn said. "Until I find a job, I've got nothing else to do."

"Is there anything we can do?" Jane asked.

Dreama bit the inside of her lip. "Actually...when Browner threatened to hang up, I kind of, sort of, used Ryder's name to get him to stay on the phone with me." She turned to Ryder. "He wouldn't talk to me, but he would talk to you."

"You're family. Of course I'll talk to him. What do you need?" Ryder asked.

She nearly teared up again by her friends' eagerness to help. "I'm not entirely sure. I guess just feel him out for me. Is he on the up and up? Is he the kind of man who would do anything to get ahead, including taking a bad plea deal for a client?"

Ryder nodded as he grabbed another helping of meat. "Not a problem. I'll call him tomorrow."

Jane grabbed Dreama's hand. "I know your job means the world to you but looking into a defense attorney goes above and beyond your parole officer responsibilities. Is there something you're not telling us?"

"No. No." Dreama shook her head vehemently before she realized she was lying to her best friend. That wasn't acceptable. Jane deserved more. "Okay, yes. I can't give you any specifics, but the evidence in his file—or rather, the evidence not in his file—suggests he might have been innocent. Based on Browner's behavior, I'm wondering if he kept that fact from my parolee."

"Excuse me for being confused, but wouldn't your parolee know if he was innocent or not?" Ryder asked.

"He lost his memory of that night. The only thing he knows is what other people reported." Careful not to break confidentiality, Dreama explained the basic facts of Cash's case, starting with the car crash that sent him to prison and ending with Browner's call to Meg.

After dinner, Ryder and Finn gave Maddox his bath, giving Jane and Dreama a chance to talk alone. In keeping with their old tradition, they each chose a pint of ice cream and, sitting at the table, ate directly from the container.

Jane took a big spoonful of her dessert and wiggled her eyebrows. "You like this guy—your parolee."

Dreama should have known Jane would see through her. "Sure, I like him. He's a nice man and he didn't deserve to go to prison if he was innocent."

"I agree, but that's not what I meant," Jane said, smiling. "You're a parole officer. Why isn't he pursuing this with a lawyer? You *like* him, like him."

Dreama rolled her eyes. "What, are we like sixteen?"

"Oh my God." Jane started to laugh. "You totally have a crush on your parolee."

"I don't..." She stopped herself. She needed to stop lying to Jane *and* to herself. "Okay, yes. I have a crush on my parolee." She inhaled a deep breath and released it. "It's more than a crush. I...He..."

Jane's jaw dropped. "Did you two...?"

"No." Not that she hadn't fantasized about it a dozen times since Friday night. She'd had to replace the batteries in her favorite vibrator twice. "We ran into each other at Club X. You know, the BDSM club. It turns out he's a Dominant and a sadist. We...let's just say we've seen more of each other than the typical parole officer and parolee would."

Jane's squeezed her hand in sympathy. "What are you going to do about it?"

There was only one answer to that question.

"Nothing."

ELEVEN

Early Monday morning, Cash stared up at the enormous tower that housed Lundquist Animal Health, which was now the largest privately held animal pharmaceutical company in the country. A flurry of what felt like tennis balls bounced around in his gut as his hands tightened on the steering wheel. *Crazy.* There was no reason for him to be this nervous. At one time, he'd considered Thomas Lundquist to be family. He'd played a pivotal part in Cash's adolescence, substituting the role left absent by Cash's father's death. How many times had the man sat at the head of the dinner table at Thanksgiving and carved the Turners' turkey?

In the time Cash had been in prison, Lundquist Animal Health had gone from a four-thousand-square-foot building and fifteen local employees to a skyscraper and nearly ten thousand employees nationwide. It was all because of Thomas's invention of Dosothysomine. Right before Cash's incarceration, the government had approved the drug for sale and distribution. The night of the accident, he and Maddie had attended the party at the Detroit Zoo, held in celebration of the drug's approval.

The drug worked much like ketamine, in that it was a dissociative anesthetic that induced a trance-like state in the animal while also providing pain relief, sedation, and amnesia. But unlike ketamine, Dosothysomine wasn't a hallucinogenic and was not processed by the kidney or liver, which meant it could be used in animals with liver and kidney ailments. Additionally, the studies had shown there were no adverse effects such as cardiac arrest or trouble breathing. The drug had revolutionized animal surgery by decreasing cost and the risks to animals.

It had been eight years since Cash had decided to cut Thomas out of his life, and judging by Thomas's success, it had been the right one. An association with a felon like Cash would have tarnished Thomas and his company's good name.

But he couldn't stay away any longer. He needed to speak with Thomas about the night of the accident. Dreama had been right. It was time to separate fact from fiction and determine what really happened that night.

Cash crossed the enclosed walkway from the parking structure into the main building. If he hadn't fucked it up, he might have obtained, and then used, his veterinarian degree to work for Thomas. He could've been doing so much good for animals.

After stopping at the guard desk to get a guest badge, he rode the elevator up to the CEO's top-floor office. Once there, a receptionist behind a shiny desk awaited him.

She looked up at him with a practiced smile. "Can I help you?"

"I have an appointment with Mr. Lundquist. My name is Cash Turner," he said with a confidence he didn't feel. It had taken some finagling on the phone this morning, but he'd managed to secure an appointment once Thomas had been informed by his secretary that Cash had wanted to speak with him.

"Yes, Mr. Turner," she said, standing. "He's just finishing with an appointment." She motioned to the three armchairs in waiting area. "Please, have a seat. Can I get you something to drink?"

"No thanks," Cash said. "I'm good." He took a chair in the waiting area and picked up a magazine from a side table.

A few minutes later, he tossed it back on the table and instead drummed his fingers on his thigh as an outlet for his nervous energy. He didn't know what he was going to say to Thomas. Cash wouldn't apologize. It had been the right thing to do even if Thomas wouldn't agree.

Chin down and a phone at his ear, a man with too much gel in his brown hair and wearing a pin-striped gray suit strode past Cash. The guy seemed familiar, but Cash couldn't place him. Cash shook his head and chuckled. No one he personally knew would wear such an ugly suit. The man was so slick looking, Cash guessed that he was probably some kind of lawyer or banker.

The receptionist got up from her chair and stepped out from behind her desk. "Mr. Turner. Please come with me."

He followed her down a hallway until she opened a door and motioned for Cash to go inside.

Thomas Lundquist came toward Cash, greeting him more warmly than he'd expected. "Cash? My God. You've turned into a man. It's so good to see you, son." Thomas gave him a thump on the back and then pulled him in for a hug.

"Good to see you too," Cash said, his throat thick with emotion. Until now, he hadn't realized just how much he'd missed Thomas. It was strange to see the new wrinkles on his face and the gray in his hair.

"I'm sorry I kept you waiting. My meeting with my investment banker ran over."

Cash suppressed a smile. It didn't surprise him that the guy out in the lobby had turned out to be an investment banker.

Thomas closed the door and brought them to a seating area arranged in front of a wall of windows. His old boss took a spot on the couch and sat back, his legs and arms spread as he got comfortable.

Although the city of Windsor, Canada, was located miles away, the building was so tall, Cash could see it from up there. But while the view was impressive and reeked of privilege, the rest of the office was typical Thomas, a man who cared more about science than economics.

Piles of paperwork littered his desk and stacks of files were scattered around the floor. There was no framed artwork. Instead, Thomas's walls were covered by whiteboards, all with different formulas written on them. The office was the equivalent of a mad scientist's lab, but without all the chemicals and test tubes.

Thomas himself was a small, mild-mannered man in his midfifties who had devoted his entire life to improving the health of animals. Before Dosothysomine, none of the drugs he'd created had been approved by the U.S. Food and Drug Administration, but he'd refused to quit, never once losing hope, and his determination had paid off.

"I came to apologize," Cash said, sitting on a chair next to the couch. "I know you did your best to help me and rather than thank you, I cut you out of my life. But I want you to know I did appreciate everything you did for me. I was in a bad place at the time, and I didn't want to take you down with me."

"I know." Thomas wrung his hands. "But you shouldn't have made that decision for me. Your protective nature has always been both your greatest strength and your greatest weakness. My business and I would've been fine. I wish you would've allowed me to help."

Cash didn't believe that for a second. If Thomas was captain of a sinking ship, he'd go down with it.

"If the offer is still good," Cash said, balling his fists on his lap to keep himself from drumming his fingers on his thigh, "I could use your help now."

"Of course. Whatever I can do."

Cash steeled his nerves. No matter what Thomas had to say, Cash needed to hear it. "I need to know more about what happened the night Maddie died."

Thomas's brows rose. "Yes. Sure. What do you want to know?"

"You told the police I'd been drinking champagne that night."

"Yes. I'm sorry but I couldn't lie." His voice was filled with regret.

"You have nothing to be sorry for," Cash said, reassuring Thomas. He would have never asked Thomas to lie for him. If Cash had drunk that night, he had to accept the consequences of his actions. "How much did you see me drink?"

Thomas rubbed his forehead with his knuckles. "I don't know...two? You had a glass when you first arrived and another during our toast."

Cash's pulse quickened. Maybe Dreama had been right. There was no possible way a big guy like him could've gotten drunk off two glasses of champagne. "Two. You're sure it was only two?"

"No." Thomas stood from the couch and looked out the window, giving his back to Cash. "It was a long time ago and it was a crazy night. It could have been the same drink or you might have had several in between." He turned around. "What is this about?"

Cash spread his hands wide and rested his elbows on his knees. "Maybe nothing." Thomas's hazy recollection didn't do much to help Cash, but it didn't hurt him either. There was still hope. "My parole officer...she thinks it's possible that I wasn't intoxicated at the time of the crash."

Thomas pressed a hand to his heart. "My God, Cash. That...What made her think that?"

"My Breathalyzer was under the legal limit, and my defense attorney never mentioned it."

"Why would he have kept that from you?" Thomas asked.

Wasn't *that* the million-dollar question. "I don't know." Cash got up and joined Thomas at the window. "There's something else. The toxicology report from the hospital is missing from my file."

Thomas scratched his head. "It's your own medical record. You should be able to order it from the hospital."

"Already done." He'd called the hospital on his drive over here. "They said under the HIPAA laws, they have thirty days to send it, but it will probably only take a week."

In seven days, Cash would have the evidence that might clear his name and ease his guilty conscience. All these years, he'd blamed himself for Maddie's death and the loss of their unborn son, Joshua. If he hadn't been intoxicated, why had he driven the car into the concrete wall?

A part of him worried the answer to that question would be equally horrifying.

Whatever the reason, he needed to know. He couldn't move on with his future until he had closure with his past.

"Damn it, it's my fault," Thomas said. "I should have pushed harder, convinced you to get a real attorney and not one of those public defenders."

That was pure Thomas. Taking the blame when he'd done nothing to warrant it.

Cash clapped Thomas on the back. "I was an adult and it was my decision to stick with the public defender. It's not your fault I didn't listen to you and Rebecca."

"Then listen to me now." Thomas gripped Cash's shoulders. "Allow me to take this off your hands and pay for an attorney to look into it for you. I'm in the position to pay for the best. Money is no object. Let me make a couple calls and see what I can do."

Cash could see this was important to Thomas. "Thank you. I'll take you up on that offer, but the last time I trusted an attorney, it may have cost me eight years of my life. I'm not going to make that mistake again. Even if you hire someone for me, I won't stop my own search for the truth. I owe that much to myself... and I owe it to Maddie and our child."

"I get it," Thomas said. "But you're wrong. You owe yourself much more than the truth. You owe it to yourself to move on with your life and not waste all your time being stuck in the past. Maddie was a sweet girl."

"Yes, she was," Cash said, the lie as natural as breathing by now.

"But it's been eight years since Maddie died and you've been given a second chance. Use it," Thomas said, returning to the couch. "What are your plans now?"

Cash sat beside Thomas. "I'm not sure. I'm working for Rebecca at the shelter."

"What about going to vet school?"

He could just imagine what the school's admissions committee would think when they read Cash had a record for involuntary manslaughter. "No one is going to accept an ex-con."

"That's horse shit and you know it," Thomas said. "What's the real reason?"

"I'm just not sure if being a veterinarian is what I want to do," he told Thomas. "I don't know what I want anymore."

"Well, if you do decide it's something you want to pursue, I have some connections at Edison University. I could put in a word for you."

"Thank you. It's decent of you to offer, but if I do decide to go to vet school, I want to get there on my own merits."

"Let me tell you what I've learned after being in business all these years," Thomas said. "You can't let a setback prevent you from achieving greatness. It's time you fought for what you really want. You want a job here? It's yours. You want me to get you into vet school? No problem. I'd even help you pay for it. You're meant for great things, Cash. I always knew it. Don't allow one mistake to keep you from claiming your destiny."

Destiny? What did Cash know about destiny? Before the accident, he'd been so sure he knew what he wanted to do with the rest of his life. Now he didn't even know what he wanted to eat for lunch.

Before Maddie, Cash had had his whole life planned out. He wanted to go to Michigan State University's veterinarian school, work for someone else for five years, and then open his own practice. He'd imagined himself married to a woman sweet and wholesome on the outside but dirty and kinky on the inside. He'd wanted a house in the suburbs filled with kids and dogs, preferably somewhere near his family.

The idea of attending vet school didn't appeal to him like it had before the car accident. His parents were both dead and his fantasy wife had turned out to be a mirage. He was a widower and had lost a child. Everything he'd once envisioned for himself had crashed and burned eight years ago. He was no longer that naïve young man.

There was only one thing he was certain he wanted, and it was the one thing he couldn't have.

Dreama.

TWELVE

Dreama felt like a teenage girl waiting for her date to arrive. She'd seen parolee after parolee this morning, but there'd been no sign of Cash. He was on the schedule, but the last time she'd glanced at the computer, he hadn't checked in yet. Every time she opened the door to the waiting room, she expected to see him sitting there in one of those uncomfortable chairs, legs spread with his elbows on his knees. And every time, she was disappointed.

Disappointed.

She couldn't ever recall a time when she'd been so eager to see someone. Cash Turner wasn't a date. He wasn't her boyfriend or her Dom.

He was her parolee.

She shouldn't be this excited to see him, and yet adrenaline was pumping through her blood, making her heart race and her palms sweat. It was absolutely ridiculous.

As the hours passed, she began to worry he wasn't going to come. Her mind started to wander as she led one of her

other parolees to her office. Maybe Cash had changed his
mind and decided to ask for a new parole officer. Maybe
he was uncomfortable with the fact that she'd seen him
naked.

Maybe she needed to get a grip.

Finally, at eleven-thirty, his name appeared on her computer. She saw two more parolees before she called him
back. It took everything she had to act normal.

She avoided eye contact, and even though they wouldn't
be shaking hands, she wiped her palms on the sides of her
skirt. "Follow me, Mr. Turner."

Walking beside him, she didn't speak or even look at
Cash. She was afraid that if she did, one of her coworkers
could pass by them in the hall and deduce immediately how
she felt about him. Sometime between the waiting room
and her office, her pulse had skyrocketed to the moon and all
her female bits had woken up as if she'd mainlined a double
shot of espresso to them. It was a good thing she was wearing a suit jacket over her blouse or everyone would know
the exact size of her nipples.

Cash's scent tantalized her. He smelled delicious. Sweet
with a hint of spice, like a warm, fresh apple cider donut.
When she was younger, she'd suffered from a bout of iron
deficiency that made her crave non-edible items like laundry
detergent and gasoline because of their scents. Luckily, she'd
been old enough to know not to eat them. That's how she
felt now, only she craved Cash.

She led him to her office and closed the door behind
them. He stood in the middle of the room, eating up the

space with his magnetic presence and filling it with the scent of baked goods.

Heart pounding, she rested her back against the door. "Hi."

Cash rocked back on his heels. "Hi."

His sneakers looked brand-new, a clean white with the logo in black. They were a vast improvement over last week's grungy ones. Again, he wore jeans, but this time, he'd matched them with a long-sleeved gray Henley that accentuated his eyes. Her hands tingled with the desire to explore all the muscles hidden underneath.

And that wasn't the only thing tingling.

She rolled her bottom lip into her mouth. Seriously, she needed to get it together. "How was your Sunday?"

His sexy lips curled up at the sides. "Good. Yours?"

"Good." She nodded way too many times to be normal. "This is weird. Don't you think this is weird?"

On the desk, her cell phone buzzed with an incoming call. Deducing it was probably her mother calling, she ignored it. She'd already spoken with her this morning on the way to work. Anything she had to say could be left in a voice mail.

"It's only as weird as we make it." He took a giant step closer to her. If some other man did that, she'd probably be curled into the fetal position. She wasn't sure when it had happened, but she trusted Cash to keep the boundaries. "We're just talking, Dreama. Nothing about Friday night should change that."

"Right," she said, catching herself nodding again. She

gestured to him to sit and took her chair behind the desk. "Right. I got the results from last week's urine test." She slid it over to him. "It came back clean."

He perused the paper and returned it to her. "How does the random testing work?"

"You'll receive a text requesting you visit the lab that day for the test," she said, sticking the results in his file. Her phone buzzed again, and this time, she confirmed it was indeed her mother calling. She opened her desk drawer, dropped the phone inside, then closed it. When was the woman going to accept that Dreama was an adult with adult responsibilities?

"And now that we've gone over your test results," Dreama said, "we can move on to more pressing matters. I spoke with my friends over the weekend. Ryder agreed to meet with Browner about offshore investments, and Finn, his attorney brother, is going to look into Browner's cases to see if anything unusual pops out at him."

While discussing their plans to look into Browner last Friday night, Dreama had told Cash all about her friendship with Ryder McKay, heir to the multi-billion-dollar McKay Industries, and his marriage to her best friend, Jane.

Cash chuckled. "I can't believe your friends are a bunch of billionaires."

Neither could she. Money wasn't a big deal for her. As long as she had enough to live comfortably, without her parents' help, she was satisfied. She was pretty certain that if she did have billions, she wouldn't spend it on herself. She'd use the money to help others. But like having the ability to eat her weight in chocolate and not gain a pound, being a billionaire would never become a reality.

"Trust me, they don't live like billionaires," she said, thinking of their modest home. "If you met them, you'd understand. They're some of the most down-to-earth people you could ever meet."

"I believe you. I'm a complete stranger with a criminal history and yet they're willing to help. That says more about them than anything else could." He leaned forward, placing both hands flat on the desk. "Anyway, you're not the only one who's been busy. I ordered my medical records from the hospital. It was surprisingly easy. The woman on the phone said I should have them in a week."

With them practically begging to be ogled, Dreama studied his hands. His long fingers tapered to clean, clipped nails and the tops of his palms were covered with a light dusting of fine brown hair. She could almost feel his hands between her thighs, forcing her legs open and dipping into where she throbbed for him. He wouldn't be gentle or treat her as if she were made of glass. He'd use his physical strength to demonstrate his dominance over her and leave purple fingerprint-shaped bruises on her skin. That way, his mark would remain with her even when they were apart.

She crossed her legs to quell the rising arousal, but it didn't help. "And then we'll know. But in the meantime, we should still talk to the witnesses who reported you'd been drinking to help your legal case if you're going to get the conviction overturned. I read through your file again this morning and jotted down the names of the other witnesses," she said, looking at the notes she'd taken. "Kevin Sanders and Jay Moran. Do you know them?"

Cash squinted as he sat back in his chair. "Yeah. Sanders was the research director at Lundquist Animal Health and Jay Moran owned a chain of veterinary clinics throughout Michigan. But..."

"What?"

"Sanders and I worked in the same building, but I don't remember meeting Jay Moran. I just know his name because he did some of the clinical trials for the company."

From what she'd read in her online research about the celebration, Lundquist Animal Health had rented out the zoo's events pavilion, which held up to five hundred people. It seemed odd that out of everyone at the event, a stranger would give a statement about Cash to the police.

"Is it possible you met him the night of the accident?" she asked.

He ran his hand over his scalp. "Yeah. I guess."

"What was the last thing you remember from that night?"

"I remember driving to the Detroit Zoo. I don't recall arriving."

"The notes in your file indicate the accident occurred just after ten p.m. and that the event at the zoo began at eight," she said. "So, that gives us a two-hour gap to fill."

"I spoke with my old boss yesterday. He said he thinks I only drank two glasses of champagne, but he couldn't be certain." Cash shifted in his chair and folded his arms over his chest. "Dreama, I don't see why all of this is important.

If my blood test shows I wasn't intoxicated, wouldn't that be enough to overturn a conviction?"

"Apparently, no. Finn McKay told me it's really difficult to do it." *Difficult* was putting it mildly. Finn had used the words *nearly impossible*. "The first hurdle is that you pled guilty. The court asked you if you comprehended your rights, which included waiving the right to appeal the conviction. Your new attorney would have to prove that Browner withheld vital facts about the evidence against you. It would be Browner's word against yours and Browner is never going to cop to malpractice. We're going to need as much proof as possible to help win your case. But even if the toxicology report and all the evidence still point to your guilt, don't you want to know what happened during those missing hours?"

"Honestly?" Cash covered his face with his hands and dragged them down. "Maybe I don't."

She understood his apprehension. There was a part of her that wished she'd blocked out all her memories of her attack. Sometimes, it was better off to remain in the dark. But in Cash's case, she couldn't see how the truth could hurt him worse than not knowing. "There's a therapist. Her name is India and she specializes in treating crime victims. My cousin Isabella went to her for a while, and after my attack, she counseled me in the hospital. I could call her and see if... I don't know... maybe there's something she could do to help you remember."

Before he had the chance to respond, Candice's voice came through the phone's intercom. "Dreama? I'm sorry to interrupt, but there's an urgent call for you on line two. It's your mother."

Grr. If it was anyone other than her mother, she might be worried there was an emergency. But she'd jumped to the wrong conclusion too many times in the past to consider it a possibility. Her mom had probably watched a show about this season's flu epidemic and wanted to make sure Dreama had gotten her immunization.

She rolled her eyes. "Can you tell her I'm in with a client, Candice, and I'll call her back on my lunch break?"

"She already said it can't wait," Candice said, familiar with Dreama's mother's frequent calls.

"Okay. Thanks, Candice." Dreama sighed. I'm sorry," she said to Cash. "My mom..." She'd already briefed Cash about her mother's anxiety. Now he was witnessing it in person.

She picked up the receiver and pressed line two. "This better be an emergency."

"Dreama, baby," her mother said quietly. "I didn't want you to hear it from someone else. Are you sitting down?"

Shit. She'd never asked her to sit down before. Dreama let out a shaky breath. "Oh my God. Is Dad okay?"

"Everyone is fine. At least in our family."

Dreama sighed in relief. *Thank goodness.*

"There was a story on the news," her mom continued. "A young woman was murdered in your city."

Frustrated by her mother's dramatics, Dreama raked her fingers through her hair. "That's terrible, Mom, but what does that have to do with me?"

"This girl. She was beaten to death with a baseball bat."

Dreama didn't hear anything else her mother had to say. She wasn't even sure if her mother was still talking. It was all just static in her ears. She thanked her mom for the information and hung up.

Acid rose in her throat as her mind flashed to another time and place. She could see herself lying broken like a china doll on the carpet and the man in the ski mask above her, a bloody baseball bat in his hand.

It wasn't him. The man who'd attacked her was gone. Ryder had seen the dead body. The police confirmed it. But what if they were wrong about the identity of her attacker?

What if the man who'd almost killed her was still alive? "Dreama? What is it?" Cash asked, his voice sounding as if it were coming from the far end of a tunnel.

Still, his voice was enough to jar her from memory and to bring her back to the present. She blinked away the black dots swimming in her vision and focused on Cash sitting across from her. "Nothing. Just my mother being her typical overprotective self."

He stood and rounded the desk, then crouched beside her chair. "Yeah, I'm not an idiot, Dreama, so don't take me for one. Talk to me," he said gently.

"That *was* my mom. I wasn't lying about that. She called to tell me that someone died."

Her mother probably thought telling her about the murder was the right thing to do, but like Cash with the night of the accident, Dreama wasn't sure if she would have been better off not knowing.

Cash's eyes expressed sympathy. "I'm sorry for your loss."

She swiveled her chair to face him. "I didn't know her."

"Then...I'm confused."

Cash had already witnessed three of her anxiety attacks. He'd proven himself worthy to know why.

"Just over a year ago," she said, her voice wobbly, "a man broke into my apartment. I wasn't supposed to have been there, but I'd stayed home from work that day with the flu. I was in my bedroom, my cell phone dead, so I grabbed the only thing I had on hand to protect myself...a baseball bat. He snatched it out of my hands and used it on me." She waved a hand up and down her body. "All of this. My scars. My pain. My panic attacks. It's all from the attack. If Ryder hadn't found me when he had, I might have died."

Cash's face turned red and the corded muscles in his neck grew taut. "I hope that fucker is in prison," he said on a growl, "so I can tell my buddies still in there to teach him a lesson on what happens to men who beat on women."

"He's dead," she informed him. "Or at least, I thought he was. My mother told me a local woman was murdered with a baseball bat." Her chest tightened and it became harder to get air into her lungs. "What if the police were wrong and someone else was responsible for my attack? What if he comes back to finish the job?"

"Don't panic, sweetheart. Chances are, it's probably a coincidence. There's no reason to think this attack has anything to do with yours." He looked her right in the eyes. "Friday night, I promised I wouldn't let anyone hurt you again. I intend to keep that promise."

Her rational side agreed that it had to be a coincidence.

But she couldn't discount her intuitive side, which whispered in her ear that this attack had everything to do with her.

The office door flew open. Still crouched beside her, Cash vaulted up to full height and leapt backward, clearing as much space as possible between himself and her chair. Meg took one step into the room, her lips pressed tightly together and her arms folded over her chest.

If a parole officer had a good faith belief that another parole officer's life was in danger, she didn't require permission to enter the room. In all the years Dreama had worked there, only once did a situation require a supervisor to forgo the common courtesy of knocking.

Meg had no right to barge in there and she knew it.

But she also knew how to cover her ass. "Dreama, I was concerned something was wrong since you've been in here so long with this parolee." Her brows rose. "Did I interrupt something?" Meg spoke the words as if they were a statement of fact rather than a question.

Although her limbs were shaking and the panic still had its tentacles wrapped around her lungs, Dreama got up from her desk. "We were just finishing up. It ran over because I had to take a phone call."

Meg didn't hide her sneer. "Personal phone calls are not permitted during work hours," she reminded her, suggesting to Dreama that she knew the identity of the caller. "You have a room full of parolees who have better things to do than wait for you, and I'm sure Mr. . . . ." Meg looked at Cash. "I'm sorry. What is your name?"

He shoved his hands into his pockets. "Cash Turner."

"Mr. Turner," Meg continued, "deserved to have your full attention and not have his time wasted while you spoke on the phone. I'm sure it won't happen again. Am I understood, Ms. Agosto?"

"I apologize, Ms. Wilson," she said, pasting on the most insincere smile she was able to muster. On the bright side, her resentment toward Meg reduced some of the lingering anxiety over her mother's phone call. "Since you're so concerned that I not waste my parolees' time, I think I should accompany Mr. Turner to the waiting room and call back my next appointment. Don't you agree?"

Dreama squared her shoulders and took a step toward the door. She didn't buy Meg's lame excuse for charging into her office without permission.

Was it possible Meg suspected something because of the phone call she'd received from Browner last week? Or did Meg know more than she was saying?

Dreama couldn't underestimate her. If there was one thing Dreama had learned throughout the years of working with Meg, it was that she was willing to play dirty to get what she wanted. And she'd made it clear that what she wanted was to fire Dreama.

No matter who got hurt in the process.

THIRTEEN

Cash hefted a bag of dog food over his shoulder and carried it back to the kennels. He hadn't been on the schedule today, but his sister had called him in when Nancy hadn't shown up for work. With what Dreama had told him still fresh in his mind, he needed the distraction.

Thoughts of her being beaten with a baseball bat made him sick. His offer to have his prison buddies take care of the son of a bitch who'd attacked her had been real. He didn't care that it was illegal. Anyone who would beat a woman, especially Dreama, deserved to be taught a lesson.

The recent murder of a woman with a baseball bat had to be a coincidence. He'd looked up the story on his phone, but the police hadn't released a lot of information about the crime. Not even the victim's name since her family hadn't been notified yet.

Part of him felt guilty, but he hadn't been able to stop himself from Googling Dreama's name. It turned his stomach to read the details of her attack and to see her reduced to just another victim of violence. No one who knew Dreama would ever see her as a victim. The woman was a survivor and nothing less.

He opened the door to the kennels and rested the bag of dog food against the wall. He then strolled down the aisles to see if any had been adopted over the weekend and to familiarize himself with any new dogs. With the exception of Duke and Harvey, who were somehow managing to sleep through the racket, all the others stood at the front of their cages, barking their heads off.

He'd come to know some of these dogs pretty well over the last several days. Chewbacca with her long fluffy hair, Barney with his dopey grin, Buck with his frequent sneezes, the dogs were some of the best animals he'd ever come across. They deserved so much more than being stuck in a cell for the crime of being unwanted.

If Cash had the means, he would adopt each and every one of them so that they had the freedom to run around and play. They'd never live behind bars again.

From what Rebecca had told him, every Sunday, parents with young kids on their heels came to the shelter seeking to adopt a new pet, but ultimately, most left empty-handed. Families in their county wanted a healthy, non-shedding puppy. Two-thirds of the dogs at the shelter were a Lab/pit bull mix, and families with young children tended to be apprehensive about adopting them. The other third of the dogs had health issues, shed, or were deemed too old. But a few lucky dogs were fortunate to find their forever homes with good people who understood the commitment of animal ownership.

Among the barking was a familiar whine. Cash walked over to Butch's kennel and crouched down in front of the dog, who was giving him sad puppy dog eyes. "Hey, Butch. What's going on?" Still whining, the dog butted his nose against the cage door, inviting Cash to pet him. Maybe Butch missed Dreama. "I'm sorry, boy. She's not here today."

"Saw you at the club on Friday night," said Buddy from behind him. "How'd you like it?"

Startled, Cash jumped to his feet.

So, it had been Buddy leaving the club the other night.

Shit. Had he seen Cash and Dreama together?

Cash looked around to make sure no one was listening. "It was enlightening."

"Didn't think I'd ever see you on that end of a whip," Buddy said.

Cash didn't owe the guy an explanation, but something compelled him to give one anyway. "I wanted to know what it was like."

Buddy looked at him as if he'd suddenly grown two heads and a set of horns. "Who the fuck cares? If you do it right, it should hurt like a motherfucker. There's nothing like a girl crying as she takes everything you have to give. Both of you knowing it's *you* who holds all the power in your hands. Thought you were a man. Not a fucking pussy sub."

Cash's hands curled into fists. He wasn't an expert in BDSM, but he knew enough to know that what Buddy was describing sounded more like abuse. From what he'd learned in his session with the Dominatrix, subs were no pussies. They were strong as hell. And the power he was talking about? That came from a sub's trust in his Dom. It was a fucking power exchange, not a theft. With his dangerous beliefs, Buddy was a threat to all unsuspecting subs.

He could also be a threat to Dreama. If he had witnessed Cash and Dreama together, what would he do with that information?

At the same time, Buddy could have seen the person who'd tried to mow down Dreama. Come to think of it, where had Buddy disappeared to after he left? There was no one outside other than Cash and Dreama...and whoever was driving that car.

"Hey," Cash said, ignoring Buddy's admonishment. "I left right after you, but I didn't see you. Where'd you go?"

He smirked and gave Cash a wink. "Picked up a girl who lived nearby and walked back to her place."

Cash had only seen Buddy, but it was possible the girl had walked out the door already. "After you left, did you happen to see anybody hanging around outside the club?"

"No, but I wasn't exactly looking around," Buddy said, squinting at Cash as if trying to see through him.

Before Cash had the chance to question him further, Rebecca came storming through the door. Her nose was red and tears streamed down her cheeks. "The police are here."

"What? Why?" Buddy asked.

Rebecca swiped under her eyes. "Nancy was murdered. They need to speak with all her coworkers."

The words were like a punch to his gut. He didn't know

her well, but she was a sweet woman and a hard worker. What the hell was in the water around there? That was two murders he'd heard about today.

Poor Rebecca. His sister had such a big heart, she would cry over the death of a perfect stranger, but she and Nancy had worked together for more than two years. This had to be hitting her hard.

He hooked his arm around Rebecca's back and pulled her in for a hug. "Are you okay?" he whispered in her ear.

"No, but I have to be." She sniffed into his shoulder and stepped out of his arms. "The police are going to use my office to do the questioning. I have to go into surgery."

The last time he spoke with a cop had been after the accident. Cash hadn't been in his right mind, overcome at the time with grief and guilt. He'd been honest with the officer, telling him everything he remembered . . . and didn't remember. He'd withheld only one secret, the same secret he kept today. The last words he remembered uttering to Maddie were "I want a divorce."

In Nancy's case, he had nothing to hide, but he wasn't certain the police would agree. While in prison, he'd spoken to several guys who'd insisted they'd been done wrong by the cops simply because they were in the wrong place at the wrong time and had a criminal history.

Rebecca reached out and rubbed the spot between his brows with her thumb. "Don't worry. It's not as if you're a suspect."

How had she known what he was thinking? *Right.* His damned divot.

She gave him a quick kiss on the cheek and left.

Wearing a somber expression, Buddy crossed his arms. "Your sister is wrong. We're ex-cons. That automatically makes us suspects. We might be innocent until proven guilty but in the cops' eyes, we're just a bit less innocent than everyone else." He took a step toward Cash and lowered his voice. "Don't offer them more than you need to and don't lie. If they ask about a particular person or place, start your answer with the phrase 'to my current recollection.' That way if they find evidence to contradict your statement, you can argue you remembered it wrong. And if you want to hide something, just tell them you don't remember."

Cash gave him a curt nod. "You've done this before."

"Yeah. A time or two. Most of the times I had nothing to do with the crime they were investigating. Other times..." Buddy's lips twisted up in a grin that scared the pants off Cash. "Don't worry your head about it. Your sister wouldn't have hired me if she thought I was a danger to anyone here, right?"

Yeah, but Cash doubted Rebecca had asked Buddy's opinion on sadomasochism and misogyny. Most of the time, Buddy seemed like a nice guy. He got along with everyone at the shelter and always completed his tasks without complaint. Then other times, he tended to do or say things that creeped Cash the hell out, like his crude comments about Laci, his misguided beliefs about power exchanges, and the fact he'd snuck up behind Cash a few times without making his presence known. If the police arrested Buddy for abusing a woman, Cash would believe it. But murder?

Then again, although he'd left Club X before Cash and after Dreama, Buddy was nowhere to be found when the car attempted to hit Dreama. Was it possible that Buddy had been the one who'd tried to run down Dreama the other night?

What reason would Buddy have to try and hurt Dreama? Or Nancy for that matter?

Cash needed to know more about what happened to Nancy. "Mind if I go first?"

Buddy jutted his chin toward the door. "Have at it."

He strode down the hall to Rebecca's office. After getting out of prison, keeping his head down had been his grand plan. Now here he was a week later, and he was about to be interrogated by the cops.

He knocked on the half-open door, pushing it fully open. Inside, a plainclothes man sat in a folding chair, iPad in his lap, with an empty folding chair across from him.

Not just a cop, but a detective. With a head of silver hair, a face of weathered skin, and weariness in his eyes, the man definitely wasn't a rookie.

"I was told you wanted to speak with me?" Cash asked as he lumbered into the room and sat in the empty chair.

"I'm Detective Henry. Can I get your name?" asked the detective, typing on his iPad.

That was new. Eight years ago, the cops had written out their notes on a pad of paper.

"Cash Turner," he responded, wondering if the detective had already done his homework on Cash's background.

"Thank you for sitting down and talking with me today, Mr. Turner. I just have a few questions to ask."

Cash nodded. "Sure."

"How well did you know your coworker Nancy Balsom?"

"Not well at all. I just started here last week." Cash folded his fingers into his palm to keep himself from tapping his thigh. "Can I ask what happened to her?"

Detective Henry lowered his iPad to his lap. "Ms. Balsom was murdered. According to what we've determined so far, sometime between Friday night and Saturday morning, she was beaten to death with a baseball bat. You wouldn't know anything about that, would you?"

* * *

Dreama stepped into her apartment and quickly engaged both door locks. She'd been a nervous wreck all day. She wished she still smoked, but she'd quit before Maddox was born.

This anxiety was different than the kind that led to one of her panic attacks. She wasn't experiencing any flashbacks or the burning sensation that came with being touched. Since her mother's call, it was as if a million tiny ants were crawling around under her skin, and she had a feeling it wouldn't go away until the cops caught the latest bat-wielding maniac.

Logically, she knew the chance of it being the same monster as the one who'd hurt her was minuscule, but that didn't stop her from worrying that he'd come after her. She couldn't get her brain to slow down or focus on anything other than the murder. The appointments after Cash's had been disasters.

She'd been completely distracted and had spent the time between clients refreshing the browser on her phone to see if the article about the murder had been updated. It was after seven and nothing new had been reported.

This night called for reinforcements. After dropping her stack of mail onto the family room's coffee table, she strode to the kitchen and pulled out a bottle of wine from her refrigerator. Forgoing a glass, she took several chugs of it straight from the bottle to calm herself. Then she grabbed her quart of rocky road ice cream from the freezer, snatched a bag of potato chips from the counter, and brought it all with her to the couch.

Damn it. This was her home. She should feel safe here. She was so tired of allowing her fears to rule her. It had already run her from her own bedroom. She was still sleeping on the couch.

Tools like the visualization exercises she'd learned in therapy with India hadn't helped her anxiety. Cigarettes, wine, and junk food were all poor substitutes for what she really needed—an intense session with a sadistic Dom. Pain and submission grounded her and allowed her to escape herself for a little while.

If only she could.

After stuffing her face with chips dipped in ice cream and drinking half a bottle of wine, she shuffled through her mail. She chucked the junk mail into one pile and the bills in another until she came to a large manila envelope with no return address. Frowning, she slid her finger under the envelope's flap and pulled out the contents.

Her stomach churned and acid rose into her throat.

It was a photograph of her crossing the road in front of Club X, with Cash following not too far behind. Her hands shook as she flipped the picture over.

Whoever sent it had written out a message in a deep red marker. The color resembled fresh blood spilling from a vein.

Stop looking into Cash's case or next time my car won't miss.

Terror seized her, squeezing her around her neck. As if the photo were a rattlesnake about to strike, she released it from her fingers. The picture landed facedown on the carpet.

Friday night's attempt to run her down hadn't been a random act of violence. Cash had been right.

Whoever sent this photograph had tried to kill her. If she didn't do what they wanted, they'd try again.

She'd already suffered at the hands of one psychopath. She wasn't eager to do it a second time.

She snatched her phone from her purse and dialed 911. But she didn't press Send. Her fingers hovered over the button.

Inside, she was screaming with a dozen different emotions and they were all clamoring to be released. Her mind didn't know how to process it. While receiving the photograph terrified her, it also pissed her off. How dare he threaten her life as a kind of blackmail for her silence! If anything, she was even more determined to learn the truth about Cash's accident. She would not allow this asshole to intimidate her.

Other than the police, there were a number of people she

could call for help. Her parents or Jane and Ryder would be here in an instant. But there was only one person she wanted.

Mind made up, she dialed his number and hit Send. "I need to see you."

FOURTEEN

Adrenaline pumping hard through his system, Cash knocked on Dreama's door. After receiving her phone call, he'd left work and hightailed his ass over to her apartment building. Poor Rebecca was working late at the shelter, preferring to keep herself busy rather than deal with Nancy's death.

Cash had spent ten minutes with Detective Henry answering questions that gave Cash the impression the police didn't have any leads as of yet. Since he never spoke with Nancy outside of her giving him his duties for the day, he didn't have much to offer. Contrary to what Buddy had led Cash to believe, Detective Henry hadn't as much as batted an eyelash when Cash told him he'd recently gotten out of prison.

From what Cash could glean from the questioning, Detective Henry was still building a timeline for the murder, but sometime between Friday night and Saturday early morning, Nancy was beaten to death in her home. A bloody baseball bat had been left at the scene.

For the rest of the day, Nancy's murder was all his coworkers could talk about. Seemed as though everyone had an opinion, but no one had any real proof. Someone mentioned she'd gotten out of an abusive marriage last year and that her ex-husband had probably killed her. Another person believed Nancy had interrupted a home invasion and had died as a result. Laci insisted that Nancy had told her she had a date Friday night and that Nancy had acted dodgy when Laci pressed for details about the guy.

Any one of their theories could be true.

As for Cash, he couldn't get the coincidence of the baseball bat out of his head. If the victim had been a stranger, he could've believed it. But for it to be Cash's coworker? Was it possible Nancy's death was related to Dreama?

He hadn't mentioned it to Detective Henry or to anyone else. As of now, it was mere conjecture on Cash's part. But since Cash was the only tie between Nancy and Dreama as far as he knew, it would make Cash a suspect.

Until Cash learned more details about Nancy's death, he was keeping his mouth shut.

But what should he tell Dreama?

He was trying to figure that out when Dreama's door swung open. She was in her suit from earlier, a sexy-as-hell navy jacket and a skirt that molded to her curves and gave him the urge to ask her to bend over just so he could see the material stretch over her luscious ass. Beneath that buttoned-down professional exterior of hers hid a wildly seductive temptress. She was both the devil and an angel all tied together in one fucking spectacular package.

He moved inside her apartment before any of her neighbors saw him and stripped off his coat. "I left the fake name you gave me with the guard in the lobby."

Her call had shocked the hell out of him. After learning about Nancy, he'd gone back and forth as to whether to call Dreama. He'd just punched out of work when she'd called and asked him to come over. He didn't know why. She'd refused to tell him anything over the phone, insisting they talk in person.

Earlier when she'd walked him from her office to the waiting room, she'd pretended she was fine, but she hadn't fooled him. She hadn't been fine at all.

Although she was calm and collected at the moment, her eyes were glassy as if she'd been crying.

"I'm sorry I asked you to lie to the guard and say you were Ryder McKay," she said, taking his jacket and hanging it up in the coat closet. "I thought it would be better not to have any written evidence of your visit here."

"I get it," he said, kicking off his wet shoes and leaving them by the door.

The guard in the lobby hadn't blinked when Cash had given Ryder's name or when Cash signed in as Ryder in the guest registry. Hopefully, Dreama's friend didn't make an unannounced visit tonight.

She turned from the closet and faced him. Her lips were trembling and her skin was about two shades paler than usual. But there was also a quiet determination about her in the steel of her spine and the rigidness of her jaw.

He fought the impulse to take her in his arms, hold her

tight, and promise her whatever was wrong, they'd face it together. "What's going on, Dreama?"

She squared her shoulders and gestured with a tip of her head. "Come with me."

He followed her farther into the apartment, noticing that although she was still in her suit, she'd taken off her pantyhose, leaving her shapely legs bare.

Her place was kind of a mess and for some reason, he found it endearing that she hadn't tried to hide it. Clothes hung off the back of the couch, pillows and a comforter lay on the carpet, and mail and some junk food covered the coffee table. Her apartment was like a window into Dreama's soul. And he liked it. He liked it a lot.

Cash averted his eyes when she bent over to pick up something on the floor. As much as it pained him, he sensed now was not a good time to ogle her ass.

She thrust whatever it was in his direction. "Here."

He snagged the item out of her hands. At first, he wasn't sure what he was looking at. It was a grainy 8 x 10 black-and-white photograph. As he examined it more closely, he recognized the figures as him and Dreama. "This is from outside Club X."

"Turn it over."

Stop looking into Cash's case or next time my car won't miss.

Fuck. He'd always heard the expression *shivers down the spine*, but until now, he'd never experienced it. While he appreciated Dreama's dedication to helping him, he wouldn't forgive himself if something happened to her. "You need to call the police."

It was the rational thing to do.

Which is why Dreama shocked the hell out of him with her next word.

"No."

*   *   *

Dreama had given herself five minutes to cry and panic over the photo before she'd shut it down. She wouldn't allow herself to be a victim again. That meant she needed to stay in control and take a logical approach. Whoever sent her the photo intended on scaring her, and she'd be damned if she gave in to emotional blackmail.

Cash's jaw dropped in response to her refusal to call the police. "No? What do you mean, no? This photo is obviously a threat." He held it out to her. "Look at the angle. The person who took the picture was most likely the driver who tried to mow you down."

"I know." She'd figured that out on her own. "But as of Friday night, there were only a couple of people other than you and me who knew that we're looking into the evidence of your case—Stephen Browner and my boss, Meg. And as much as Meg despises me, she wouldn't follow me to a club and try to run me over or send me this photo to get me to drop the matter. She'd just fire me."

Cash remained quiet as her words sank in. "That leaves Stephen Browner."

"Right." She plopped herself down on the couch and patted the cushion beside her. She understood why Cash would want to call the police, but she had to convince him it was the wrong thing to do. Right now, his shoulders were up to his ears. If they were going to solve this mystery, they needed to look at things calmly, rather than based on emotion.

He took her up on her implied offer to sit next to her on the couch. "He already called your boss once. If he wanted you off my case, why wouldn't he send this photo to her? Why almost kill you with a car?"

"I don't know why he didn't send it to Meg," Dreama said, noticing the black bra she'd worn yesterday resting on the couch cushion behind her. She quickly tossed it over the side and out of view. "Maybe because it would implicate him as the person behind the wheel?" There were pieces of the puzzle missing, but she was certain they were on to something. "Besides, we don't know that the driver ever intended to actually hit me with his vehicle. It could have been a scare tactic."

"Whether he meant to hit you or not, you're clearly in danger." Cash surged to his feet. "That's why you need to report this to the police."

She shook her head. "I'm not calling the police. If I do, there's no doubt Meg will fire me and you might never learn the truth." She wouldn't allow anyone to stop her. Not even Cash.

She'd become a parole officer to help people. What better way than to prove Cash might have been innocent? Besides, she wasn't doing this just for him. Because of her phobia of touch, she needed to prove to herself that she wasn't going to live her life in fear, and that's exactly what she'd be doing if she gave in to the photographer's attempt at emotional terrorism.

"The photo only shows we were at the club at the same time," he pointed out. "We weren't even together in the picture."

"We could swear up and down that it was a coincidence, but it won't matter to Meg." She was just waiting for a reason to fire Dreama.

Cash blew out a breath and ran his hand over his head as he sat back down. "Is this job worth more than your life?"

"No," she admitted. "But if I give in to him, what's to keep me from giving in to the next bully I go against? And the next?"

He dropped his chin to his chest and let out a loud sigh. It gave her optimism that he had understood why she wouldn't call the police. "What if I ask for another parole officer? That should appease Browner for the time being, right?"

"Meg would want to know why. She'd use it against me somehow, probably tie it to my prying into your case."

His eyes narrowed on her. "You say you won't let bullies intimidate you, but that's exactly what you're doing with Meg. You're giving her more power than she deserves. Stop worrying so much about Meg and focus on what you need to do for yourself."

Strands of her hair fell across her face as she looked at him. What he didn't understand was that by helping him, she was already focusing on what she needed to do for herself. "You're right that I worry too much about Meg. But that doesn't change how I feel about going to the police. Please, just give me a few more days," she pleaded. "Finn is still planning on researching Browner's record and Ryder has an appointment with him tomorrow. As far as Browner's concerned, he'll think I've dropped it."

Cash was silent for a long time, so long she was sure he wouldn't agree.

"Fine," he finally said. "As long as the threats stop, I'll keep you as my parole officer. But one more threat and we're calling the cops."

"Deal." She smiled as she waved her hand. "I'd shake on it but..."

But that was one fear that had her in its grip.

She couldn't control her phobia of a man's touch, but at least she wasn't giving in to all her other fears. And she was afraid. Afraid that she'd lose a job that meant so much to her. Afraid whoever had sent her the photo would try to hurt her. Afraid the man who'd attacked her with the baseball bat was still out there. She couldn't deny all of that. But helping Cash—just being around Cash—made it easier to be strong.

Cash clasped his hands together. "How are you doing otherwise? You were pretty shaken up after your mom's call, but you seem fine now."

She shook her head. "I know she thought it was best to hear it from her, but honestly, a part of me wonders if she wanted me to be scared in order to convince me to move back home with her."

"Would moving in with her be so bad?" he asked.

Dreama's fingers curled into the palms of her hands. Her mother treated her as if she were a toddler, incapable of taking care of herself. "When I got out of the rehabilitation center, I stayed with my parents. One day I realized that I was hiding there and if I remained there for much longer, that meant my attacker had won because I was too afraid to live on my own." She hopped up from the couch. "I refuse to let my fear get the best of me."

It was damned hard to do, especially with all the anxiety she'd experienced since her attack. That's why it was so important for her to fight against it and not give in.

She slid her hand over her collarbone and down between her breasts. His eyes tracked her hand and his tongue slid across his lower lip. Even though she and Cash couldn't touch, his reaction gave her a thrill.

"The old Dreama loved to touch and be touched," she said. "She found power and strength through her submission. I miss it, Cash. It's like losing a limb. I'm not a stranger to anxiety, but before my attack, I had an outlet for it. I've tried every conventional method of beating my phobia, but nothing's worked."

Silent, he stood from the couch and walked away from her. When he reached the wall, he flipped around to face her. "There was a dog brought to the PAWS program who wouldn't allow anyone to pet his head," he said. "Anywhere else on his body was fine, but go near his head and he'd bite. Before he'd been rescued and taken to the shelter, his owner had burned his face with cigarettes. My sister asked me to help desensitize him. We bonded pretty quickly. Leon—that was the dog's name—was as sweet as could be and smart too. Every day, I moved my hand a little closer to his face, and if he didn't snap at me, I'd give him a treat. It took three weeks before he let me pet the top of his snout."

She had no idea what he was talking about. "That's a great story, Cash. But I'm not a dog."

"No, but the psychology is the same."

"What are you suggesting?"

He squared his shoulders and stared into her eyes. "You said conventional therapy hasn't helped. What if you tried something unconventional? Let me help you beat your phobia. Let me Dominate you."

Her pulse began to race and she wasn't yet sure whether it was from fear or excitement. "How? You can't even touch me."

"You know better than me that Domination doesn't require touch," he said. "We'll build up to it. Start slow and desensitize you just like I did with Leon."

She'd learned about desensitization in one of her psychology classes, but it had never occurred to her to try it.

She dragged her fingers through her hair and went behind the couch, where she paced the length of it, picking up clothes along the way. There were a lot of things to consider. Would she even want Cash to dominate her?

Watching her, he rested his back against the wall and folded his arms. The thought of him standing over her with a flogger in his hand shot heat throughout her core.

No problems there.

She dropped her clothes into a pile by the couch, then cleaned the junk food off the coffee table and carried it into the kitchen. Suddenly parched, she grabbed two bottles of water and returned to the family room. They needed to talk this out.

Standing in front of Cash, she thrust a bottle in his direction. "If we do this, we're crossing a line we can never uncross."

Of course, they'd already crossed the line the moment they'd gotten themselves off in front of each other at Club X.

He snagged the water from her hand. "No matter how long we fought this thing between us"—he lowered his head, delivering both a promise and a threat—"you and I were inevitable."

FIFTEEN

Dreama shivered even as Cash's words lit a fire inside her.

Cash had called them inevitable.

Maybe he was right.

She'd only met him last week, but it felt as if she'd known him forever. There was a connection between them she couldn't deny. Her throat was dry and her body was pounding with arousal. She stared up at him, unable to speak in that moment.

"Think about my offer. You don't need to make the decision tonight," he said gently. He pushed himself off the wall. "I should go."

She wasn't sure about much at the moment, but she did know him leaving was the last thing she wanted.

He turned from her, but before taking a single step, she finally found her voice. "What if I said I don't want you to?"

Her heart hammered wildly as he spun around and faced her.

"I don't need to think about it," she said, feeling confident that she was making the right decision. "I want you to Dominate me." She flung off her suit jacket, then unbuttoned the top of her sheer white blouse. "Stay."

Time and time again, he'd proven himself to be protective, first defending her to the security guard in her office building, then pushing her out of the way of a speeding car, and again tonight, trying to convince her to report the photo to the police. She'd witnessed his affinity for dogs, and he spoke of his sister with true affection in his voice. Cash Turner was the last person she should fall for, but she had come to trust him more than anyone else in her life.

This was happening.

She popped another button on her blouse, giving him a sneak peek of her cleavage.

"What do you think you're doing?" he asked, his eyes narrowing.

She was confused. "Don't you want me to … you know … undress?"

"No, not tonight. Tonight, we're going to keep our clothes on and talk."

That was his idea of domination? "We already know each other," she said somewhat petulantly. She wasn't going to make it easy for Cash to top her. He had to earn her submission. She didn't see how he was going to accomplish that through a conversation.

His eyes darkened. "You know me as your parolee. You might even know me as your friend. But, sweetheart, you don't know the first thing about me as a man. Lesson number one, I make the rules, and unless you choose to use your safe word, you will follow those rules. Try to top from the bottom and I'll punish you."

She smirked. He was forgetting she was a masochist.

His expression hardened. "I'm guessing you're the type of sub who acts like a brat in order to get a punishment. Don't think you can manipulate me, Dreama. The minute you do, I'll end the scene. I'm not the kind of man who takes control from a woman. This only works if you give it to me willingly." He moved closer to her. "Trust me, Dreama."

Her toes curled into the carpet as heat rushed to her pussy. No other Dom had ever confronted her about her brattiness. Most of the guys had liked that about her because that gave them an excuse to spank, flog, or paddle her. But Cash was right. She'd been topping from the bottom, manipulating them into giving her what *she* wanted. That meant she'd never really given over her control. Cash wasn't going to let her get away with it and that turned her on more than any touch.

"I do trust you," she said. "I wouldn't try this with you if I didn't."

He sat on the couch and patted the spot beside him. "Then let's go over your limits."

"What's the point of going over my limits if you can't touch me?" she asked, sitting.

"The point is I don't want to do anything to cause you any psychological, physical, or emotional damage. You've been in this lifestyle longer than I have. I'm surprised you would consider doing a scene without expressing your limits."

The disapproval in his tone caused shame to spread throughout her chest. Already she wanted to please him. "Normally I wouldn't, but I assumed if you couldn't touch me, the limits were already set."

"What's your safe word, Dreama?" he asked.

"Marathon." To remind her that life was a never-ending battle for the finish line. "But I've never used it."

Cash scooted a bit closer to her, leaving only a hair's distance between their thighs. It should have unnerved her to have him sit so near, but instead, she relished the heat radiating from him. Her core clenched as her arousal simmered. "You have nothing to prove to me. If you don't feel safe or if anything I do scares you, use it. I won't judge you if you do. Tonight, I won't touch you with my hands...or anything else. But in the future, how would you feel about me using a flogger or a cane?"

"I...I'm not sure. I hadn't even thought about it." The sight of those items at Club X hadn't scared her, but she had only been an observer and not a participant. Using an impact toy on her could potentially throw her into a full-blown panic attack. Her mind might perceive a cane as a baseball bat. Then again, her fear seemed to be limited to physical contact between her body and a man's, especially his hands. "It might be okay," she added. "I'd be willing to try."

"What about my mouth?" he asked, drawing her attention to his lips. "What if I slowly lick my way around your body...suck on your nipples...and fuck your pussy with my tongue?"

Yes please. A year ago, she'd be pleading with him to make all of that a reality. Even now, her body felt damp as if she could actually feel his tongue traveling over her skin. Her nipples beaded behind the lacy fabric of her bra. Her clitoris throbbed and her core ached. But the thought of it also made her scars burn and her heart race in terror.

"No. I can't . . ." She wasn't surprised to hear the quiver in her voice. "Not yet. It's a hard limit."

If she were speaking about this to anyone else, she might have been embarrassed. What kind of masochist couldn't handle a tongue on her skin? But Cash didn't look at her any differently than he had before her answer.

"No contact between my body and yours. Got it," he said as if he were merely ticking items off his list. "How about bondage? Ropes? Chains? Cuffs?"

If done properly, she loved bondage, and thankfully, the thought of it didn't invoke any fear. "Maybe. As long as you can bind me without touching me."

"Hmm. I'll have to get creative." His wicked grin fired another round of heat through her pelvis. "I'll tell you my limits. Even if you were ready, I won't use anything I don't have experience with or feel comfortable using. I've only got one training session under my belt with the Dominatrix. That means no canes or whips for a while. But like I said, we're not even gonna take our clothes off tonight. Instead, we're going to do a trust exercise." He stood and pulled his cell phone from his pocket.

She hadn't done a trust exercise since grade school when a group of girls had to catch her as she fell backward. It wasn't any fun back then and she couldn't imagine it being fun now. Still, she was willing to give Cash the benefit of the doubt. "Okay."

"Stand up." He pushed her coffee table back a couple of feet to give them more room. "Ever play 'mirror image' before?"

"I don't think so."

He fiddled with his cell phone until music began to play and then placed the phone on the table. "I learned it in a drama class I took in high school." Before she could ask why he took drama, he added, "It counted as an English credit and was an easy A."

The song he put on was one of her favorites. Slow, sappy, and likely to stay stuck in your head for hours afterward. She wouldn't have pegged Cash as a fan of the artist or his music, especially since the singer didn't have his breakout hit until Cash was in prison.

He beckoned her with a crook of his finger. "Come closer and stand opposite me." Elbows bent, he held his hands up at the level of his chest with his palms facing her. "When I move, you mirror my action."

She moved in front of him, feeling as if a bunch of tennis balls were ricocheting around in her stomach. "You won't touch me?"

He lowered his head to look her straight in the eyes. "I promise."

She lifted her arms and copied his stance as if she were his reflection in a mirror. Only a couple inches separated his palms from hers.

Her hands shook and her legs felt like gelatin. Apparently, her brain trusted him, but the rest of her body was still apprehensive.

She swallowed the glob of fear in her throat. "Did you get to listen to music in prison?"

Cash moved his left hand to the left as Dreama mimicked his movement with her right hand. "I had a special tablet for prisoners that allowed me to download music and audiobooks, play games, read the news, and rent movies. But the selection of media was limited."

As a parole officer, she probably should have known that, but the subject had never come up before. When she had gone to the prison for pre-parole meetings, she'd focused on their future rather than their current situation. She regretted that now. She'd thought it was better to concentrate on things they could change and not fixate on things they couldn't. She helped them with the transition to the outside world, but how could she really do that if she didn't know what it was like for them on the inside? Getting to know Cash this week, she realized her parolees deserved better from her. Ignoring the years spent like dogs in a cage didn't mean those years didn't happen.

Humming, Cash swayed from side to side to the beat of the music. She followed his movements, stepping left when he stepped left and swinging her hips from side to side. They were dancing without touching, hands and feet so close together, their body heat joining together even when their skin could not. Cash set the rhythm, led her body's tempo, and compelled her to mirror his motion. She imagined he fucked much like he danced, all confident and controlling, with one hundred percent of his attention concentrated on his partner.

The warmth of arousal flowed through her pussy, making her insides clench and release in anticipation of being filled and causing her panties to dampen. The temperature of the room hadn't changed, but suddenly, she became overheated and feverish.

"Do you feel that?" he asked as a new slow song came on.

She didn't have to ask what he meant. "Yeah. I do."

"Good. That's good," he said huskily. "I want you to describe it to me."

"Heat."

"Use your words, Dreama. I want to know exactly what's going on in that body and mind of yours."

How could she describe something she barely understood herself?

"It's like I'm heavy, so heavy my feet are sinking into the floor, only at the same time, I'm weightless and floating in the air. The room is whirling around me, so quickly it's just a blur of colors and shapes. All my senses are heightened."

"Are you scared?"

His palms were now mere millimeters from hers, but the last thing she was feeling was scared. "No. I know you won't touch me."

He stopped moving and dropped his arms to his side. His gray eyes were as dark as the sky in a thunderstorm. He dipped his head, his mouth drifting closer and closer to hers. "Do you trust me?"

She wasn't scared that he'd kiss her. He'd promised not to touch her and he'd keep that promise.

She was scared that she'd never get the chance.

"With my life."

His lips hovered over hers. "Then tell me a secret."

* * *

Cash hadn't intended to ask for her secrets. The words had spilled from his lips before he could stop them. All he knew was that he'd never felt closer to anyone than he had while dancing with Dreama. It wasn't just sexual, although the sight of hardened nipples poking through that sheer white blouse of hers currently had his mouth salivating. It was far more complicated. If he couldn't use his fingers or his tongue, then he needed to find some other way to explore her. He wanted more than her body. He wanted to know everything about her—all her thoughts and her fears and her dreams.

Her gorgeous breasts rose and fell with every heavy breath. She gazed up at him with pure lust in her eyes. It made him feel invincible, as if he could climb Mt. Everest so long as she continued to look at him like that.

She wrung her hands. "I haven't slept in my bed since I moved in here."

"What? Where have you been sleeping?"

"On the couch."

That explained the comforter and pillow on the carpet.

"Why aren't you sleeping in your bed?" he asked.

She rubbed her arms as if she was cold. "You're supposed to feel safe in your bed, safe enough to close your eyes and trust that no one will hurt you, but it's also where you're most vulnerable."

He recalled her story about the attack. She'd been sick in bed when the man had broken into her apartment. "You've had your trust violated. I get it." She deserved to feel safe, and he could be the one to give that to her. "Do you want me to stay here for a little while until you fall asleep?"

She hesitated. "It's probably not a good idea."

"It's a terrible idea." They could add it to the list that included not telling the police about the photograph and the attempt on Dreama's life, and their Dom/sub relationship. "But what's one more?"

Deciding, she gnawed on her bottom lip. "Yes," she finally said. "I want you to stay." She gathered the comforter and pillow in her arm and motioned at him with a tilt of her head to come with her.

He picked up his phone from the coffee table and shot a quick message to Rebecca so she wouldn't worry. He had no idea what he was going to tell her about where he went tonight. His sister would know if he lied to her.

As Dreama shut off the family room lights, he stuck his phone back into his pocket. He must be insane to think he could lie in a bed with her and not touch her. Every moment he spent with her made it harder and harder.

And that wasn't the only thing getting harder.

But his desire to touch her was more than sexual. He wasn't sure why, but the need to take her into his arms and soothe her felt as necessary as breathing. Words weren't enough to explain what she was beginning to mean to him. If she could only put her hand on his chest, she could feel how fast his heart was beating whenever she was near.

He followed her into her bedroom where he got another glimpse into Dreama's soul.

Dreama's room was like a bohemian oasis. Purple beads hung over the archway between her room and the bathroom, and she had an honest-to-God lava lamp on top of her dresser. He hadn't seen one of those since his first and only year at college. Her bedspread was an explosion of bright colors, and there was a stuffed unicorn by the top of the bed-frame. *Cute.*

A huge box by her bed marked *toys* caught his eye.

What kind of toys?

"Help yourself," she said, gesturing to the box. "I know you're dying to see what's in there."

He dropped to his knees and lifted the box's flaps. Inside he discovered enough sex toys to fill the shelves of an adult store. Most items he recognized. She had a collection of vibrators and dildos, lube, butt plugs, and nipple clamps. Anything she would need for self-pleasure.

He pulled out a metal piece that was in the shape of a question mark with two small steel balls at the end. What the hell was it?

Dreama knelt beside him. "The orgasm I'd had at Club X was my first in more than a year. Between my lack of arousal and living at my parents, there was no need to unpack my toys. I opened this box Friday night after I got home. Underneath the couch pillow where you were sitting earlier, you'll find my favorite. It's gotten quite a workout these last few days." She smiled and sighed wistfully as her fingers caressed a glass dildo. "I have missed my vibrator collection. I've had a longer relationship with them than any man, and they don't mind that I prefer a little variety in my pussy."

He chuckled, amused by her unabashed love for her masturbatory aids. He held up the odd-shaped toy. "And this?"

"Oh. That's an anal hook." She winked. "But it's not for me."

He dropped it back into the box.

She laughed. "Don't worry. I promise not to impale your ass with Captain Hook."

"Captain Hook?"

"Because of its shape," she said as if it was obvious. Then she laughed again. "I'm just kidding. I've never used it on anyone but myself. One of my first Doms gave it to me to use for posture training. But it can also be used in bondage."

His mind immediately went to a dark and dirty place where Dreama was harnessed in place by the anal hook connected by rope that went around her torso. His heart and cock throbbed in tempo. He rubbed his hand over the front of his jeans and as discreetly as he could, shifted himself.

He was proud of how calm he remained. Especially when inside, his heart was pounding a staccato beat against his breastbone and heat was curling around his groin.

He had to be a masochist. How else to explain he was

about to sleep in bed with a woman he wanted but couldn't touch? Only a masochist would agree to that kind of torture.

"So...bed. How do you want to do this?" he asked.

"We could use my extra bedding as a wedge between you and me. I brought the one in from the family room and there's more on the top shelf of my closet."

"Sure." After standing, he opened her closet and reached up, snagging a couple of bright bedspreads. He turned around just in time to catch her checking out his ass.

She winked at him again, delightfully unapologetic for her actions, and pulled a pair of pajamas from her dresser. "Be right back. Make yourself comfortable."

Dreama disappeared into the bathroom, leaving him alone in her room. With his dick being strangled behind his boxers, there was no way for him make himself comfortable. Tonight wasn't about him or his dick. He'd gone nine years without pussy. He could control himself for another few hours.

In the middle of the queen-sized mattress, he created a barrier with two of the blankets. Unsure of which side she preferred, he settled on the front edge of the bed.

A minute later, the bathroom door opened and Dreama strolled back into the room. She'd changed into a modest pair of pink silk pajama shorts with a matching short-sleeved top and had put her hair up in a messy bun. Her face was scrubbed clean of makeup. She looked younger that way.

Choosing the right side of the bed, she slid under the

sheets and tugged the comforter up to her chin. "Ready for bed?"

"Sure," he said, his voice coming out a little more gruffly than normal. He flipped off the light and with only a sliver of light coming in through the window, made his way to his side of the bed. He stood there, a hand at the button of his jeans.

"I meant it when I told you to get comfortable. You can take off your pants if you need to," she said. "It won't bother me."

He gritted his teeth. *Sure. Why not?* He unbuttoned his jeans, shoved his pants down his legs, and kicked them off, leaving him in his boxers. Settling himself on top of the covers, he placed his head on the pillow and threw a blanket over himself. When his eyes adjusted to the darkness, he turned his head and found Dreama on her side, watching him.

"Hi," she whispered.

"Hi," he replied, flipping to face her.

He couldn't believe he was lying in bed with Dreama. It seemed surreal to him that less than two weeks ago, he'd been sleeping on a prison cell cot.

"What was it like for you in prison?" she asked, as if she'd read his mind.

Sometimes, at night, he'd wake up in his sister's house and forget where he was. He'd forget that he could pee in a bathroom behind a closed door.

"Lonely," he answered. "It's weird, because you have no privacy. And yet, I'd never felt more alone."

SIXTEEN

The next day, Dreama had a little more bounce in her step. Not even the long-ass staff meeting had brought her down. The pain from her scars was still there, as was her limp, but she had more energy than she could remember having in months. More significantly, she had hope.

When she'd awoken this morning, Cash had been gone, but he'd stayed long enough last night for her to fall asleep in her own bed. Something as simple as that wouldn't mean much to most people, but it meant everything to her. With Cash by her side, she could finally overcome her fears.

After work, she drove straight to Jane's house for dinner. Ryder and Finn both had information about Browner to share and they wanted to do it in person. She was eager to hear what they'd learned.

Nervous excitement effervesced in her belly as if it was filled with bubby soda. Cash was coming over again later, and she really wanted to be able to give him some good news.

Standing on Jane's porch, Dreama had just lifted her fist

She was quiet for a moment. "I have another secret to tell you. I've never slept in bed with a man before."

"What do you think so far?"

She lit up the room with her smile and it was all he could do to keep from stealing some of that light for himself. "I think I could get used to it."

to knock when the door swung open. Smiling, Jane took a step back. "Come on in."

Dreama practically bounced as she moved inside the house. "I slept with my parolee," she announced to Jane with a smirk on her face.

And it had been the best night's sleep she'd had in more than a year.

Maddox ran toward her, his cheek covered with something that looked like ketchup. "An Dweama."

Aunt Dreama. She'd never enjoyed hearing her name more.

She bent down and snatched him up into her arms. "You smell delicious. I'm going to eat you up." She made a hungry growl and kissed him all over until he let out a loud belly laugh.

"You had"—Jane glanced at her son—"S-E-X?" she whispered. "Putting aside the matter that he's your parolee, how did that work if he couldn't touch you?"

"We didn't have sex," Dreama said, not bothering to spell out the word. It wasn't as if Maddox understood what it meant. "We slept—actually slept—in the same bed." She handed Maddox to Jane, then removed her coat and boots.

Jane shook her head and brought Dreama to the kitchen. "I don't know what to tackle first. You've never slept in the same bed with a guy before. You had rules about it."

Ah, yes. Her list of rules.

Never spend the night.

Never invite him to hang with friends.

Never make plans for more than one week out.

And most importantly, never, ever, introduce him to the parents.

She'd invented the rules to prevent any expectations about their future—or more specifically, their lack thereof. Sex had always been easy for her, but once emotions got involved, things got messy and complicated—mainly because she didn't get emotional over men.

She'd never been in love. She wasn't even sure she was wired that way.

Dreama grabbed a shiny red apple from the fruit bowl on the kitchen counter. "Safe to say I've chucked the rules out the window when it comes to Cash."

Jane put Maddox in his high chair, where he attacked the rest of his chicken nuggets and ketchup. "Cash, huh? Sexy name."

"Sexy man." *Sexy ass. Sexy smile. Sexy, large hands.* A sigh escaped her. "He's helping me with my phobia."

Jane poured a glass of white wine and handed it to Dreama. "Is he some kind of therapist?"

"Yeah. Sort of." She took a large sip. "Okay, not really. He's using a technique he used for a traumatized dog."

The sides of Jane's lips twitched. "What is he working on first? Teaching you to sit or how to roll over?"

Dreama couldn't help smirking. "More like he's teaching me to beg. He's acting as my Dominant."

Jane grabbed the bottle of wine and, perhaps realizing she was pregnant and therefore couldn't drink, handed the sucker over to Dreama. "Wow. Are you sure you trust him? I know you think he was innocent—"

"Yes. I trust him completely."

"Aren't you worried someone will find out and you'll lose your job?"

If anyone would understand, it was Jane. She'd gone through a similar dilemma not long ago when she'd helped Ryder uncover whether her employer—owned by Ryder's father—was behind the theft of Ryder's proprietary software.

"Last night, Cash brought something to my attention I'd never considered." Dreama sat at the kitchen table, leaving the wine on the counter. One glass was enough. "I love being a parole officer, don't get me wrong, but at some point, I became more focused on beating Meg than the job itself."

Jane didn't blink.

"You don't look surprised," Dreama said.

Jane plopped down in the chair beside her and rested her hands on her belly. "I lived with you for a long time. You might have mentioned your rivalry with Meg a time or two."

"Why didn't you say anything?"

"I would have if I didn't think you loved your job." Jane reached out and took her hand. "But you've always been passionate about helping people make the most of their second chance. Has that changed?"

"No."

"What will you do if you have to choose between Cash and your job?"

The thought of having to choose filled her stomach with dread. She didn't want to lose either one.

A door closed and heavy footsteps neared, bringing the scent of pizza with them. "I come bearing gifts," Ryder announced. He strolled into the kitchen carrying two large pizza boxes.

Finn followed right behind with a box of donuts. "Hey, Dreama."

Jane turned in her chair, eyes excited. "Gimme, gimme."

What had started as the enticing scent of pizza morphed into one that reminded Dreama of rotting garbage. "Oh yuck. What is that smell?"

Ryder handed one of the boxes to Jane. "That is Jane's sardine, pineapple, and mushroom pizza. Don't worry. I got a normal one for us."

Dreama missed living with Jane, but as she watched Jane dig into her pizza, she realized she didn't miss Jane's weird pregnancy cravings.

Ryder kissed the top of Jane's head and planted one on Maddox's messy cheek. "Hey, big guy. Did you miss your daddy?"

Maddox gave Ryder a huge toothless grin and gleefully shouted, "Sex."

Ryder glared at her with a raised brow. "I see your auntie Dreama taught you a new word."

What could she say?

"A good vocabulary is a sign of high intelligence," Dreama reminded him, holding back laughter.

Ryder shook his head, but she knew he wasn't really mad. She'd bet the entire contents of her wallet that he said much worse around Maddox all the time. If she was wrong, well, he could have her eight dollars.

Finn and Ryder joined them at the table with the pepperoni pizza.

"I met with Browner," Ryder said, handing her a paper plate and a piece of pizza. "He's one tenacious son of a bitch, I'll tell you that. I had to sit through an hour-long spiel of how he could turn my billions into... well, more billions. I think I glazed over about ten minutes into drinks. He mostly spent the time bragging about his extensive client list. The guy is an asshole and skirts the edge of ethics on taxes, but he didn't recommend anything that wasn't legal. I wish I had something to help you."

Darn it. She knew it was ridiculous, but she had hoped he'd be the stereotypical sleazy lawyer offering to help break fifty laws to make his client a buck.

"What about you?" she asked Finn. "Did you find anything about Browner?"

Looking thoughtful, he chewed his pizza. "Not exactly. He was only at the public defenders' office for two years before he was offered a job at his current firm. You were right that most of his cases ended with a plea deal, but his average was on par with other public defenders."

Disappointment hit her low and hard. She'd been sure Browner had something to hide. "So that's a dead end too."

"Maybe not." Finn took a second slice of pizza and dropped it onto his plate. "Browner left the public defenders' office to go work for his current firm about a month after your client's plea deal. That in itself doesn't raise any red flags. What was weird is he made partner almost immediately."

"What's weird about that?" she asked.

With two slices of that disgusting pizza still on her plate, Jane opened the box of donuts, stuffing one into her mouth and tearing another into bite-sized pieces onto the tray of Maddox's high chair. Dreama motioned for a donut. Knowing Jane, if she didn't take one now, she might not get the chance.

"On average," Finn said, "attorneys only make partner in a big firm like that after eight years."

Dreama put the chocolate-frosted donut on her plate. "How did Browner do it, then?"

"According to a friend of mine who works at a competing law firm, Browner brought a couple big accounts into the firm in his first year and threatened to walk with them unless the practice made him partner."

"What kind of accounts are you talking about?" Ryder asked.

"One of the big three auto companies and the country's largest steel mill. I confirmed that Browner started representing them the same year he started working at the practice."

"He's a decent schmoozer but he's not that good," Ryder said. "If Browner brought those companies in, he must have had friends in high places."

The question was which friends.

"You mentioned he bragged about his accounts," Finn said to Ryder. "Do you remember which ones?"

Ryder grimaced as Jane put her donut on her pizza and ate both together. "He definitely brought up the auto and steel companies, but he also mentioned representing several urgent medical care and veterinary clinics."

It was as if the heavens opened up and a rainbow began shining through the ceiling. Okay, maybe that was a bit overly dramatic, but the word *veterinary* definitely gave Dreama goose bumps. "Vet clinics? One of the people who reported that my client had been drinking the night of the accident owns a bunch of vet clinics."

Finn folded his pizza slice in half. "Sounds like a lead to me."

Maybe it wasn't a great lead, but it was the only one she had. The problem was now that she had it, how was she going to follow that lead without getting herself killed?

* * *

Fresh from the shower, Cash heard his sister talking to her cats as he wrapped his towel around his waist. The house that had seemed so big to him as a child had gotten a lot cozier now that he and Rebecca were adults. He couldn't deny it was an improvement over a prison cell, but lack of privacy was definitely becoming an issue. A couple of nights ago while on the way to the bathroom, he'd overheard a quiet buzzing coming from her bedroom. There were some things a person did not want to think about when it came to their sibling, and masturbation was one of them.

Then last night, he'd stumbled home at two and found

Rebecca awake with insomnia, wondering where the hell he'd been. He hadn't lied exactly. He'd simply skirted around the truth, explaining he'd been on a date. Thankfully, she'd been too tired to bother with follow-up questions, but knowing Rebecca, they were coming.

Between his training with the Dominatrix at Club X and his sessions with Dreama, he would be out late most nights. He didn't know what to tell Rebecca about where he was going. His sister didn't need to know about his sexual penchant for domination. But he also wouldn't lie to her.

Dressed in a pair of comfortable jeans and a black T-shirt, he went into the kitchen to grab a quick bite to eat before he headed to Dreama's. He'd already spent a couple hours after work with Mistress Naomi, learning about different floggers and the various techniques that could be used with them. Just the thought of flogging Dreama was enough to make his blood pump extra hard and his head spin in circles. He felt like an eager schoolboy about to get to second base.

He opened the fridge and found a carton of leftover Chinese. Not bothering to heat it in the microwave, he dug right in, eating the sweet and sour chicken as if it were his last meal. He'd gone eight years without having the choice of ordering food from whatever restaurant he wanted. The simple act of eating leftover Chinese food was something he'd never take for granted again.

Rebecca shuffled into the kitchen wearing an old pair of pajamas and a ratty robe, her eyes red rimmed and bloodshot.

There was a reason Rebecca had chosen to work for the animal shelter rather than open her own practice where she could earn twice the amount of money. She had a huge heart. Ever since she was little, she'd been the kind of girl who'd tried to mend the broken wing of a bird and befriended the friendless in school. But she'd also been the girl who had hidden her emotions inside when she discovered that the bird could no longer fly and when the previously friendless kid dumped her for a more popular student.

At work today, she'd kept it together, but Cash knew better. She'd been as wooden as Pinocchio, her voice monotone. She wasn't taking Nancy's death well.

Maybe he should cancel his plans with Dreama and stay home tonight.

She pulled out some bread and peanut butter and robotically began making a sandwich. He leaned against the counter and waited for her to acknowledge him. When she didn't, he took it upon himself to make the first move.

"Becs," he said, putting his carton down on the counter. He turned her toward him and threw his arms around her. "I'm so sorry." She was so tiny, she fit under his chin as he rocked her back and forth. "I know I haven't been around, but I'm here for you now. Talk to me."

She sobbed noiselessly against his chest, her body shaking. Cash rubbed her back in large circles, like his dad used to do to them when they'd cried as kids.

"It's so unfair," she said, her voice muffled by his shirt. "Last week, Nancy had just gotten the good news from her doctor that the surgery and radiation on her breast cancer

had worked. For months, she'd worried she was going to die
and as soon as she learned she wouldn't, someone killed her."
She looked up at him. "Who would do such a thing, Cash?"

He wished he had an answer for her. He'd spent years
with criminals and one of the things he learned was never to
underestimate a person's capacity for evil. There were some
guys there who'd committed bad acts but regretted their
actions. Others were rotten to the core. Problem was, from
the outside, it was impossible to discern the monsters from
the men.

"I don't know, Becs. I just don't know. Bad things happen
to good people. Women are attacked in their homes, beaten
and murdered for no reason other than being in the wrong
place at the wrong time," he said, thinking about Dreama
being home sick rather than at work during her break-in.

Rebecca took a step back and frowned. "How do you
know Nancy was at the wrong place at the wrong time? Do
you know something about her murder that I don't know?"

Guilt slammed into him. He could tell himself he had a
good reason for keeping the murder a secret from Rebecca
and Dreama—there was no reason to worry them when
Nancy's murder most likely had nothing to do with
Dreama's attack—but truth was, keeping secrets was no
better than lying. Eventually, it would all blow up in his
face, regardless of good intentions...just as it had with
Maddie.

"No. I just meant it in the general sense." He squeezed
Rebecca's shoulder. "There isn't always an explanation for
why things happen." He should know. It had been sheer

luck that he'd survived the car accident while Maddie had died, taking their secret to the grave.

"I feel as if everything is falling apart. I know this isn't significant compared to what happened to Nancy, but the shelter is completely full right now and I only have until Friday to find another shelter or foster families for the animals."

"What happens if you don't?"

"The older dogs and the ones with health issues are euthanized. It doesn't happen often, but since it's after the winter holidays, less people are looking to adopt a pet. I hate this part of my job."

A lump formed in his throat as he thought of Butch. The dog was old and came with health issues. If Rebecca didn't find him a home, he would be one of the first to be euthanized.

Rebecca zeroed in on his wet hair. "You're going out?"

"Yeah. I've got another date." *Date* seemed like an understatement for what he had planned, but it was as good as any.

"I'm glad. What's her name?" she asked excitedly. "Where'd you meet her? At the shelter?" She winced, looking horrified. "Oh, please tell me it's not Laci."

"It's not Laci," he assured her, pleased to see his sister in a better mood. "It's no one from the shelter. If things get more serious, I promise to give you all the details, okay?"

"Okay." She took a giant bite of her sandwich, and with a mouth full of peanut butter said, "Oh, you got some mail. It's by the front door."

He shook his head and chuckled as he left the kitchen to get his mail. His sister was perfect and polite around everyone else. Only he was lucky enough to witness her disgusting habits like talking with her mouth full and leaving a glob of toothpaste in the sink. He might not have privacy, but at least he had a sister who he'd want as his friend even if they weren't related.

He put on his coat and snatched the envelopes on his way out the door. Shuffling through the junk mail, he stopped when he saw the hospital's return address.

Inside were the toxicology results that he'd requested.

Results that could change everything.

SEVENTEEN

Dreama tried to play it casual when she opened her apartment door for Cash. She had changed out of her professional attire and was wearing a pair of jeans and a comfy off-the-shoulder sweater. Not the sexiest clothes, but they were comfortable. She figured greeting him in fetish wear would be a little much for tonight, especially because she didn't know what he had planned.

"Hi, I was just..." *Waiting for you.* No, that would sound too desperate. She glanced at the sleeve of cookies in her hand and lifted it in offering. "Eating Oreos. Want one?"

What could she say? She'd eaten the pizza and donuts hours ago (well, two) and she had a tendency of eating junk food when she was nervous. She'd been dying to tell him about what she'd learned from Finn.

"No, thanks," he said distractedly, putting the navy gym bag he'd brought with him onto the carpet. "You were right."

She couldn't take her gaze off the bag, her imagination running wild. What was in there? Ropes? Something for another one of his trust exercises? A change of clothing? The mystery of it was torture for her.

"Wait, what?" She realized she'd been so fixated on the bag, she hadn't noticed he'd taken off his coat and boots and was standing there with something in his hand. "What was I right about?"

He smoothed out a folded piece of paper and handed it to her. "This."

Her stomach took a nosedive.

It was his toxicology report.

At the top of the page were his name, date of birth, and age. *Aw, how sweet.* His birthday was on Valentine's Day.

She scanned the rest of the page, her eyes drawn to the positives in the results column. "I don't understand. This is positive." *Damn.* She'd been hoping the test would prove he hadn't been drinking.

But wait. Her eyes narrowed on the page. There were *two* positives. She shifted her gaze to the list of drugs and matched them up with the results.

"For alcohol *and* marijuana," Cash said at the same time she saw it for herself. "The alcohol I could have believed, but not the marijuana." He scratched his head. "I suppose the hospital could have made an error and these results belong to someone else or maybe the test was defective—"

"Or the test results were rigged," she said, lowering the results to her side. It wouldn't have been easy to do, but it wasn't out of the realm of possibility.

"Or they were rigged," Cash echoed. "But there's no way to prove it."

Not yet. But this report along with Browner's failure to discuss the Breathalyzer and toxicology reports with Cash definitely raised a red flag. They were on the right track even if they weren't exactly sure what track they were on.

She gestured for Cash to join her on the couch. "I've got news too. According to Finn, Stephen Browner left the public defender's office for private practice shortly after representing you, bringing some big clients into the firm along with him, including one that owned a chain of veterinary clinics."

"You think it was Jay Moran?" He drummed his fingers on his thigh, something she noticed was a nervous habit of his.

She wished she had the ability to calm him. It was the submissive's role to take care of her Dom. If she could touch him, she'd take his hand and squeeze it. Her chest ached from her need to relieve his tension. "I don't know."

"Even if it was Moran, it could be a coincidence."

"Do you really believe that?" she asked.

He blew out a breath. "No, but if it is him, I don't have a logical explanation for why a guy I never met told the police I'd been drinking and then gave his business to the lawyer who'd represented me." He dropped his head into his hands and groaned. "I need to speak to Moran."

"No." Restless, she got up on her knees. "If he's connected to Browner, then he'll tip him off that we're still looking into your past."

"Shit, Dreama. We don't have a lot of options." Head in hands, he turned to look at her. "What do you suggest?"

They could keep digging into Browner and Moran, but as of now, they were directionless. If only they had more to go on.

She did have an idea, but it was a bit...unorthodox. "I mentioned this to you yesterday, but we were interrupted by my mother's phone call. There's a psychologist I know. Her name's India. Her specialty is treating victims of violence. I think she's also a licensed hypnotherapist."

The divot between his brows made a reappearance. "You want her to hypnotize me?"

"It's worth a shot, isn't it?" she asked. "Maybe she can help you remember what happened the night of the accident."

He stared at her for so long, she was sure he would refuse. That's why she was shocked when he gave her a single nod. "Sure. If you want me to try it, I will."

"I'll call India first thing in the morning. In the meantime, I'll have Ryder contact Browner and ask him for some references. Maybe he can confirm that Moran is one of Browner's clients."

Cash sat back, throwing his arm over the top of the couch so that his fingers stopped just short of her shoulders. Like last night, she could feel the heat radiating off his skin and warming her own. It was as if she was in front of a roaring fire after spending hours caught in a snowstorm. "You can't keep asking the McKays for help. I'm sure they have better things to do with their time."

Aside from his father's multi-billion-dollar conglomerate, Ryder and Jane owned a restaurant automation company. Finn, on the other hand, was currently unemployed as far as she knew. But even with their responsibilities, they would always have her back.

"Jane McKay is family to me and by extension, so are Ryder and Finn," she explained. Figuring it would just confuse him, she didn't bother adding that Ryder's best friend Tristan was engaged to her cousin Isabella. "There's nothing more important than family. I'm sure you feel that way about Rebecca."

His throat worked over a swallow. "I do."

Even though she'd been an only child, she'd never been deprived of family. While she had more cousins than she could possibly fit in her apartment, Cash's wistful expression reminded her that Cash and Rebecca only had each other. "Have you put your information into those adoption websites yet?"

"No." He huffed out a tight laugh. "Haven't exactly had the time these past couple of weeks."

She wouldn't push, but she had a feeling there was something preventing him. "Like I said, there's nothing more important than family. If you really want to do it, make the time."

He was quiet for a long moment. "What if I find them and they're disappointed in me?"

As much as she loved parents, she'd often felt as though she would never earn their approval. It didn't matter what she accomplished because her mom would inevitably rip it apart until she found something to worry about and her father would stay quiet on the matter in an effort to remain neutral. Her job working with ex-felons was too dangerous. *Consumer Reports* gave a low safety grade on the new car she'd bought. Worse, living alone in an apartment brought along the increased risk of another physical attack. All she wanted was the acknowledgment that they respected her choices and were proud of her.

"They won't be disappointed in you," she said quietly, shifting on the couch to angle toward him. "But if for some reason they are, then that's on them and not you. You're amazing. You could have spent your time in prison being bitter and angry. Instead, you got your degree and started a program that benefited both prisoners and dogs. Anyone would be lucky to call you family."

"Thank you." His gaze lowered to her mouth and remained fixed.

She recognized that look. It belonged to a man who was thinking of kissing her.

Just like that, the mood changed and the space between them suddenly crackled with tension. What would it feel like to have his lips on hers? She imagined he'd kiss much in the same way he'd approached their scene last night. Mindful of her comfort while never allowing her to forget for a second that he was in total control.

Heat blasted through her chest and trickled down to her core. She couldn't remember the last time she'd wanted to kiss a man this badly. While she'd fucked a considerable amount of men, she could count on one hand the number she'd kissed. To her, kissing had always been more intimate. It implied *feelings*.

So, what did it mean that she couldn't think of anything else she'd rather do than kiss Cash Turner?

It was one thing to be attracted to Cash, but it was quite another to have feelings for him. Eventually, one of them was bound to get hurt, and the thought of hurting him was almost worse than being hurt herself.

None of it mattered anyway because as much as she wanted to kiss him, there was a part of her that was still terrified of the contact. It was definitely quieter than it had been before, but it was there, like a subtle buzzing in the back of her mind.

Her pulse took off like a speeding jet on a runway. She wasn't sure how it had happened, but Cash's mouth had somehow moved closer to hers. She turned away from him, breaking the connection.

There was no scenario in which kissing him wouldn't end in disaster.

"How are you feeling about what we did last night?" he asked, confirming what her body had been telling her.

Sometime within the last couple of minutes, their roles had shifted from parole officer and parolee to Dom and sub. It reminded her that even if he had been thinking of kissing her, he would never cross that line without her consent.

"You mean the dancing with no hands thing?" she asked. "Or the sleeping thing?"

"Both."

"I wasn't scared if that's what you're asking." She had nothing to fear from Cash, at least not physically.

He stood, his gaze sliding toward his bag before resting on her. "You ready for more?"

* * *

If it weren't for Dreama, Cash would have never known there was a chance he hadn't been intoxicated the night of the accident. It didn't change the fact that he had been driving the car when it had smashed into the concrete barrier, and it didn't absolve his lingering guilt over Maddie and Joshua's deaths, but it might give him a reason to one day forgive himself for it.

No one had ever stuck their neck out for him like Dreama was doing. It awed him as much as it worried him. He hadn't loved Maddie, but he'd also never wished her harm. On the contrary, he'd married her to protect her from it.

Now that he was older, he could see how easy it had been for Maddie to manipulate him because of his protective nature. Ever since his father had died, he'd felt responsible for the women in his life. Even with Thomas stepping in to help, Cash had considered himself the man of the house. It had been his duty to keep his sister and his mom safe.

Maybe that was part of the reason he was drawn to sexual domination. In daily life, it simply wasn't possible to control the people or situations around him. Only when it came to sex could he expect it.

With Dreama, he was beginning to develop an overwhelming need to protect her both in and out of the bedroom, no matter what it cost him. What happened within these walls had nothing to do with their everyday roles. It was the only time he had the power to keep her completely safe, and he didn't plan on wasting a minute of it.

Dreama's pupils dilated right before him, her eyes darkening and smoldering with heated interest. "What did you have in mind?"

He could get used to the way she looked at him. It made him feel worthy and desired. "I was thinking we could introduce a toy or two. I promise, there won't be any contact between my skin and yours."

At least not yet.

She didn't blink. "I trust you."

He certainly hoped so because he planned on testing that trust tonight. "Go to your room and stand in front of the bed."

Her lips twitched right before she pivoted on her bare feet and flounced to the bedroom with an obvious sway to her hips that pulled his gaze straight to her ass. That outfit of hers was killing him. Whether she was wearing one of her starchy suits or a corset, she always looked sexy, but seeing her in a pair of relaxed jeans and a baggy sweater made her seem like the girl next door, a girl who was very much a woman in the bedroom.

Cash gave her a couple of minutes to anticipate what he had planned for her. Tonight wouldn't only test her trust in him. It would also test his self-restraint. If he didn't get a taste of her soon, he was likely to combust. But his first responsibility was to Dreama and the limits they'd set. That meant he'd have to get creative. It was fortunate that he had perfected his imagination during those long eight years without a woman.

He picked the duffel off the floor and swung it over his shoulder. Everything he needed for tonight's scene was in that bag, as well as a change of clothing and his toiletries for the morning.

Adrenaline coursed through him as he crossed into her bedroom. Dreama was waiting just as he'd ordered. Only she had gone one step further, assuming a submissive pose, standing with her legs apart and her hands behind her back. His groin tightened, stealing the blood from other parts of his body. It was a heady feeling to have such a strong, capable woman surrender to him.

He wouldn't let her down. Not if he could help it.

But the time for coddling was over.

"What's your safe word again?"

Her eyes dilated. "Marathon."

"Undress for me," he said, his voice low and rough.

It was time to push her boundaries.

EIGHTEEN

The heat in Cash's eyes and the gravelly sound of his voice instantly made Dreama wet.

But part of her was terrified.

Before her attack, she'd never worried about her body. Even though modern society would consider her fat, she'd always been comfortable in her skin. But now that skin was covered in ugly pink scars. Other than her doctors and nurses, no one had seen her naked in more than a year.

Cash would be the first.

Her hands were shaking as she caught the bottom of her sweater in her hands, pulled it over her head, and dropped it on the floor. Cash stood stock-still, his gaze growing more hooded by the moment. The scars on her arms and upper abdomen didn't appear to have diminished his appreciation of her body at all. If anything, he looked hungrier for her. It gave her the courage to keep going.

With her gaze trained on Cash, she reached behind her and unhooked her bra. Slowly, she peeled the straps down her arms until the lacy fabric floated to the floor. Cash's mouth parted and his tongue moistened his lips, leaving them as shiny and juicy as ripe fruit. The air wafted over her breasts, bringing out goose bumps, and her nipples tightened into hard little buds.

She threw back her shoulders, becoming more confident every moment.

"God, you're gorgeous," Cash said, his voice coming out scratchy and raw. "I've never seen a more beautiful woman."

Her hands slid down the sides of her rib cage, coming to rest at the button of her jeans. "Does that mean you want me to continue?"

He swallowed hard. "Fuck yeah."

She flicked open the button and unzipped her jeans, then slid them off her legs. *Here goes nothing.* Now clad in only a lacy black G-string, she bent over, giving Cash a full view of her ass as she removed them.

When she straightened, the sight of Cash nearly knocked her off her feet. It was more than the way he unapologetically ate her up with his eyes. It was in the way he seemed to be reining in his desire for her, evident by the fists at his sides and the considerable bulge at the placket of his jeans.

Heat swelled in her lower belly.

He moved closer, his gaze sweeping over her like a gentle wind. Each and every one of her scars was visible, but his body language didn't change. He studied them in the same manner as he did the rest of her—with passion, heat, and longing.

His acceptance compelled her to map out her scars,

beginning with the ones on her arms. She wanted him to know her. *Really* know her. And her scars weren't only healed incisions. They told the story of what she'd endured. "He shattered the bones. The surgeon was able to reset them, although I needed plates and screws in my forearms. When it rains, my elbows ache. Otherwise, they don't cause any problems."

His silence gave her permission to continue.

"My legs, on the other hand, hurt every day. They're stiff when I get up in the morning and shortly after, they start aching. That pain is actually manageable, although it gets worse as the day progresses. It's the scars that hurt the most. I have scar neuropathy. Sometimes, it feels like there's a knife slicing through my skin. I take over-the-counter pain relievers for it, but it only takes the edge off. Luckily, it doesn't bother me every day."

She had to give Cash credit. He remained quiet even as the knuckles of his fists turned a purplish red.

She ran her hands over the smattering of small scars on her upper abdomen. "I suffered internal bleeding. My heart actually stopped beating for a minute on the operating table. They had to remove my spleen and"—her hands slipped lower—"I required a full hysterectomy."

That was the first time she'd spoken those words out loud. It was freeing, as if talking about it had instantly healed a festering wound.

"You know what I see when I look at you?" Cash said, striding toward her. "I see lush, womanly curves, and full breasts tipped with nipples I want in my mouth. I see softness that will cradle my cock perfectly and silky flesh I can't wait to touch. On your sweet pink pussy, I see gleaming moisture that I dream about tasting, and on your body, I see the marks of a survivor, ones I someday plan on worshipping with my tongue. And do you know why, Dreama? Because they're all a part of you. You know I find you beautiful, but *beautiful* isn't strong enough to capture the way I see you. You're more than beautiful. You're everything that's right in this world."

No one had ever said anything like that to her before. Her heart seemed as if it had suddenly expanded in her chest, filled with adoration for Cash. Standing there, naked and vulnerable before him, she felt like a goddess. "Thank you."

"You don't need to say thank you," he said. "Not when you can show your gratitude. Lie down on the middle of the bed, faceup, legs spread and arms stretched out overhead in a V."

Lust washed away her anxiety as she put herself into position. Her pussy throbbed, her arousal dripping down her inner thighs. He hadn't even started the scene, but if she didn't come soon, she was going to cry. She was so turned on that if she'd been with any other Dom, her fingers would be inside her. But she respected Cash too much to disobey.

A shirtless Cash stood to the right of her with a flogger in his hand, looking positively sinful and every bit in his element. As if promising things to come, he ran his fingers over the thick knotted leather strands.

She trembled, jealous of the flogger that got to experience Cash's caress.

His gaze fixed on the spot between her legs. "How wet are you?"

"So wet."

"Use your hands and show me your pussy," he ordered. "I want to see how wet you really are."

Spreading herself like that was an incredibly intimate act. It embarrassed her, even as it excited her. Humiliation was one of her kinks.

"Tonight, I want you so wet, you're swimming in it." He lifted the flogger into the air.

* * *

Cash's cock was so hard, it was excruciating. Dreama's submission was like plunging whiskey directly into his veins, giving him a hot rush of pleasure and making him feel high.

He felt as if he could do anything. *Be anything.*

Her eyes were unfocused, her pupils like a full moon. She looked as high as he felt. Her gaze fell to the flogger in his hand and she smiled as if she knew what was coming next.

She didn't.

"Flip to your stomach," he ordered.

Having a naked Dreama on her stomach, unable to see what he was about to do to her, was a fantasy come true. The flogger's weight was heavy in his hands.

His need to touch her creamy skin and taste her wet pussy had become an obsession. The flogger would enable him to do both.

Starting at the base of her neck, he swept the ends of the

flogger over her skin, substituting the leather for his finger-tips. She gasped, her rib cage jumping as if she'd hiccupped.

He continued his exploration of her skin, dragging the falls over the curve of her shoulders, down the length of her spine, and across her shoulder blades. Teasing her by skipping her delicious rounded ass, he trailed the leather down her thighs to her ankles.

She restlessly ground her pelvis into the mattress. Another time, he would punish her for it, but tonight was about conditioning her to equate his touch with pleasure.

Cash caressed the cheeks of her ass with the falls, making sure to touch every inch of it. As if begging for more, she bucked upward and quivered as he teased her crack with the ends of the buttery leather.

"Time to turn over and show me that wet pussy of yours, Dreama," he ordered, grabbing a couple of disinfectant wipes from his duffel and cleaning the flogger.

She groaned as she flipped to her back. Her lips glistened as if she'd been licking them, and that wasn't the only part wet. Her pussy was absolutely drenched.

His mouth watered at the image of her splayed out on the bed for him. He wanted to feast on her, to bite those tempting breasts and eat her pussy until she screamed his name.

To give his aching cock a bit of relief, he unsnapped his jeans and quietly drew down the zipper. Then he returned to his exploration of Dreama's body, only this time on her front. He used the flogger in lieu of his fingers, running the falls across her neck, her tits, her belly, and her legs.

Only when she whimpered and trembled did he decide it

was time to give them both some relief. Her skin was slick with perspiration.

He'd kept her on the edge for long enough.

It was time to finish it.

Dipping the leather between her spread thighs, he coated the strands with her arousal.

"Watch me," he commanded.

Her eyes popped wide open.

Finally giving himself what he craved, he brought the wet leather to his lips and licked it clean. Like the woman, her taste was sharp and strong on his tongue. "I knew you'd be delicious."

She watched him with glazed eyes as he flipped the flogger in his hand and sucked the handle into his mouth. Once it was good and wet, he positioned it directly upon her swollen clitoris and stroked it. He tightened his fingers around the wrapped leather of the handle to keep himself from touching her. "You have my permission to come."

He slid the handle inside her pussy and moved it in and out of her a few times before returning to tease her clitoris. Over and over, he continued that pattern, alternately fucking her with the handle and manipulating her clit.

His cock pulsed with need and his heart banged a rapid beat in his chest. He hadn't even exerted himself and sweat was dripping down the side of his face. Imagining his cock inside of her warm, wet pussy, he thrust his hips in tempo with the flogger.

When her body shook and arched in climax, he couldn't restrain himself any longer. On the razor's edge of control, he tossed the flogger onto the floor and climbed onto the mattress, perching himself above her. He shoved his jeans and underwear down to mid-thigh. His cock sprang from its confinement, the head of it already soaked with pre-cum. "My turn, baby."

Sleepy eyes watched him as he gripped the base of his cock and stroked himself from root to tip. His need to come went beyond the physical.

He needed to brand her with a part of himself.

"Don't forget that it was my hand wrapped around that flogger," he reminded her. "Who made your pretty pussy ache, Dreama?"

Her gaze sharpened. "You."

Fire licked at his balls as he moved his hand faster and faster. "And who took that ache away? Who made you feel good?"

"You." She smiled. "Cash."

His name on her lips was all it took for heat to shoot down his spine, then up the length of his cock. Spurts of come splashed across her flushed breasts, marking her as his.

She just didn't know it yet.

NINETEEN

Ten minutes early, Dreama shook the snow out of her hair before walking into India's waiting room. Just as she'd assumed, India had been booked solid for the entire month, but when Dreama had explained Cash's unusual situation, India had agreed to stay late to see him tonight.

That morning, she'd opened her eyes and found Cash still asleep beside her. Even with a comforter and pillows between them, she felt the warmth permeating from his body. It was the first time she'd woken up with a man in her bed. She'd broken one of her rules, but for some reason, it didn't bother her.

The more time she spent with him, the harder it became to see him as her parolee. She couldn't allow herself to forget that what they were doing within the four walls of her apartment was ethically wrong. But why did it feel so right?

Tonight, she'd have to remember to act completely professionally around him. Although India wouldn't report her to Meg, Dreama didn't want to put her in an uncomfortable position. It wasn't common for a parole officer to attend therapy with a parolee.

It was Dreama's first time seeing India in her actual office. All of her previous sessions had been in the hospital and rehabilitation center. She was supposed to have set up an appointment upon her release from rehab, but she'd never called, making excuse after excuse to herself as to why. There wasn't enough time. Therapy couldn't help. It was better to focus on the future than the past.

The truth was she'd been scared. Talking to a therapist accessed painful memories and forced her not only to confront them head-on, but also to find solutions to deal with them. Although she was a trained social worker, the whole process had overwhelmed her. Rather than face it, she'd made justifications as to why she didn't require therapy, but thanks to Cash, she had begun to reconsider. After all, if she was willing to risk her career to prove his innocence, shouldn't she be willing to risk as much for herself? Maybe she'd make an appointment for herself soon.

Dreama sat on the couch as she waited for Cash to arrive. She'd left him a voice mail earlier today letting him know she'd made the appointment and he'd texted her later that he'd gotten it. What if he changed his mind and wasn't coming? Last night, he'd seemed open to trying hypnosis, but she'd understand if he was too scared to face his past. If anyone understood, it was Dreama.

She couldn't believe how far she'd come in only two nights of Cash's domination. Watching him lick her climax off the flogger's strands was one of the hottest things she'd ever seen in her life, second only to watching Cash stroking himself off. The moment his tongue lavished its attention on the leather was the same moment her desire to touch him eclipsed her fear. She'd been *this close* to begging him to fuck her when he'd fisted his cock and gave her the show instead. Just thinking of his hot cum splashing on her breasts made her grow wet between her legs.

She was practically squirming in her spot as a snow-covered Cash stomped inside the waiting room, bringing with him some appreciated cold air. "Sorry I'm late. It took me an extra twenty minutes to get here because of the weather." He unwrapped the cable-knit black scarf from around his neck and unzipped his coat.

"No problem," she said a little breathlessly, thanks to her arousal.

The intensity of his gaze pinned her in place. It took her back to last night when she'd sworn he'd been thinking of kissing her. And she had to wonder, if she didn't have the phobia, would she risk kissing him here in public, where anyone could witness it? How much was she willing to gamble when it came to Cash Turner?

Luckily, Dreama didn't have long to think about her answer before India's door opened.

"Dreama," India said, grabbing both her hands and squeezing them. "It's wonderful to see you again."

She gave India a sincere smile. "You too."

Although she was in her thirties, India could easily be mistaken for a flower child from the seventies. Despite the freezing temperature outside, she had on a flowy turquoise skirt, a sunflower-yellow off-the-shoulder blouse, and Birkenstocks. Like the previous times Dreama had seen her, India wore her black hair in a long braid down her back, no makeup, and dangling beaded earrings.

India released her hands and turned her attention to Cash. "And you must be Mr. Turner. Please, come inside."

Bathed in soft lighting, her office was an explosion of reds and golds and greens. Sparkly throw pillows enhanced the otherwise plain hunter-green couch, colorful blown-glass figurines lined the back of her desk, and in the corner of the room by the bookshelves sat a bongo. Among the photographs on the walls were ones of India riding a camel in the desert, hanging off a mountain, and skydiving with her arms outstretched. It looked as though she'd lived a million adventures in her lifetime.

Dreama was a bit envious. Other than visiting extended family in a handful of nearby states, she'd never traveled anywhere. Then again, she preferred to be suspended in ropes over jumping out of an airplane. Before her attack, she'd taken plenty of risks and enjoyed life to the fullest without ever leaving the state.

"Have a seat." India settled onto a love seat and Cash and Dreama sat on the couch across from her. They made some small talk while Cash filled out a few forms. After, India said, "I understand you're trying to regain the memories of a particular night. You were in a car accident?"

Cash tapped his thigh with his fingers. "Yes."

Dreama could tell Cash was nervous, and once again, she wished she could console him physically.

"Did the hospital mention a concussion or do a CT scan or MRI of your brain to determine if there was a brain injury?" India asked.

"Yeah, my doctor said I had gotten a grade three concussion from the accident," Cash said. "I had a CT scan, but they didn't find any swelling or any other abnormalities. I was told that my memory loss was probably the result of the concussion and that it was possible I'd never get it back."

India nodded. "The brain is an amazing thing. Your doctor didn't lie. A concussion or other head injury can cause permanent memory disruption, but there are several other reasons as well. Drugs and heavy alcohol consumption of course can trigger blackouts and memory loss. And then there are times a trauma can be so overwhelming, our minds reject the information. Until we come to terms with the traumatic event, we cannot remember. It's a way for our brains to protect us from something too painful to accept."

Cash stopped tapping. "But otherwise, it is possible I could recover the memories?"

"Yes, it's possible, but there are no guarantees," India said, crossing her ankles. "It's been eight years since the accident?"

"Yes."

India briefly pressed her lips together. "Normally, I would prefer to use psychotherapy to slowly recover the memories and determine if there's an emotional, psychological, or even psychiatric component to the amnesia. But if you'd like, I can try hypnosis with you."

"Does hypnosis really work?" Cash asked, doubt evident in his tone.

"It does. In addition to having my doctorate in psychology, I'm an experienced certified hypnotherapist." India smiled reassuringly. "I promise you, I won't make you bark like a dog. In fact, I can't make you do anything you don't want to do. You remain in control the entire time."

Dreama knew next to nothing about hypnosis. "How does it work exactly?"

"All hypnosis does is put you into an altered state of consciousness," India explained. "Some people think of it as that place between wakefulness and sleep, but I've always thought of it as tuning in to our internal voice. Have you ever been so deep in thought that you didn't hear someone speaking to you?" she asked Cash. On his nod, she continued. "That was you focusing on your internal voice. It's my role as your hypnotherapist to guide you to that place. If the memories are still accessible, that's where you'll find them."

Cash leaned forward. "I want to try it. Now."

India gave him a nod, then looked at her. "Dreama, you should probably wait in—"

"No," Cash said forcefully. "I'd prefer her to stay."

His words filled Dreama with warmth. It meant that he trusted her. Looking at India, she silently pleaded to stay.

"Fine," India said. "If you believe it will help you relax to have her here."

"It will."

India turned off the lamp beside her. "Then let's get started."

* * *

Cash couldn't believe he'd consented to allowing a stranger to hypnotize him. Before tonight, he didn't even believe in it. Hell, he still didn't believe it could be done. After he'd gotten Dreama's message earlier, he'd almost called to cancel. But then he'd remembered how excited she'd been when he'd agreed. Since the day he'd met her, she'd proven her bravery to him over and over again, first by soldiering through the pain of her physical scars and next by working with him to conquer her emotional ones. By refusing to give up on him, she was risking her career and, more importantly, her life. He couldn't bear the thought of disappointing her.

So, despite his reluctance and his doubts, he was here. If there was even the slightest possibility of hypnosis working, he owed it to himself...and Dreama...and hell, even to Maddie, to give it a shot.

The sound of waves crashing against the surf played softly as India dimmed the overhead lights. "Close your eyes," she said quietly.

Just having Dreama beside him eased his apprehension. For a man who thrived on control, turning his power over to a hypnotherapist wasn't easy for him. He might not trust India—after all, he didn't know her—but he did trust Dreama. He took one final glance at Dreama before shutting his eyes.

India's soft, soothing voice rolled over him. "I want you to breathe in through your nose and out through your mouth."

He followed her instructions and relaxed against the

couch, feeling all the tension leaving his body as he inhaled and exhaled in a rhythm that matched the ebb and flow of the ocean's waves.

"Good," she said, her words sounding as if they were floating around him. "Now I want you to picture yourself at the top of a staircase. I'm going to count backward from ten to one. Each number, you will move down another step, relaxing your body and taking another breath in through your nose until you reach the bottom step."

Within the darkness, a lit wooden staircase appeared directly in front of him, each stair covered with carpet as white as freshly fallen snow. Looking at the bottom, all he could see was the glow of a brilliant orange light. Step by step, he descended the staircase, his bare feet cushioned by the plush carpet. The light seemed to be talking to him, but he couldn't understand what it was saying. As he approached it, a single word became louder and louder. *Cash.* The light was calling out to him, inviting him to enter it. At the end of the staircase, he walked into the warmth and comfort of the light and waited.

"Very good," India said. Her voice sounded as if it were coming from miles away. "Cash, I'm going to ask you to talk about a night from long ago. It's the night you went to the zoo for a party. Do you remember that night?"

"Yes," he said automatically.

"Good. Tell me about getting ready for the event."

Suddenly, the light disappeared and he was standing in front of the mirror of his old apartment bedroom, dressed in his rented tuxedo. If they didn't leave soon, they'd be late.

"I hate this tuxedo. I've been in it for five minutes and I'm already sweating."

"What else do you remember?" India asked.

Behind him, the details of his bedroom became clearer. Dressed in a light blue gown, Maddie was sitting at the edge of their unmade bed, tears streaming down her face.

He'd done that to her. He hadn't meant to tell her tonight, but he couldn't hold it in anymore. So, when she'd asked him if he loved her, he'd finally told her the truth.

"No. I don't love you," he'd said. "I never have. Our marriage was a mistake. I want a divorce."

"Maddie...She's crying." What he'd thought would be his salvation had turned into one of his biggest regrets. The shame of it continued to haunt him to this day. He'd wanted to be free of her, and he'd gotten his wish. "I don't want to talk about it."

"You don't have to," India said gently. "What did you do after you were ready?"

Maddie's makeup was fixed and she was smiling. He knew then she would never let him go. She'd find a way to keep him by her side. She always did.

"We left for the zoo," he told India. "I just wanted to get it over with."

"What over with?"

"The night. Everything." Maddie's incessant chattering about their future. She wanted to paint Joshua's room. They needed to buy a crib. Cash should drop out of college and work for Thomas full-time so that they could afford a house. She was pretending he hadn't asked for a divorce. "I put on the radio." To get Maddie to stop talking. It worked. "We're at the zoo." He parked in the lot by the main entrance.

"What do you see?" India asked.

"A huge white tent filled with people. There's a band playing soft jazz on a stage at the front of the tent. Waiters carrying glasses of champagne. There's a bar in a corner with a long line." Thomas spared no expense for the party. Maddie was in heaven. Cash would rather celebrate with a cold beer at the bowling alley. This wasn't his scene. "I don't really know anyone. I need to congratulate Thomas." And to get away from Maddie. She wouldn't let go of his arm.

India's voice cut through the noise of the party. "Do you find him?"

The images flash in and out. He's no longer in the tuxedo. Now he's outside his own body, watching it all like a movie. "I leave Maddie with some woman she knows from yoga class and go look for him. Michael from work tells me Thomas is getting ready to give his speech and is behind the stage."

"What do you do then?"

There's a wall of white in front of him. He doesn't see anything anymore. "I don't remember."

"Do you stay with Michael? Go back to Maddie?" India asked.

At the mention of Maddie's name, the wall of white parts in the middle. "I go behind the tent to find Thomas." He sees himself walking around the perimeter of the tent, but he stops when he hears some conversation coming from around the corner. "There are two men talking. I don't let them see me, but I listen. I don't like what I'm hearing."

The Cash he's watching has clenched fists and a pounding heart. He's angry.

"Who are the men?" India asked.

His own heart began to race. "I don't know."

"Pretend you have a pair of binoculars and you can see closer," India directed. "Can you make out their faces?"

"No." Not if he wants to keep his hiding spot. If he moves closer, they'll see him. "It's too dark."

"What about their voices? Are they familiar?" India asked.

He listened closer. "One is familiar. The other is new."

"Do you know whose voice it is? What are they saying?"

A red and black danger sign popped up in front of his face and the music playing inside the tent drowned out the two voices of the men. But he'd heard enough to know it wasn't right. He had to warn Thomas. "No, I don't...I don't remember."

"What happened after you heard them talking?"

The space around him turned black. He didn't even see tuxedo Cash anymore. "It's all blank. I don't want to remember it."

"Why?" India asked.

He tried to push away the darkness in his mind and see through it. His heart was beating too fast and the warmth of the orange light was gone. He felt as if he were encased in ice. He had to leave. He had to tell someone. "It hurts too much. I don't want to stay here."

"You see the staircase? It's right in front of you, but before you leave, do you remember drinking champagne?" India asked.

His throat was dry. He thought back to all he'd seen. "No."

Cash followed the sound of India's voice up the steps until he reached the top. Feeling the couch underneath his fingertips, he opened his eyes.

To some degree, the hypnosis had worked. He couldn't believe how easily India had gotten him to remember bits and pieces of that night. It felt as if he'd actually traveled back in time. But at the same time, he was disappointed. As skeptical as he'd been about hypnosis, he'd hoped he'd remember everything leading up to the accident.

He ran his hand down his face and realized he was sweating. "That was a bust."

"Not really," Dreama said, angling toward him on the couch. "You remembered more than you did before hypnosis."

His frustration lingered over not being able to recall what he'd overheard that night. "Nothing that's going to help."

India leaned forward, resting her elbows on her knees. "I don't know you, Cash, so I'm not capable of making a full assessment based on one session, but I can give you my gut impression. I don't think you're dealing with a brain injury. I believe the details about that night are there, available for you to access, when you're ready to face them."

"You think I'm choosing to forget that night because I don't want to know?" Cash stood from the couch, his fingernails poking into the skin of his palms. "That's bullshit. I wouldn't be here if I didn't want to know what happened."

India tilted her head and put both hands up in a defensive manner. "Forgive me. That's not what I'm trying to imply. The brain can repress events it perceives as a threat. The night ended in tragedy. It's possible there's a part of you that wants to protect you from reliving it."

"Then why wouldn't he remember everything up to the crash?" Dreama asked. "He recalled almost everything until he overheard the two men speaking."

Something tugged at his mind. Although he hadn't seen them, he thought he'd recognized a voice. He hadn't heard it in years, so he couldn't be certain, but he knew one way to find out.

Like that night, he needed to speak with Thomas.

"I don't know," India said, rising from the love seat and moving closer to him. "But I wouldn't give up hope. Now that you've begun the process of recalling that night, it's possible you'll start to remember other pieces as well. Give it time."

Time.

They should have plenty.

So, why then did it feel as if they were running out of it?

TWENTY

The next morning, Cash slid into the restaurant booth across the table from Thomas. "Thanks for agreeing to see me."

Thomas poured a creamer into his coffee. "My secretary had already canceled my appointments for this morning, so it's no inconvenience. Besides, I never say no to macadamia nut pancakes."

After his session with India, he'd needed some time alone to process everything. He'd told Dreama he wanted to sleep apart for a night. He'd missed having Dreama beside him, but in the end, he'd made the right decision. He'd barely slept, too busy replaying his recovered memories over and over in his head.

As he'd lain in bed, other things had come back to him, like the music that had been playing and the smell of animals in the air. But still, there were memories that remained out of reach, as if they were locked in a filing cabinet in his brain and he only needed to find the key to open it.

He wondered if India was right and that part of him didn't want to know what happened that night. Even while hypnotized, there were things about Maddie he still refused to say out loud. He'd never told a soul about her suicidal threats and the ways she'd manipulated him into staying with her. Her parents were both alcoholics and had severed ties with her when she went off to college. They hadn't even come to their wedding. Maybe that was why Maddie had clung so tightly to him. She'd been looking for someone to take care of her, and he'd been too young to understand she needed psychiatric care and not a boyfriend.

If he hadn't told her he wanted a divorce, would that night have ended differently? He must have asked himself that question thousands of times throughout the years, and he still didn't have an answer, because every time he started down that path, the same wall that had blocked him during hypnosis slammed down, separating him from coming too close to the truth.

Maddie had been mentally ill. Was it possible she had somehow caused the accident? He'd come out of the hypnosis with a lingering sense of betrayal. What would be worse than finding out Maddie had intended for him to die along with her?

At the same time, he couldn't discount the theory that Browner had something to hide.

Cash had lied to Dreama last night. He had learned something significant from the hypnosis. He was almost positive that the familiar voice he'd overheard the night of the accident belonged to Kevin Sanders, one of the witnesses who claimed to have seen Cash drinking. But until he was sure, he didn't want Dreama to know.

That's why Cash had called Thomas early this morning and asked to meet for breakfast.

"I need to ask you about Kevin Sanders," Cash said after the waitress took their order.

Thomas couldn't have looked more surprised. "Sanders? What about him?"

Cash flipped a creamer over in his hand, weighing how much he wanted to tell Thomas. "The night of the accident, I might have overheard a conversation between him and another person."

Thomas pinched the bridge of his nose. "I'm confused. You said before you didn't have any memory of that night."

"I'm starting to remember."

"After all these years?" Thomas asked. "Did something happen to cause your memory to return?"

Cash hated to admit it, but he didn't have much of a choice. "I saw a shrink. She hypnotized me," he mumbled.

If Thomas thought it was ridiculous, thank goodness he kept his opinion to himself. "What do you think you heard?"

"That's just it. I don't know." Frustrated, Cash took a giant gulp of his coffee. "I was on my way to see you when I heard two men talking. I stopped to listen, but it was too dark to see them. One of the voices was familiar."

Thomas frowned. "And you think it was Kevin Sanders."

Sanders was one of three who'd given a statement to the police that Cash had been drinking. When would

Sanders have witnessed it if the man had been outside the tent?

As Cash ruminated on that question, the waitress came by and topped off their coffee mugs, promising their pancakes would be up shortly.

"That night, did I mention anything to you about overhearing a conversation?" Cash asked.

"No, but to be fair, I might have not given you a chance." Thomas grimaced. "I was running around quite a lot that night. In fact, right after our toast, I went onstage to give a speech."

"I don't remember our toast." If Thomas wasn't inside the tent prior to their toast, how could he have seen Cash drinking the first glass of champagne?

Thomas put his mug down on the table and sat back, folding his arms over his chest. "Kevin Sanders still works for me. He's vice president of operations now. I'll talk with him. See what he remembers."

"You don't have to do that. I'll get the information some other way." Thomas was a scientist, not a detective. If Sanders had something to hide, Cash didn't want to put Thomas in his crosshairs.

"If it's important to you to remember that night, it's important to me. Don't worry." Thomas gave Cash a look that said he understood his apprehension. "I'll be as subtle as I can when I ask him about it."

What was the worst that could happen? If Sanders was working with Browner, he already knew Cash was digging into his past.

"Thank you," Cash said, appreciative of Thomas's offer.

But he was still wondering how Thomas could have witnessed him drinking before the toast. "You said you saw me drinking twice at the party."

Thomas wrapped his hand around his mug. "When you and I shared a toast and then again later."

That wasn't what he'd told Cash previously. "I thought you saw me drinking before our toast."

Thomas nodded as he lifted the coffee to his mouth. "That's right. Sorry. It's been a long time."

Cash couldn't fault him for forgetting a detail or two. Not when there were huge chunks missing from his own memory. Even so, the inconsistency left him unsettled and for the first time, he considered Thomas wasn't being completely honest with him.

"It's weird," Cash said. "My toxicology report came back positive for alcohol and marijuana."

Thomas raised one silver brow. "Marijuana?"

"Before you ask, no, I didn't smoke or otherwise use marijuana." At least he knew that much. "I think the report was doctored in some way."

Deep lines materialized on Thomas's forehead. "Why? What purpose would someone have to alter your results?"

Wasn't that the million-dollar question.

"I don't know, but I'm not going to stop until I find out."

* * *

Dreama's car slid along the ice as she pumped the brakes. It had been steadily snowing since last night and forecasters predicted they'd get another three inches before lunchtime. At least the freezing rain had stopped. The area's school districts had closed for the day, but unfortunately for her, government offices remained open. Still, she'd called her clients to give them an opportunity to reschedule their appointments for another day and they'd all taken her up on the offer. That left her with this morning free to perform the obligatory random parolee home checks.

Parking in the driveway, she wrapped her scarf around her neck and got out of the car. The house was an adorable redbrick Tudor with white shutters and a large picture window on the first floor. Christmas lights hung from the branches of a small tree adjacent to the home's oversized front porch. Thank goodness the sidewalk was clear. With the weather exacerbating her nerve pain, walking was extra difficult this morning.

Her stomach tumbled as she limped toward the front door. She didn't know why she was so nervous. She completed home checks all the time. Oh, who was she kidding? This one meant more to her because it was for Cash. Although the parole office rules restricted her from giving advance notice of her visit, he'd mentioned last night that he wasn't scheduled to work this morning.

After his hypnosis session, he'd walked her to her car and suggested they sleep apart that night. As much as she'd hoped to have him in her bed again, the hypnosis had left him visibly unsettled. Retrieving some of his memories from the night of the accident had obviously taken a toll on him. She didn't blame him for needing to be alone to process it all. It was unfortunate that he hadn't learned anything that could help him. Hopefully India was right and he'd remember more with time.

As for sleep, it hadn't come easy last night, but she was proud to say she'd slept alone in her bed for the first time since moving into the apartment. To anyone else, that wouldn't mean much, but to her, it was a major accomplishment.

Shivering from the cold, she slowly and carefully climbed the porch steps and rang the doorbell. Wind whipped the snow at her back and every time she exhaled, the condensation from her breath created clouds.

The door opened and a woman appeared. "Can I help you?"

"My name is Dreama Agosto," she said, pulling her card from her coat pocket and handing it over. "I'm Cash Turner's parole officer, and I'm here to do a random home check."

The woman glanced at the card. "Cash isn't here. I'm Rebecca, his sister."

"Is he at work?" Dreama schooled her expression, not wanting to give away her disappointment over his absence. Although she had to admit to herself, she was intrigued to finally meet the sister he'd spoken so much about.

"No, I think he's running some errands. I'm not sure when he'll be back."

"As part of his parole, I'm expected to search the house for prohibited items like alcohol, drugs, and weapons. It's not necessary for him to be here. Would you mind if I came in? It should only take a few minutes." Legally, she didn't require permission, but in her experience, she found people responded better if they believed they had a choice.

Smiling wide, Rebecca waved her inside. "I don't mind at all. You must be freezing. Come on in."

If Cash hadn't already mentioned he and Rebecca were adopted, she might have wondered how two siblings could look so different. While Cash was her gentle giant with his large hands, gray eyes, and light complexion, Rebecca was short and small-boned, with brown eyes and radiant dark skin.

Dreama stepped into the house, getting her first glimpse into where Cash not only currently resided, but also where he'd grown up. She removed her coat and tugged off her snowy boots.

"Can I get you something to drink?" Rebecca asked. "Coffee?"

Warming up, Dreama's toes tingled. She discreetly massaged her thigh, hoping the pain would decrease now that she was inside. "I don't want to be a bother."

Rebecca beamed. She was so warm and friendly that it immediately put Dreama at ease. "It's not. I was just about to get a cup for myself."

Anything hot sounded like bliss at the moment. "Well, then sure."

"How do you take it?"

As long as it was coffee, Dreama would drink it. "Black is fine."

Rebecca pointed to the closet. "If you'd like, you can

hang up your coat in there. Feel free to look around while I get our coffee."

As Rebecca disappeared around the corner, Dreama hung up her coat. Turning toward the family room on her left, she nearly jumped when a white cat without ears darted past her. She laughed quietly. According to what Cash had mentioned, there should be another one lurking around somewhere.

Dreama started her search in the adjacent family room. The space was cozy with a pale blue couch with an oak coffee table in front of it and a flat-screen television on the wall across from it. On the left side of the room there was a small bookshelf. She knelt beside it, checking out the titles. The novels were a mix of thrillers, romance, and science-fiction. All appeared worn, as if they'd been read several times.

Beyond the family room was the dining room made up of a rectangular six-seater table and china cabinet. The home's layout was similar to her parents' house located twenty minutes away, only theirs was a traditional colonial rather than a Tudor. In her head, she could almost imagine a younger Cash sitting at the table with his sister and parents.

After passing by the kitchen, she stopped in the hallway to check out the numerous photographs on the wall. As she looked at the wedding photo of Cash's parents, her throat thickened. Even with her overprotective mother, Dreama was fortunate to have parents who were alive and well.

"Here's your coffee," Rebecca said, yanking her out of her musings and handing her a steaming mug.

Dreama took a sip of her coffee, unable to pull herself

from the photographs. It was as if Cash's life story was all there on the wall for her to see. There were photos of him dressed up as Batman and Rebecca dressed as Catwoman, both holding trick-or-treat pumpkin baskets, and the whole family at Disney standing with Mickey Mouse.

"How old was he there?" she asked, pointing at the photo of Cash in a football uniform, together with his team, holding a trophy.

Rebecca lovingly touched the photo with her fingertip. "Twelve, I think. He was good, so good he earned a scholarship to college."

With his solid build, she didn't doubt it. Her gaze drifted over to a picture from Cash's wedding. Wearing a tuxedo, he held Maddie's face in his hands as if he was about to kiss her. It might have made her jealous if it wasn't for the expression on his face. This past week, Dreama had learned what Cash looked like when he wanted to kiss her, and it was nothing like the one in the photograph.

"That's Maddie. Cash's late wife," Rebecca said.

Dreama's cheeks heated when she realized she'd been staring at that wedding photo for much too long. "She was beautiful."

"Mmm. That's about all she was," Rebecca muttered.

"You didn't like her?"

Rebecca sighed and tilted her head to the side. "I can't say I ever got to know Maddie very well, but what I did know . . . Let's just say my mom and I tolerated her for Cash's sake." She turned to Dreama. "There was something not right about her."

"What do you mean?" Dreama asked. Cash hadn't spoken much about Maddie or his marriage.

"I don't know exactly. He wasn't affectionate with her, but she was constantly hanging onto his arm. In the time they were together, I don't think I ever had a conversation with her without Cash by her side, and he was always tense around her. He has this nervous habit of—"

"Tapping his fingers," Dreama said, realizing too late that in finishing Rebecca's sentence, she'd shown an overfamiliarity with Cash.

"Yes." Rebecca's lips curved up. "But you're not here to listen to gossip about Cash's marriage."

Maybe Dreama the parole officer wasn't, but Dreama the woman was eagerly gobbling up every bit of information about Cash that she could.

"You know, Cash didn't mention that his parole officer was a woman," Rebecca continued, her grin growing by the second. "The one who did the home inspection before Cash's release had been a bald older gentleman."

Dreama did her best not to blush. "Reassignments are common." She had a feeling Rebecca saw straight through her. "I should probably finish my inspection. I'm sure you have things to do." Dreama turned around to head toward the kitchen when a photo on the opposite wall of a toddler with a toothy grin and gray eyes caught her attention. Confused, she walked over to it. "Why do you have a photo of Maddox?"

"Maddox?" Rebecca frowned. "That's Cash. I think he was about two at the time."

Dreama's pulse shot into the stratosphere. Cash had seemed familiar to her from the moment she'd first looked into his eyes.

Now she knew why.

Every male McKay shared the same unique gray eyes.

Cash Turner was the missing McKay heir.

TWENTY-ONE

Staring at her reflection in the bathroom mirror, Dreama put a huge smile on her face as she rehearsed delivering the news to Cash. "Funny thing. Turns out, you're Ryder and Finn's brother."

Her smile changed into a scowl. *Ugh.* It didn't sound better no matter how she said it.

She turned away from the mirror and stomped to the kitchen for reinforcements. Cash would be at her apartment in five minutes, and she had no idea how to tell him that he was a McKay.

She tugged on the bodice of her fetish wear. Her leotard didn't leave much to the imagination. She'd made it out of a sheer nude fabric similar to pantyhose, with strategic places covered in bright silver sparkles. Hopefully, telling him while she was wearing it would soften the blow.

She'd called Jane earlier and casually brought up the topic, then inquired into the status of their search and what their private investigator had discovered so far. Over the summer, he had gotten a lead that gave them a birthdate and the name of the adoption agency. Unfortunately, the adoption agency had closed twenty-five years ago and their records had gone missing, presumed to have been dumped in a landfill.

But the birthdate had been all Dreama had needed.

Valentine's Day. Almost thirty years ago. The same day Cash was born.

That alone wasn't enough to conclude he was the missing McKay brother, but add in those unique gray eyes of his and Dreama had no doubts.

Dreama pulled out a tub of chocolate chip ice cream from the freezer. Keeping the secret about Cash from Jane hadn't been easy. She needed advice in the worst way and Jane was typically her go-to person for it. Between Cash being fresh out of prison and their investigation into the accident, maybe now wasn't the best time to throw a major life change into the mix. Although he'd expressed an interest in finding his birth parents, he hadn't taken any action as of yet. To her, it indicated that he wasn't quite ready for the information.

At the same time, how could she sit on something so monumental? Being a McKay meant more than just acquiring two brothers; it also meant acquiring about a *half-billion dollars.*

She shoved a large spoonful of ice cream into her mouth. Cash deserved to know. There was no other choice. She had to tell him. As to the best way? Perhaps it was best to rip it off like a Band-Aid, quick and without warning.

At his knock, she shoved the carton back into the freezer, dropped the spoon into the sink, and hurried to let him in. *Like a Band-Aid.* Taking a deep breath, she opened the door, prepared to blurt out the news before she lost her nerve.

"I think Thomas is lying to me." Carrying his duffel bag, Cash stormed past her without so much as a glance.

"Funny thing," she mouthed to herself. So much for ripping off the Band-Aid. The news would have to wait. She shut the door and followed him into the other room. "What did he lie about?"

An agitated Cash paced along the length of the room. "I met him for breakfast to ask him again about the night of the accident. He told me we shared a toast before he made his speech to the guests and then he saw me drinking another later. But the last time we spoke, he said he'd seen me drinking before our toast."

Cash was so upset, he'd failed to acknowledge her half-naked state. She tried not to take it personally as she rested her back against the wall. "It was eight years ago. He might be confused. Did you ask him to clarify?"

"Yeah. He said he'd misspoken the last time."

She shrugged, not seeing the problem. "Well, then that's probably true. I mean, why lie about it?"

"I don't know. But how could he have seen me drinking before the toast if he wasn't even in the tent?"

Okay, she'd be the first to admit that was a little suspicious, but in the grand scheme of things, it was probably insignificant. Cash hadn't acted anything like this when he'd learned about his negative Breathalyzer or when he'd received his toxicology report. Until tonight, he'd remained even-keeled and rational in spite of everything they'd uncovered.

"You don't know if everything you remembered through hypnosis is one hundred percent accurate. Maybe more time passed between your arrival at the party and the time you went to find him. Or maybe after you overheard the conversation, you went back inside the tent."

Cash stopped pacing. "You're right." Head hanging, he gripped the back of the couch with both hands. "I think regaining some of my memories threw me for a bigger loop than I'd anticipated."

She understood that all too well. Whenever she experienced one of her panic attacks, it was like going through her tragedy all over again. "That must have been difficult for you."

"I was thinking about what India said. What if there are things I don't want to remember?" he asked quietly.

She strode toward him. "Am I pushing you too hard? Do you want to call off our search into your past?"

He shook his head. "If Thomas is lying to me for some reason, I need to know why." His rib cage expanded as he took a deep breath. "We're getting closer to the truth. I feel it in my bones."

Standing directly behind him, she reached out her hands, wanting terribly to console him and remove his torment. She would wrap her arms around his waist, rest her cheek against his back, and use her body as a means of comfort. It was such a simple act. Her fingers were twitching with need. He'd worn an off-white sweatshirt that looked so soft, she could almost feel it pressed against her skin. And he smelled delicious, like oregano and basil. Those were practically pheromones to the Italian in her.

With his chin to his chest and his shoulders hunched, her gentle giant looked broken. If only she could figure out a way to put him back together again.

She didn't think telling him about his parentage right now was going to help. That info was going to have to keep on ice for a while until the time was right.

But maybe there was a way to take his mind off things, if only temporarily.

"Cash?" she said softly. "Let me help you." The greatest gift she could give to him was her submission. If unleashing his sadistic side relieved his inner turmoil, the masochist in her would gladly accept it. "Use my body for your pleasure. I can take it." She lowered herself to the carpet, spreading her thighs apart and leaning forward, splaying her arms out in front of her in offering.

He slowly turned around. His eyes widened as he finally noticed her and what she was wearing. A muscle jumped in his cheek as his jaw tightened. He stared at her as if he was a predator about to devour his prey. "Tell me your safe word." He caught the bottom of his sweatshirt in one hand and yanked it over his head before dropping it onto the floor without a care. She salivated over the way his obliques twisted and tightened from the action. "Because you might need it tonight."

Her pussy clenched at his threat. It had been so long

since she'd experienced real erotic pain, the kind that made her lose herself in subspace. "Marathon." But she doubted she'd need it. She trusted that Cash would respect her limits and wouldn't give her more than she could handle.

Wearing jeans low on his hips, he flicked the button undone. She stared at the bulge behind the fly, wondering if that impressive erection had led to the decision to unbutton those jeans. Maybe *she* was the sadist because she wanted him uncomfortable, aroused, and desperate. She wanted him to feel at least a little of what she was feeling.

All her senses sharpened on him.

Legs spread, she waited patiently for instruction as he walked around her in circles. The minutes ticked by, him saying nothing, revealing nothing. She couldn't ascertain his next move. It put her on edge. She felt like she was a poor helpless gazelle caught in the crosshairs of a hungry lion, knowing it was not a question of *if* he'd strike but *when*. Her breasts grew heavy and achy. A sliver of fear darted through her middle, making her body tremble.

Her breathing grew shallower and more rapid with every minute that passed. The air became thick with anticipation. She could practically taste it on her lips. Her fingers tingled on her thighs. She wanted to touch him.

Holy shit, she really wanted to touch him. There wasn't an ounce of fear at the thought of it. What did it mean? Had she conquered her phobia?

He stopped to stand behind her. "I can't tell, Dreama. Is your pussy dripping for me?"

"Yes, sir."

"Take your clothes off and then get on your hands and knees," he ordered. "I want to see for myself."

Dizzy with lust, she peeled off her leotard and got into position, keeping her gaze trained ahead as she waited for further instructions. She felt his heat behind her.

"Spread your legs wider. As much as you can," he said gruffly.

A few moments later, warm air blew on her pussy. *Oh Lord, did that feel good.*

She hung her head and saw him lying on his back, faceup with his head directly underneath her pussy. He lifted his neck off the floor and crudely inhaled, smelling her. "Unfortunately, there's no evidence. I'm disappointed."

She called foul as to his assertion of a lack of evidence. Even without personally checking, she knew her panties were drenched. He was playing with her, and she loved it. Heat gathered in her belly. She could barely catch her breath as she waited to see what he'd do next.

He slid out from underneath her and got to his feet. "I promise not to touch you with any part of my body, but that's the only thing I'm promising. Because I'm going to hurt you, Dreama. You can count on that." He circled around to her front, dangling a black silk blindfold. "Crawl to your bedroom."

Crawling might seem demeaning to some people, but she adored everything about it. The slight humiliation, the submissiveness of being low to the ground, the way the position drew her Dominant's attention to her ass.

She swayed her hips as she made her way to the foot of her bed.

Once there, Cash dangled the blindfold in front of her face. His bag was on the floor beside him. "Take it and get on the bed. After you put it on, lie down on your back with your head on your pillow."

Heart pumping wildly, she mounted the mattress, slipped the blindfold over her head, and tightened the strap. Even with her eyes open, she only saw darkness. She lay back, following Cash's instructions. Her mind ran through various scenarios of what implements Cash could use with her on her back. A cane? A crop? She squeezed her thighs together to quell the rising ache.

"Bad girl," he hissed in her ear. "I saw what you just did. You're already due for a punishment. Don't make it worse for yourself."

The worst punishment would be no punishment at all.

"Bend your knees, spread your legs, and put your feet flat on the mattress," he ordered from above her.

She quickly complied, feeling the air waft over her wet pussy. The position left her open and on display for him. Perfect for cropping or flogging. She tried not to squirm as a wave of arousal pulsed through her core.

"Arms over your head and elbows bent," he said. He was ensuring he had full access to her body, with nothing in his way. "I'm going to restrain your hands to your headboard. You're going to feel the metal cuffs wrap around you, Dreama, but I'm not going to touch you with my hands. Remember to use your safe word if you need it. And, Dreama, you definitely might need it."

A delicious chill passed through her, making her shiver. Smooth metal snaked around her wrists. She yanked at them, testing their strength. Her arousal multiplied at the knowledge she was helpless.

"Don't forget to breathe," he warned, a second before there was a pinch on her breasts, only a couple inches from her areola.

Her eyes rolled back in her head. "Son of a bitch!"

"Quiet!" Cash demanded. "No speaking or I'll use a ball gag on you."

He had a ball gag? *Ugh*, she hated those. They tasted like rubber and made her drool like a Saint Bernard. "What did you just put on my breast?"

He chuckled. "Clothespin."

She gasped as a second pinch joined the first. Tears formed behind the blindfold, but she didn't mind. Cash needed to hurt her and she needed the release. It was the beautiful symbiosis of a sadist and masochist.

Both spots throbbed and every time she inhaled, the clamp tightened. She concentrated on holding still as he attached the next clamp, but her body involuntarily jerked from the pain of it, making it even worse.

Oh God. If it hurt this much going on, what was it going to feel like coming off when all the blood rushed back in?

He worked in a circular pattern, adding more and more clamps to her breasts. They felt as if they had swollen to ten times their size. After a while, the individual throbbing morphed into one giant beating heart, and she no longer knew whether she wanted to arch up or shrink away.

Her breasts weren't the only parts throbbing. Cash hadn't done a thing to it yet, but her clit pulsed relentlessly. She was so sensitive, just the air felt like a finger's caress. If only he'd allow her to close her legs, she could squeeze her thighs and create pressure to ease the ache. Testing him, she slowly brought her knees closer together.

"Stop, Dreama," he said darkly. "Keep those legs spread wide for me." Warm breath fanned her face. "Is your pussy jealous of your breasts? Give me a minute and I'll rectify that for you," Cash threatened.

Or was it a promise?

Would he really use the clamps on her pussy?

Did she want him to?

"You might want to hold your breath for this next one," he warned.

The clamp caught her nipple between its teeth like a dog chomping on a bone.

A scream tore from her throat. Her entire pussy started pulsating as if her heart were beating inside of it. Pain flowed over her in hot colorful waves of reds and blues, and hot thick syrup vibrated in her veins. Her limbs tingled, and she felt as if she were floating above the mattress.

Sweet subspace.

When he finished clamping both her breasts, he started on the skin of her pussy. *Two, four, ten* of them were attached to her labia.

She was one giant exposed throbbing nerve.

"I wish you could see yourself, Dreama," Cash murmured. "These clothespins look so beautiful decorating your body. I'm going to take a picture of you with my memory, so whenever I close my eyes, I'll see you like this."

She heard the slapping sound of Cash's hand working his cock and her mouth watered at the thought of him shoving it between her lips. She turned her head toward him and opened her mouth in invitation.

"*Fuck, fuck, fuck,*" he chanted. "Dreama." Hot liquid splattered across her cheeks, chin, and lips, and she licked up every earthy drop she could. "You've been a good girl," he crooned. "It's your turn now. One more clothespin. You'll take it for me. Won't you, baby?"

She tried to speak but couldn't, so she willed herself to nod. Her entire body trembled as Cash trapped her clitoris between the vicious teeth of the clothespin. Bright stars exploded in her eyes.

"Ready, baby?" He rolled a smooth wooden object between her breasts.

A cane? Oh no. The clothespins must be strung together.

"One, two?"

"Wait," she begged.

He didn't finish counting. On three, she felt him swipe the cane at the clothespins on her breasts. All at once, the clamps on her breasts, her nipples, her pussy, and her clitoris, released.

Blood rushed back into the tissue, bringing the most intense pain she'd ever experienced. Her toes curled into the bed and her nails bit into her palms as the orgasm hit her. Waves of exquisite pleasure tore through her pussy, and her inner muscles contracted around nothing, over and over again.

She shivered as smaller aftershocks rocked through her.

The room came into focus. Somehow, Cash had removed her blindfold and the cuffs from her wrists without her knowing. His handsome face filled her view.

"Can you sit up?" he asked, a bottle of water in his hand.

She nodded and hoisted herself up. Her jaw just about dropped to the floor as she took in his magnificence. Cash was completely naked. If she had created him with her own hands, she couldn't have done it better.

After taking the water, she gulped it down and watched as he tipped his own bottle to his lips. Her gaze ate up the way his fingers wrapped around the plastic. She wanted them wrapped around *her*.

She wasn't afraid.

What did it mean? Had she beaten her phobia?

She couldn't be sure. Not until she tested it out and did what she'd wanted to do since meeting him.

Finished with her water, she put the empty bottle on the nightstand and got to her feet.

Her hands were trembling, but not from fear. "I need you to do something for me," she said to him. "Keep your hands at your side."

He nodded, his divot making another reappearance. He

put down his bottle next to hers and dropped his arms to his sides.

Without an ounce of trepidation, she stepped closer to him.

Standing on her tiptoes, she tilted up her chin, and after taking a final breath, pressed her lips to his.

TWENTY-TWO

Holy shit, Dreama was kissing him.

Cash's pulse ratcheted up a hundredfold. Holding his breath, he didn't move a muscle, even though he was dying to take control. He'd been tested plenty in his lifetime, but never more than in this moment. She tasted sweet, like the cookies she loved to eat. He wasn't typically a sweets eater, but for Dreama, he'd always make an exception.

When her small hands settled on his chest, he was prepared for her to push him away. Instead, her fingers dug into his skin and her tongue slid between his lips, intensifying the kiss. He groaned as he curled his fingers into his palms to keep himself from touching her. Her hands were so damn soft and her lips fit perfectly against his. Tasting her mouth, feeling her skin on his skin, was like experiencing a bit of heaven on earth.

All too soon, she pulled her lips away and took a step back from him. Her pulse was throbbing on the side of her neck. He couldn't take his eyes off it. The spot taunted him with its frantic beat. He wanted to press his mouth up against it and feel its vibration on his lips and his tongue. He wanted to suck on that spot until she wore his mark and bite into her flesh until she shuddered beneath him. Would she finally let him?

"I want to try something," she whispered. "But first I need you to agree."

He didn't hesitate. "Whatever it is my answer is yes."

She smiled. "You don't know what I'm going to ask."

"It doesn't matter." Her warm breath caressed the skin of his chest. "If you want it, and it's in my ability to give it to you, it's yours."

She gestured to the handcuffs at the headboard. "I want to touch you, but I'm still a little apprehensive about the thought of you touching me."

Understanding, he sat on the edge of the bed. "You want me to be the one in handcuffs this time."

She nodded.

He hated that he had to say the next words, but he had to confirm that she was of sound mind to give consent. "Are you sure you're not just riding a high after our scene? I don't want you to do anything before you're ready. You have to be one hundred percent certain that you're able and willing to make this decision."

"Thank you for checking." She moved toward the bed. "I'm certain I want to try, but I'm not sure how far I can take it."

"Take it as far as you're comfortable." He lay back on the bed where Dreama had been only minutes before. The spot was still warm. "Don't worry about me. As you know first-hand, I can take matters in my own hands when necessary," he teased.

A small smile played at her lips and her lids grew hooded.

He lifted his arms over his head. Her knees hit the mattress and as she secured his wrists to the headboard, her breasts hung like an offering in front of his face. It took all his willpower to keep from sucking one of those nipples into his mouth.

She secured the metal around each wrist with an audible click and then straddled his legs. He hissed as wet heat soaked his skin. Although he'd just come not five minutes earlier, his cock was as hard as a goalpost, and like a player, just as eager to score.

Staring into his eyes, she positioned her palms against the skin of his lower abdomen. Her lips trembled as she fanned out her hands and explored the area above his groin.

She was going to kill him.

But what a way to go.

* * *

Dreama would give anything to make Cash hiss again. The noises he made drove her wild. Being a submissive, she'd never considered taking the lead during sex, but having Cash at her mercy right now, she could see the appeal.

Leaning forward, she pressed her lips to his chest. He moaned and pulled at his hands as if he had forgotten he couldn't touch her. The need to drive him crazy with lust emboldened her to go further. She lapped at the taut flesh, tasting salt and spice and a flavor that was quintessential *Cash*.

Heat singed her skin, but it was a delicious heat that warmed her all over. There was no pain. No fear. Nothing but smooth skin and hard muscle beneath her lips.

Now that she had tasted his skin, she couldn't stop herself from wanting more. She raised herself off his legs and scooted forward. His eyes darkened as she rested her wet core on the area above his hips. Leaning forward, she dragged her teeth along the underside of his jaw and traced a path down his throat with the tip of her tongue, enjoying the way his Adam's apple moved up and down as her mouth worked over it.

Cash was breathing hard and fast, his face lined with tension. It couldn't be easy for him to give up control, but she definitely planned to make it worth his while.

She rained gentle kisses across his pecs and then down over his ribs, memorizing each and every muscle along the way. She licked his nipple and lightly bit down, relishing his tremors beneath her before moving to the next and doing the same. His breaths became more ragged as if he was having trouble getting enough air into his lungs.

She moved lower again, careful to stay above his pelvis. His cock was fully erect, its curve toward his stomach. Her pussy clenched with the need to take that hard cock inside of it. But she wasn't sure she was ready for that. Not because she was scared of the physical act—she wasn't—but because she needed to protect her heart. She'd never been in love before, but it would be all too easy to fall for Cash. But this was supposed to be about helping her conquer her phobia. Things were complicated enough between them without throwing a thing like love into the mix.

Smiling at him, she dragged her finger lightly over the crown of his cock and then down his length, stopping at his balls, where she cupped them in both hands and squeezed.

Cash growled and pulled against the handcuffs. "Fuck. I want to touch you so badly right now."

"I want that too," she whispered. "But not yet. Let me make you feel good tonight."

"You already are."

She moved forward again and, holding on to his shoulders, leaned into him, needing his mouth. She nibbled on his bottom lip, and on a roar, he took control of the kiss, plunging his tongue into the depths of her mouth. Creating friction on her clit and sparking a fire between her thighs, she rocked against his skin. Her labia and clit were still tender from the clothespins, making every grind of her pussy against him count. She lit up inside, desire sweeping through her.

Cash's chest rumbled. "You." *Kiss.* "Are." *Kiss.* "Killing." *Kiss.* "Me."

She laughed against his mouth. "Sorry." *Kiss.* "Not." *Kiss.* "Sorry."

She curled her hands tighter around his shoulders, digging her nails into his skin. Her mouth felt bruised, swollen, and her body felt electrified. Kissing Cash was better than chocolate—and she fucking loved chocolate. He tasted like ice-cold water on a hot summer day. She couldn't get enough. His lips were firm and supple, and his tongue eager and thorough. If he could get her this hot and bothered by kissing her lips, what would it be like to have that talented mouth between her thighs?

Tension built inside her core. Her body quaked as she teetered on the precipice of climax for what felt like a bazillion minutes but was probably more like three seconds. Then finally, an explosion of heat blew outward from her clitoris, consuming everything in its path. Her pussy clenched over and over as the orgasm tore through her.

She fell against him, unable to breathe, or move, or think. Cash pressed gentle kisses on her cheeks as her body continued to shudder with strong aftershocks.

After a minute or two, she slowly became aware that she'd left Cash's needs unattended.

But not for long.

She slid down his body until she lay between his legs.

"Hey," he said softly. "You don't need to do this for me."

"I'm not." Making her point clear, she licked her lips. "I'm doing it for me."

Cash's expression grew heated as he stared at her mouth. Smiling, she looked up at him as she wrapped her fingers around the base of his cock. He groaned and arched into her hand.

His cock was as massive as the rest of him. It wasn't only the impressive length that mesmerized her, but also the width. Her thumb didn't even come close to touching her other fingers. She wasn't certain she could get the thing into her mouth.

But she sure was going to have fun trying.

"Are you going to suck it or just hope I spontaneously climax from you looking at it?" he said hoarsely. "Because I have to tell you, Dreama, I'm so close to coming, that's a fucking possibility."

"I'm not sure it will fit in my mouth," she quipped.

"It'll fit. This cock was made for you."

She almost believed that.

Opening her mouth wide, she slid her lips over the top of him. He groaned as she worked her way down his length with her tongue. She knew if he'd had his way, his hands would be fisted in her hair and he'd be controlling the depth and pace of the blow job. And although a huge part of her wanted that, too, there was something strangely empowering about being the dominant one right now.

She forced herself to take him farther into her mouth, until the tip of him bumped into the soft palate. Then she slowly dragged her lips all the way up, stopping only before he slipped from her mouth. Salty liquid squirted onto her tongue, and she lapped it up eagerly. She felt his cock throbbing beneath her tongue.

Picking up the pace, she bobbed her head up and down his shaft, taking more and more of him each time until he was halfway down her throat. She swallowed repeatedly, creating a vacuum around his girth, and with one hand at the base of his cock, she used the other to massage his balls.

"If you don't want me shooting down your throat, you

better move now, because I'm about to blow," Cash warned through gritted teeth.

Her answer was to squeeze his balls harder.

Two seconds later, a gush of liquid heat ran down her throat. She continued to swallow, choking, gagging, unable to breathe, as she accepted every drop he had to give. Eventually, his cock softened and slipped from her mouth.

Trying to catch her breath, she rested her head on his thigh. She'd thought she could protect herself from falling for Cash.

She'd been wrong.

TWENTY-THREE

Driving to work, Cash rubbed the faint marking on his wrists where the cuffs had bit into his skin and smiled, recalling how he'd gotten them. The marks were a small price to pay for having Dreama's hands and mouth on him.

God, what she could do with those hands and her mouth.

He'd never experienced anything better. He couldn't wait to finally touch her.

As he pulled into the parking lot of the shelter, Cash's residual high from last night disappeared like mist. There was a police car in front of the animal shelter.

What if something had happened to Rebecca? He hadn't seen her since yesterday morning when he'd told her he was going out to run errands. When he'd returned from his breakfast with Thomas, she'd already been at work and she hadn't come home before he left for Dreama's.

Pulse racing, he quickly parked and sprinted toward the building, prepared to hear the worst as he went bursting through the front door.

Buddy stood up from behind the receptionist desk, a grim expression on his face. "Hey, man, your sister's been trying to call you."

Cash bowed his head and breathed a sigh of relief. *Thank goodness, she's alive.* He pulled his phone from his coat pocket, dismayed to find it dead. "Rebecca's okay, then?"

"Yeah," Buddy said, his brows dipped in confusion. "She's obviously upset, but you know Rebecca. She can hold her shit together."

Cash latched on to one word. "Upset. Why is she upset?"

Buddy ignored the ringing phone and came out from behind the desk. "Haven't you turned on the news? The police found Laci's body in her driveway early this morning. She was killed the same way as Nancy. Death by baseball bat."

He suddenly felt as though he was going to be sick.

Baseball bat.

Dreama.

Had she been right? Had the police accused the wrong perp? If it was the same guy who'd almost killed her, why go after the women Cash worked with?

"Where's Rebecca now?" Cash asked.

Buddy rubbed his knuckles down his face. "I think she brought the detectives to her office."

The door to the back flew open and Rebecca walked out, strain evident from the flatness of her lips and the lines around her eyes. "I've been calling you for hours." She tapped her fingers against her upper thigh. "The police need to talk to you."

He slid a glance at Buddy. Nervous tapping wasn't Rebecca's habit. It was Cash's. Something was up but she couldn't talk in front of Buddy. Cash gave her a nod. "Sure."

They left Buddy to man the lobby and went in the back. Instead of going straight to Rebecca's office, she pulled him into one of the exam rooms.

Her mouth was tight with tension. "Where have you been? I must have left ten messages for you since the police got here at seven this morning."

"I'm sorry. My phone was dead."

"Detective Henry has been asking all sorts of questions about you."

"What kinds of questions?"

"Where were you last night? What was your relationship with Nancy and Laci? Have I noticed any changes in you?" She wrung her hands together, twisting her fingers until her knuckles turned pale.

He placed his hands on her shoulder and leaned down to look her in the eye. "Don't worry, Rebecca. I didn't kill Nancy or Laci."

Except that wasn't exactly true. He might have not been the one wielding the baseball bat, but he couldn't say with certainty that they weren't murdered because of him. When it had just been Nancy, he'd been willing to believe it was a coincidence. Now he could no longer ignore the similarities between their murders and Dreama's attack. Someone was targeting the women around him.

The question was why?

And who was next?

"You don't have to convince me that you're innocent,"

Rebecca said. "But you didn't come home last night. So I panicked. I told Detective Henry that you were home all night with me and that we stayed up late watching the televised *Star Wars* marathon until three. I also told him I saw you this morning before I left. When you didn't answer your phone, I said that you'd forgotten to charge your phone."

Shit. He'd been at Dreama's all night.

Rebecca had lied to the police to protect him. He couldn't go in there now and admit she'd been lying. His sister could get in trouble.

But how could he keep the odd connection between Nancy's and Laci's deaths and Dreama's attack a secret? He supposed he could tell the detective that Dreama had been the victim of a baseball bat attack a little over a year ago, but it would probably seem odd for Cash to know that fact about his parole officer.

And if he did tell the truth about his alibi, Dreama would lose her job.

What the hell was he going to do?

He kissed Rebecca's tear-soaked cheek and headed to her office, where Detective Henry was waiting.

He turned the doorknob and pulled the door open. "Detective Henry. Sorry to keep you waiting. I didn't realize anyone was looking for me. As you can see, my phone's dead." He handed his cell to the detective in order for the man to confirm it.

"Mr. Turner. Please, have a seat." He gestured for Cash to sit across from him. "What was your relationship with Laci London?"

"We're coworkers. Nothing more. I've barely even spoken with her. She and I had one conversation when I began working here," he said, leaving out that she'd cornered him in the closet and propositioned him for sex.

"When was the last time you saw her?" the detective asked, folding his arms.

"Um..." He had to think about it. "I didn't work yesterday, so... Wednesday."

"Have you ever been to her house?"

Cash frowned. "Like I said, we were just coworkers. I have no idea where she lives." He shook his head. "Lived," he said, correcting himself.

"Interesting. Because I got an anonymous call this morning from a witness that says he saw a man fitting your description leaving Ms. London's house shortly after midnight last night. Would you like to amend your statement?"

Was the detective telling the truth or was he trying to capture Cash in a lie? Either choice was discomforting.

"No, I would not like to amend my statement," Cash said calmly. Resisting the urge to drum his fingers, he laid his palms flat onto his thighs. "As I said, I've never been to her house."

Detective Henry sat back in his chair and folded his arms across his chest. "Where were you last night around midnight?"

Cash didn't pause. "I was home with my sister. There was a *Star Wars* marathon on. As you probably know, I've spent the last eight years in prison. I was past due for a *Star Wars* fix."

The detective's eyes narrowed on him as if he doubted the veracity of Cash's alibi. "Can you think of any reason why someone would kill two of your coworkers?"

Cash's stomach twisted into knots. "No."

If someone was targeting women at the shelter because of him, Rebecca was a prime target. But it all came back to Dreama.

How could he keep both Rebecca and Dreama safe?

* * *

Dreama's desk phone trilled, startling her out of her thoughts. Recognizing the extension, she swiftly answered. "Good morning, Ms. Wilson." Calling Meg by her formal name tasted sour in her mouth.

"Come to my office," Meg said, then hung up.

Dreama stuck her tongue out as she slammed her phone down. "You forgot to say *please*."

Like that was ever going to happen.

Knocking on Meg's door, Dreama pasted on a fake smile. At Meg's command for her to enter, she went inside. "You wanted to see me?"

"Have a seat, Dreama," Meg said, crossing her arms over her chest and sitting back in her chair. "How have things been going for you?"

"Good," she answered cautiously. This "nice" version of Meg was throwing her. She sat, but she refused to get too comfortable. It was only a matter of time before Meg slid the knife into her back.

Meg smiled and Dreama wasn't ashamed to admit she was frightened. "Not too overwhelmed by your caseload?"

"No, not at all."

"I'm happy to hear that. I know that things have been tense between us, but I'm hoping we can find a way to get past it."

"I'd like that too."

"Wonderful. There's a supervisor's position officially opening up next month in our satellite office. They've asked me to put in my recommendation. I'd like to give them your name."

Dreama's mouth gaped. She was absolutely flummoxed. A supervisor position was everything she'd worked for. It meant more money, increased benefits, job stability, and more importantly—she'd no longer answer to Meg. "Thank you. I'd really appreciate that."

"Of course, before I do that, you'll have to prove to me you're ready for the job. I'm sure you think that this desk should have been yours, but even if you hadn't been attacked, they would have given the job to me anyway. A supervisor position is much more demanding than what you're used to. That's why I thought it would be prudent to give you some additional duties before I recommend you."

Dreama allowed Meg's words and their hidden meaning to sink in. "Let me guess. You want me to do some of your work for you?"

"It's the perfect way to prepare you for what it will be like when you're a supervisor." She paused, adjusting her glasses. "Unless you think you can't handle it."

Dreama wasn't an idiot. She knew this was more than a test. It was Meg who couldn't handle her workload. She needed Dreama's help and instead of admitting it, she'd packaged it as a way to help Dreama.

She'd call Meg's bluff. Even if Meg was lying and there wasn't an open supervisor position, Dreama would prove she could manage whatever Meg threw at her. "You have yourself a deal," she said.

If in a month Meg didn't recommend Dreama for a supervisory position, Dreama would go over Meg's head and report that Dreama had been completing Meg's work for her.

Either way, there was no way Dreama could lose.

The rest of the day was a blur of activity. Every time she had a moment to breathe, Meg would give her some other task to do. Her poor mother was probably having an apoplectic fit since Dreama had ignored all eight of her phone calls. Frankly, Dreama didn't care what her mother was worried about this time. She needed to learn not to bother Dreama during work hours.

In addition to the appointments with her parolees and the usual documentation that came with them, Dreama had written two memos in Meg's name and prepared the office's monthly statistical report. Seeing she'd be working late, Dreama had quickly texted Cash earlier in the day to ask him to come over after nine. It was good planning because while she normally finished work between five and six, she didn't get out of her office until eight that night.

In the end, working extra hours was going to be worth it. Dreama would get that supervisor's position and beat Meg at her own game.

It was another cold and snowy drive home, but Dreama was more content than she had been in a long time. Not even the ache in her legs could bring her down. Everything in her life seemed to be coming together for her. She had the new opportunity to advance her career, had mended her friendship with Jane, and with Cash's help, was on her way to completely beating her phobia.

Forcing the memories of last night out of her head today had been incredibly difficult. She could practically still taste Cash on her lips. Having his mouth on hers had been one of the more erotic experiences of her life.

The only thing that could ruin it, other than Meg finding out about them, was her secret about Cash's parentage. She still didn't know how to approach the issue with him. Last night, she hadn't gotten the chance, but she couldn't keep the information from him any longer. He deserved to know. She'd find a way to tell him tonight.

In her apartment lobby, she waved to the guard.

"Good evening, Ms. Agosto. I've got a package for you back here," he said, getting up from his chair and bending over to retrieve something.

Huh. She wasn't expecting anything.

The guard stepped out from behind his desk, a long white box tied with a red bow in his arms. "Looks like someone sent you roses."

Warmth bloomed in her chest. The last time she'd gotten

flowers was college graduation, and those were from her parents. She'd never received flowers from a man.

Cash must have sent them.

When the guard transferred the box to her, she was surprised by the weight of it. "Thank you."

Upstairs in her apartment, she set the box on her coffee table and removed her coat, shoving it off her shoulders and leaving it on the couch. She was too excited to worry about keeping her place clean. Besides, Cash was probably used to her messes by now.

After kicking off her boots, she dropped to her knees and slid the pretty ribbon off the box. Maybe she'd answer the door for Cash wearing the bow—the bow and nothing else.

Giggling to herself, she lifted the top off the box.

She stared at the object inside, not sure what she was seeing. It took a moment for it to sink in.

Her stomach cramped and bile climbed her throat.

Cash hadn't sent her flowers.

Cash hadn't sent this at all.

In place of the long-stemmed roses she'd expected lay a wooden baseball bat.

This wasn't a gift of endearment.

It was a death threat.

TWENTY-FOUR

Growing more and more concerned, Cash knocked on Dreama's door again. She had to be in there. The guard downstairs had mentioned she'd just gotten home a few minutes ago. There was probably a good explanation as to why she wasn't answering—maybe she was in the shower—but his stomach was roiling with unease. His concern intensified when he wrapped his hand around the doorknob and found the door unlocked. He pushed it open and stormed inside. "Dreama?"

Relief washed through him as he immediately spotted her on the carpet between the couch and the coffee table. "I've been knocking for five minutes. Why didn't you answer?"

Remaining as still as a statue, she didn't acknowledge having heard him. She was on her knees, still in her work clothes, staring at the box in front of her.

Beside him, Butch whined, trying to break free of Cash's hold on his leash. Cash crouched down and unhooked the leash from the dog's collar. "Go get her, Butch."

Butch's tag jingled against the metal of his collar as he padded over to Dreama. He bumped his nose up against Dreama's side, announcing his presence and signaling he wouldn't mind if she petted him.

Cash came around the couch, getting his first view of what was inside the box. *What the hell?* Someone had sent her a baseball bat.

He knelt on the floor, Butch between them. "Dreama, where did you get this?"

"Downstairs," she said, still staring at the bat. "I thought you sent me flowers."

Anger swelled before giving way to acquiescence. He would let the past die and stop his search for the truth. Whatever he'd overheard the night Maddie died, it wasn't worth risking Dreama's life. "We've let this go on long enough. You have to call the police and file a report. Tell them about the car that tried to run you down two weeks ago, the photo sent to you that was taken outside Club X, this baseball bat. *Everything.*"

She shook her head. "I can't."

"Yes, you can."

"Someone probably sent this as a joke," she said flatly.

He wanted to take her over his knee and spank some sense into her. "You don't honestly believe that, do you?"

"No, but what else am I supposed to think? The guy who hurt me is dead."

He had done this to her—him and his secrets. "This isn't about you," he admitted. "It's about me. The woman who was recently killed with a baseball bat. That was my coworker, Nancy. Last night, another one of my coworkers, Laci, was murdered the same way."

Her face lost its coloring. "What?"

He lifted himself off the floor and sat on the couch. "The police came by the shelter to speak with me. This was the second time, but it seems like they're narrowing down their list of suspects. A witness reported they saw a man fitting my description leaving Laci's house late last night."

Something about the way Detective Henry had phrased that had bothered him all day. Cash was six foot three. With less than 4 percent of men being taller than six foot two in this country, the chance that the killer was around his height seemed highly unlikely. Either the cop had lied to him in the hope that Cash would suddenly confess or someone had intentionally given Cash's description.

Dreama's coloring began to return. She joined him on the couch. "You were with me the whole night."

He sighed. "Rebecca lied and told them I was home with her."

"You know I met her," she said, absentmindedly petting the top of Butch's head. The fact that she hadn't asked about the dog's presence yet showed that she was still in shock. "I came yesterday morning to do your home visit, but you were out. She's sweet. She's also very smart. I think she suspects something is going on between us."

Cash covered his face with his hands. Rebecca had taken him in when he'd gotten out of prison and how did he repay her? He'd not only put her in the position where she felt as if she had to lie to the police to protect him, but he'd also placed her life in danger.

He dragged his fingers down his cheeks. "She won't say anything if we don't want her to, but, Dreama, I think we're going to have to stop our investigation and tell the police about us. The closer I get to the truth about what happened the night of the accident, the more I put you and Rebecca at risk."

She angled toward him. "You think it's Browner?"

"Or Kevin Sanders. Jay Moran. Or Thomas. Hell, it could be all of them. I might have had some champagne for a toast with Thomas, but after remembering pieces of that night, I'm almost certain I wasn't drunk and it seems unlikely Moran, Sanders, or even Thomas saw me drinking inside the tent." He'd gone over and over it. He still had no idea what he'd overheard that night, but he knew whatever it was had resulted in the deaths of three women.

He wouldn't allow it to be four.

Dreama scratched Butch under his jaw. "I thought you were close to Thomas at one time. Do you really think he could be capable of murder?"

"No, but that doesn't mean he isn't." Cash couldn't discount the fact that everything came back to what happened at Lundquist's party eight years ago.

Dreama gave him a little smile. "Should we talk about the elephant in the room—I mean, the dog?"

"I was wondering when you'd mention it," he said, relieved she was no longer in shock. "I can't possibly protect both you and Rebecca at the same time. That's why I brought Butch."

Her brows dipped. "Did you adopt him?"

He rubbed Butch's back. "Not exactly. He's for you. To keep you safe."

"Cash, I told you, I can't have a dog in my life right now."

He decided to go with a different angle. "He's got nowhere else to go. If I didn't get him out of the shelter, Rebecca would be forced to euthanize him to make space for a younger, healthier dog."

She narrowed her eyes suspiciously. "Why can't you take him?"

"Rebecca has her cats." He leaned toward her. "And it would make me feel better to have him with you."

"Fine. I'll take him for now, so long as you try and find a more suitable owner for him."

"Deal," he said, knowing there was no one more suitable than Dreama. He'd bring up the dog crate and all the supplies from his car before he left. Butch had already bonded to Dreama and it wouldn't be long before Dreama bonded to him. Besides, she could protest all she liked, but he'd heard the wistfulness in her voice when she told him she'd wanted a dog as a child.

She looked down at her lap. "I don't think we should report this to the police."

He opened and shut his mouth a couple of times to keep from saying what was on his mind. It didn't work. "Are you insane?"

"We still don't have any evidence," she pointed out. "This will only give the cops more ammunition to use against you. Think about it, the bat was sent as a warning. Whoever delivered this to me still hopes we'll drop our investigation. He's using me as collateral. Otherwise, he would've just killed me already. If we go to the police, who's to say they'll even listen to me? If anything, it would strengthen the case against you and we could lose our shot at finding out the truth about what happened."

She'd crafted a rational, well-thought-out argument.

But he was calling bullshit. "All that is true, but I don't buy that's your only reason. What aren't you telling me?"

She bit down on her lip. "There's an open supervisor's position. Meg is going to recommend me for it."

Was she kidding? He jumped to his feet, startling Butch. "You're willing to risk your life for a job? I thought we discussed this already and that I'd gotten through to you."

She popped up from the couch and strode away from him before flipping around. "Don't you get it? Do you know what it's like to have a mother who thinks you're not good enough—not smart enough—to make it on your own?" She put her hand on her chest. "Because I do."

He stayed quiet, knowing now was a time for listening.

"I have attention deficit disorder," she said. "Before my diagnosis, I did terrible in school. I thought I was stupid, and rather than find out why I had trouble learning, my mother coddled me. She said that it was okay if I didn't get good grades or go to college because I could live at home and work at my aunt and uncle's bakery like so many of my other cousins. She told me someday I'd marry a man who would take care of me and protect me. That my real job was to support my husband and raise children. I don't judge anyone for choosing that life if that's what they want. But that was never my dream and it hurt that my mother didn't know me at all."

Her eyes shone with tears. It was clear how much her mother's words had hurt her.

She took a ragged breath. "When I was finally diagnosed and got on the right medication, she didn't change her opinion of me even when I pulled straight As. So, I set out to prove her wrong. I went to college and got my social work degree." She swept her arm out, motioning to the room. "I'm a slob." She raised her chin defiantly. "While I enjoy sexual domination, I don't want or need any man to take care of me. And I'll never have children."

He got that. He really did. His mother had always supported his dreams, but he'd disappointed her. First when he'd knocked up Maddie and then again, when he'd gone to prison for Maddie's death. But unlike Dreama's mother, she'd never shown it. "So, you think if you get a promotion, she'll...what...finally accept you?"

"No. I don't know. It sounded better in my head." She ran her hand through her hair. "I realize she'll never change, but it doesn't stop me from hoping she will."

"And Meg?" he prodded. "Tell me this isn't about your silly competition with her."

"It's not silly. I deserve the supervisor's position." Her shoulders slumped. "If we go to the police, I'll have to tell them about us. My career will be over. It will prove what my mother and Meg thought about me all along."

He understood now what motivated her, but how could she not see how wrong they were? "Dreama, you have nothing to prove, but if you need a testimonial, I'll give you one. You're stronger than you give yourself credit for. After what you went through last year, you could have followed the path your mother set out for you. Instead, you moved out of your parents' house and returned to work. You fight for what's right and you're passionate about what you believe." He winked at her. "Oh, and you give the world's best head."

A tear spilled over on her laugh. "Thank you." Her eyes were red and she looked exhausted.

He still didn't agree with her about not reporting everything to the police, but for tonight, he'd let her rest. They hadn't gotten a lot of sleep this past week. He'd come back in the morning and work on changing her mind. If he could split himself in two, he would. But while Dreama was safe in a guarded apartment and had Butch, Rebecca was alone in the house with no protection.

"If you think you're okay here for the night, I should go," he said quietly. "I need to get home to my sister."

Her hand shot out and stopped him from leaving. She curled her fingers around the top of his biceps. "Could you stay? Just a little while, until I fall asleep? I can't help feeling like this could be the last time we'll be together like this."

Heat darted through him and his cock stiffened. He hoped he never got used to her touch. "I promise it won't be," he said more confidently than he felt. He smiled down at her and jutted his chin toward her room. "Come on. Let's go to bed."

Once there, she removed her work clothes and put on a set of SpongeBob pajamas while he remained dressed from the waist down. After turning out the lights, he slid under the sheets and blankets with her. Butch lay down on the carpet just inside the room.

Cash had known Butch would be an incredible watchdog. The dog reminded him of himself.

Dreama tossed the barrier of pillows to the floor. "Hold me?"

He forgot to take a breath. "Are you sure?"

She inched closer. "I'm sure."

"There's nothing I'd like more." His hand was surprisingly steady as he slowly lowered it onto her shoulder and touched her for the first time. He sighed when his fingers met the warm, soft skin of her neck. It was like coming home after a lifetime of being away.

She momentarily lifted herself so that he could slide his arm beneath her and roll her to his chest. Bliss washed over him. Dreama was finally where she belonged—in his arms. Nothing had ever felt so right.

She tilted up her chin and echoed the words he's whispered to her a few nights ago. "Tell me a secret."

* * *

Dreama's heart fluttered. She'd done it. She'd beaten her phobia. Her need to be in his arms outweighed her fear of his touch. *No.* Her only fear was never having the chance to experience it.

She hadn't lied. Call it intuition or paranoia, but she knew tonight would be their last night together, and she planned on making it count. Not with sex, but with honesty.

His warm breath blew over her skin. "I never loved Maddie."

The jealous woman inside of her was thrilled to hear it confirmed, but it also made her sad that Cash had been in a loveless marriage. "I know. Rebecca mentioned it to me."

He paused. "She never let on that she knew."

"Tell me about Maddie." There had to be a reason he never talked about her.

He sighed and held her a little bit tighter. "I confused neediness with submissiveness. By the time I realized my mistake, it was too late. She'd figured out my weakness and exploited it to her advantage. At first, she threatened to kill herself if I broke up with her. It got so bad, I just gave in to whatever she wanted. I should have told someone, but I was young and stupid and convinced I could do it on my own. Just when I'd decided I couldn't take it anymore, she told me she was pregnant."

Rebecca's words about Maddie hanging on Cash and Cash's concern about her suddenly made sense. "Why did you keep sleeping with her if you wanted to break up with her?"

"She became irrational every time I shied away from anything physical. It was easier to give in. Besides, I was a horny young guy with a willing woman in my bed. I always used condoms, but she later admitted she'd poked pinholes in them."

It didn't surprise Dreama that Cash would marry Maddie even though she'd intentionally gotten pregnant. Most men would've panicked and gone running. But Cash was different. His greatest strength was also his biggest weakness—his need to protect those he cared about.

She placed her lips on his neck and kissed him. "You're a good man, Cash Turner."

"You wanted to know a secret." His voice shook. "I'll give you one. You're wrong about me. I'm not a good man. A good man wouldn't be relieved when he heard his wife was dead, but I was. That was the first thing I felt when I woke up in the hospital and my sister told me what had happened. Maddie and Joshua were gone and I was relieved, Dreama. The feeling didn't last longer than a second, but it was there."

She put her hand on his stubbly cheek. "That doesn't make you bad. It makes you human."

"I haven't visited their grave," he admitted, guilt evident in his tone. "I never even cried."

"Crying doesn't equal grief. Give yourself time to heal." She snuggled into him. After everything he'd gone through, how could he expect so much of himself? He'd married Maddie even knowing she'd manipulated her way into it. Because despite what he believed, he was the very best of men. He'd married Maddie to protect his unborn child. "You'll go when you're ready."

With everything he lost, would he be pleased to gain two brothers?

He didn't say anything. He responded by rubbing her back. Being in his arms was like being wrapped in a cocoon of warmth. She never wanted it to end.

She closed her eyes.

And when she opened them again, he was gone.

TWENTY-FIVE

The sun was just rising as Cash pulled into his driveway. After talking with Dreama, he'd fallen asleep with her in his arms. He'd woken up a couple hours ago and quickly taken Butch out to do his business, then brought up the dog crate and supplies to Dreama's apartment. He'd thought about waking her, but she'd looked so peaceful with her hair spread out over the pillow, he'd decided against it.

He quietly walked into his house and turned to go to his room. Rebecca was on the couch, a mug of coffee in her hand. He winced, guilt eating at his stomach like battery acid. "I'm sorry I stayed out last night. I meant to come home earlier, but I fell asleep. I'm not going to spend the night out anymore. Not as long as that psycho—"

"Look," she said, jumping from the couch and simultaneously causing her coffee to slosh over the rim of her mug, "I've kept my mouth shut long enough. I'm worried about you. Where have you been sleeping every night?"

He walked to her, took the cup from her hand, and placed

it on the table. "Trust me, Rebecca. It's best if you don't know."

"I lied to the police for you," she said. "The least you can do is tell me where you really were." There was a tremble in her voice that burned him to the quick.

He grabbed her hand. "You don't think I had something to do with the murders, do you?"

"No. Of course not." She did a combo eye roll/snort that indicated she thought he was an idiot. "Give me some credit. But I *am* concerned. I don't understand why you're being so secretive about everything. Whatever it is, you can tell me. We'll face it together."

Whatever it is...

She had no idea what kind of secret she was inviting into their home.

But what was the alternative? He couldn't outright lie to her.

"It's Dreama, okay?" he admitted, throwing his arms up in the air. "I'm involved with Dreama."

God, that felt good to say out loud.

A small smile played at the sides of Rebecca's mouth.

Huh.

"You don't look surprised," he said.

Her smile grew as she shrugged. "She was more interested in looking at your baby photos than searching the house for contraband. I had a feeling then there was something between you two."

"She said you were smart."

"I really liked her."

"I do too." If he was honest with himself, he more than liked her. But he wasn't ready to go there yet.

She started to speak when a knock on the door interrupted them. The frost on the window prevented him from seeing outside. Who would be here at seven in the morning?

With her mouth downturned, she went to the front door and checked through the peephole. "It's the police."

Icy-cold dread ran through his veins.

Something told him they weren't there to ask for a donation to the Fraternal Order of Police.

On his nod, Rebecca opened the door to Detective Henry and a young female officer dressed in uniform. Cash moved to stand behind his sister.

"Good morning," Detective Henry said. "We're here to search the vehicle registered to Cash Turner."

"Do you have a search warrant?" she asked.

"Mr. Turner is on parole," said the female officer. "We don't need one."

Cash recalled some language in his parole paperwork to that effect, but never did he think it would ever be used against him.

Detective Henry stretched out his hand. "Can we have your keys, Mr. Turner?"

He fished them out of his pocket and gave them over. "Here you go. It's already unlocked."

Since the vehicle wasn't worth much, he never bothered to lock it. He had a feeling that was about to bite him in the ass.

They weren't there at seven in the morning on a hunch.

Someone must have tipped them off and it was probably the same person who'd given their witness account after Laci's death. The baseball bat had been a distraction. While he and Dreama had been worried about that, someone must have planted evidence in his car.

When the cops left to search, Rebecca turned to Cash. "Should we call a lawyer? I'm sure Thomas can find us a good one."

"No. Don't call Thomas. I'll figure something out on my own."

Rebecca's shoulders were practically up by her ears. "That's what you said eight years ago and look how that ended up."

With him behind bars.

He knew he was about to return.

"Just let the cops do their thing," he said, putting his arm around his sister and kissing her on top of her head. "It will be over soon."

But that was a lie.

Detective Henry returned to the house a minute later and cuffed Cash as he recited his rights. They'd found a bloody baseball bat in the trunk of his car, exactly where the informant had said they would.

Cash was under arrest for murder.

* * *

Dreama never worked on Saturdays, but when Meg had called her an hour ago and asked her to come in, she didn't have the desire to say no. She had no other plans for the day and it wouldn't hurt to put in some extra hours to impress Meg. Hopefully, staying busy would take her mind off things for a little while.

She hadn't heard Cash leave last night, but she had the feeling he'd just left when she'd opened her eyes. Butch was on her bed and his fur was cold, as if he'd recently been outside. Petting her dog, she'd lain there for a couple hours, a ball of nerves bouncing around in her belly. She'd fallen asleep before she could tell him about Ryder and Finn, and the guilt of it wouldn't go away.

She didn't want to be like Maddie, who lied and manipulated to hold on to him. But the longer she kept the secret, the harder it would be to explain she'd kept it for all the right reasons. And it wasn't only Cash she was keeping this from. Ryder and Finn deserved to know the truth too.

Dreama walked down the hallway to Meg's office and, noticing her door was open, crossed inside without knocking. "Good morning. What can I help you with?"

From behind the safety of her desk and computer monitor, Meg clasped her hands on her desk. She smiled much too widely for Dreama's comfort. "Last night I received an envelope at my home. Imagine my surprise when I discovered it was a photograph of you and Mr. Turner in front of a sex club."

There was a low-level buzzing noise in her ears. She shook her head to clear it. "A photo?"

Meg picked up the 8 x 10 black-and-white photo off her desk and held it out to Dreama. "See for yourself."

Dreama didn't have to see it up close. From feet away, she could determine it was the same photo sent to her earlier in the week. "No, thank you."

"Was this photo taken before or after you called that Browner attorney to inquire about Mr. Turner's case?" Meg asked snidely.

"After. But honestly, we didn't go to the club together. It was just a weird coincidence that we bumped into each other there. The person who took the photo tried to run me down with his car right after he took the picture."

Meg frowned. "Did you report the incident to the police?"

"No."

"When I came into your office the other day, Mr. Turner was standing awfully close to your desk. I got the feeling that I interrupted something. You didn't listen to me when I told you to drop your inquiry into Mr. Turner's case, did you? I knew it."

"If you had suspicions about me, why were you going to recommend me for the supervisor position?"

"You're even stupider than I thought you were," Meg sneered. "There is no supervisor position opening. I just said it to get your hopes up so I could rip them away from you. Honestly, I didn't think you'd fall for it. Imagine my surprise when you jumped at the chance to do my work for me. But having this photograph of you is even better than what I'd planned for you."

Dreama's heart sank, but at the same time, she was angry. How could the parole office give this woman so much power when she clearly didn't deserve it? Someday, Dreama would make sure they learned the truth. "I'm not stupid."

Looking triumphant, Meg strolled right up to her. "I received a call this morning from a Detective Henry. It seems your parolee, Cash Turner, has been arrested for murder and is the suspect in another. You really can pick them, Dreama."

How could they have arrested him when they had no evidence? Something must have happened after he'd left her bed this morning. But why hadn't he called her?

"Listen, Meg, I know you hate me, but this isn't about me." There had to be some good inside of Meg buried deep inside. Otherwise, why would she have chosen this career? "Cash Turner is innocent. He was innocent eight years ago and he's innocent today."

Meg tilted her head and grinned knowingly. "And you know this how?"

Dreama took a breath. "Because I was with him when those women were murdered."

Meg's brow lifted. "Your job means a lot to you, doesn't it?"

Dreama didn't know where Meg was going with this, but she had a feeling wherever it was, she wasn't going to like it. "Yes. Of course it does."

"I'm sure you'd do anything to keep it, right? You would hate to let me win." Meg took off her glasses, allowing Dreama to see the emptiness in her eyes. "What if we made a deal? I'll email a letter to my boss right now recommending you for a higher position"—she smiled, looking every bit in her element as she offered her devil's bargain—"if you agree to never to see Cash Turner again."

Dreama didn't have to think about it. "Do you honestly think I would ever make a deal with the devil? Here's your answer, Lucifer. I quit."

Meg had the audacity to look offended. "I'm going to report your illicit relationship to the county. Your career is over, do you hear me? After I get through with you, I wouldn't be surprised if someday you're back here as one of the parolees. I knew from the minute I met you that you were a loser."

Who cared if Meg thought she won some pointless competition? What did that get her? An all-expenses-paid vacation to the French Riviera?

Meg could have the job. It hurt Dreama that she wouldn't be able to help her parolees, but she wouldn't allow herself to be bullied anymore.

Dreama wasn't concerned about Meg's threats. Falling in love with her parolee might be considered unethical by the county and the state, but it was the best thing she'd ever done. And she was in love with him. She couldn't deny it and she'd never regret it.

"You're wrong. The sad part is you'd never understand why." Dreama spun on her heels and stormed out of the parole office. She'd come back to get her things from her office on Monday, during regular business hours.

She had been so worried about proving she wasn't stupid that she had acted stupidly. She should have never kept the death threats a secret. Cash had been right. She should have gone to the police. If she had, Cash might have never been arrested.

But she was going to make it right.

She had to come clean about everything.

Starting now.

After getting Finn's address from Jane, she drove straight to his new home. She would've called, but this kind of news deserved to be said in person. She parked her car and hurried to his front door, where she rang the doorbell.

Finn answered the door and yawned. His hair was a mess and he had signs of sleep still in his eyes. "Dreama? What are you doing here?"

"I need your help," she said quickly. There was no time for pleasantries. "The parolee I've been talking to you about has been arrested for murder."

He scratched his cheek, drawing attention to the fact that he hadn't shaved yet. "I'm not a criminal attorney anymore. If the police have him on a murder charge, he needs someone better than me to represent him."

He was wrong. There was nobody better suited than him.

"You don't understand—"

"The police must have solid evidence if they arrested him for murder," Finn said. "Maybe it would be best if you let it go. After what happened to you last year—"

"I know Cash Turner inside and out," she said. "He's not capable of murder. Besides, I was with him at the time of the murders. I'm his alibi."

Shock registered on his face. "Even so." He palmed the

back of his neck. "I'm sorry, I can't do this for you." He started closing the door.

She shot out her hand and stopped it. "Please, you have to."

He shook his head. "I don't understand. Why is it so important that I be the one to help?"

She told him the truth. "Because Cash is your brother."

TWENTY-SIX

Sitting on a hard bench in the temporary holding cell at the police station, Cash waited for his transfer over to the courthouse. It was hard to believe, but there was no disputing it.

Someone had set up Cash for murder.

Between the witness placing a man matching Cash's description at the scene and the blood on the baseball bat determined by preliminary tests to be Laci's, the police had enough evidence for their arrest. Cash's alibi had fallen apart because there was no *Star Wars* marathon on television the night of Laci's murder. Thankfully, they seemed to have no interest in charging Rebecca for lying to the police.

Detective Henry had interrogated Cash for two hours, but Cash had refused to answer any questions. He also hadn't asked for a lawyer. The public defender route hadn't gone so well for him in the past. This time, he'd find his own defense attorney. Problem was he had to find one he could trust, someone who wouldn't be susceptible to bribery. That wasn't going to be easy.

All of this would likely go away if he provided a solid alibi. Several times during the interrogation, he'd been tempted. But he hadn't. And he *wouldn't*. Not until he spoke to Dreama. He was still waiting for the cops to let him make a phone call before they transported him to the county courthouse for his arraignment.

Eight years ago, he'd thought he was doing what was right. He'd believed he deserved to go to prison. Thanks to Dreama, he knew the truth. He hadn't deserved to go to prison. Not then and, more importantly, not now.

But that didn't change what he had to do.

A uniformed officer appeared on the other side of the cell. "You have a visitor. I'm going to take you to the interrogation room."

Guess he wouldn't be needing to make that phone call after all. He didn't bother asking the cop for the identity of his visitor. He knew in his heart it was Dreama. As his parole officer, she would've been notified of his arrest.

Cash stood up from the bench and stretched, his lower spine already sore from the hours of sitting. This particular backache was familiar, one he'd suffered throughout his stay with the state. Sleeping on cots and sitting on cheap chairs weren't exactly conducive to a healthy back. Funny how until now, he hadn't experienced as much as a twinge since getting out of prison.

Knowing the drill, he held his arms straight out. Hard, cold steel tightened around both wrists with an unsatisfying *click*. Hard to believe that only hours before, he'd been willingly handcuffed to Dreama's bed.

He'd been naïve to think the two of them had a shot at being together. If only he'd worked harder at resisting her, she wouldn't be in danger. But resisting Dreama was like resisting the urge to breathe—totally and completely impossible.

Right from the start, she'd wormed her way under his skin and made herself at home there. He'd thought he could control the situation, control *her*, but with every glance and every conversation, he'd fallen just a little bit more until his need for her became a full-blown obsession.

Since his father had died, he'd taken it upon himself to protect the women in his life, first with his mother and Rebecca and later with Maddie. But Dreama? Dreama had made it her mission to protect *him*.

That had been his downfall. He should've switched parole officers as soon as the threats to her life began, but in his eagerness for absolution of his past, he'd succumbed to Dreama's wishes.

She'd given him hope.

Between the moment he'd left her bed early this morning and now, he'd lost that hope.

This time, he'd do whatever necessary to protect *her*.

Even if it meant hurting them both in the process.

The cop led him out of his cell and down a short hall. Police officers and other workers busily darted from room to room, none of them paying him any attention. To them, he was just another suspect. They didn't know or care that the real baseball bat—wielding psychopath was still on the loose. Then again, as long as he was in police custody, the women around him, specifically Rebecca and Dreama, would be safe.

The officer opened the door to the interrogation room. Dreama shot up from her chair. She looked exhausted. Exhausted, but still beautiful. She was wearing one of her conservative navy suits.

Was she here as his parole officer or as his lover?

And why should the answer matter?

Once inside the interrogation room, Cash was surprised when the cop removed the metal from his wrists. Something must have happened because that wasn't procedure. Earlier, Detective Henry had kept Cash handcuffed to the table.

Dreama clenched and unclenched her fists, but other than that, she didn't move from her position at the far side of the six-foot table. Vibrating with tension, she reminded him of a shaken bottle of soda pop—ready to blow.

"We'll be monitoring the room," the officer said. He nodded once before turning to leave. "You have ten minutes."

As soon as the door closed, Dreama launched across the room and hurled herself against his chest, burying her face into his shirt. "I'm sorry this happened. It's all my fault."

He opened his mouth to protest her claim when her words permeated. She'd just given him the opening he needed. It would be easy to pin the blame on her, then use it to drive her away.

But he just couldn't do it. Not like that. He understood what it was like to live with the guilt over something he couldn't change. It wasn't her fault he was in here or that

Nancy and Laci were dead. The responsibility lay solely in the hands of whoever had framed him.

But that didn't mean he wouldn't find another way to end things with her.

Knowing it might be the last time he had the chance, he held on to her tightly, memorizing the feeling of having her in his arms. "How is it your fault? You're not the one who's framing me for murder."

She peered up at him. Her eyes were bloodshot as if she'd been crying. Seeing her in pain over him was like a wrecking ball to his gut. It was as if he were looking at his sister and his mother eight years ago. He'd failed them. Failed Maddie and Joshua. He couldn't fail Dreama.

"If I had just listened to you from the very beginning," Dreama said hoarsely, "right after the car tried to run me down, none of this would have happened."

He plunged his hands into her soft hair and cradled the back of her head. She needed to understand that it wasn't her fault. He'd been a willing participant. "We can't change the past. We can only go from here." His heart ached with imminent loss.

"I told the police you were with me in my apartment at the time of the murders," she said, laying a hand on the side of his neck, over his pulse point. "They're going to confirm the alibi with the guard. I told them you signed in as Ryder, so they're bringing a photo of you. Finn thinks that will be enough to get them to drop the charges for now."

That explained why he wasn't handcuffed to a table. "Finn?"

Her gaze darted away before returning. "I asked him to represent you."

Cash's experience with Browner had left him apprehensive about using an attorney, but Finn McKay was Dreama's friend. Plus, he'd already been helping Cash to uncover the truth about his past, proving that Cash could trust him. "Let him know it will take me a little time to pay for his services, but that I'm good for it."

Her gaze dropped down to the floor as she nibbled on her bottom lip. "He's not charging you."

She was nervous.

"That's generous of him," he said cautiously. "Why would he do this for me?"

She wouldn't look him in the eyes. "I've been keeping a secret from you."

"Tell me." He rubbed her shoulder, concerned by her behavior. "Whatever it is, I'm sure I'll understand."

Her rib cage expanded and fell as she took a deep breath. "When I was at your house, I saw a photograph of you on the wall. You were about two. I thought it was Maddox, Ryder and Jane's child."

He had no idea why that was relevant. "Okay. Lots of kids look alike."

She placed her hands on his cheeks, her fingers sweeping across the top of his cheekbones. "No, Cash. You don't understand. All the McKay males share one thing in common. Their eyes." Tears spilled over. "I should have realized it sooner. The day we met, you seemed familiar to me, but I couldn't understand why. I felt as if I already knew you."

Understanding burned like a wildfire in his chest. He staggered backward, away from Dreama and the words that were coming.

But he couldn't stop them. "Ryder and Finn's father died last year," Dreama said. "Before he passed, he told Ryder that he'd had another son. It's you."

His voice caught in his throat as his back hit the wall. "You can't know that."

"Their brother was born on Valentine's Day the same year as you. He was given up for adoption. You have the same gray eyes, Cash. You'll still have to do the DNA tests, but I know it in my gut: you're their missing brother."

His head felt as if it was about to explode. "Plenty of people have gray eyes and were born on my birthday. That doesn't mean I'm their brother."

"Would it be so bad if you were?" she asked quietly.

Dreama didn't understand. He'd wanted to find his biological family, but on his own terms. The decision, like so many others, had been taken from him.

He shut his eyes and rubbed his temples in a feeble attempt to relieve the incessant pounding. "Why didn't you tell me sooner?"

"I tried," she said quietly. "But with everything going on, I didn't get the chance."

"You've had plenty of chances," he said sharply. "But you waited to drop this on me here, at the police station, when I'm under arrest for murder." Maybe if it was a different time and it wasn't the two men that Dreama considered family, he would've been ready for this information.

But he wasn't.

Just like he wasn't ready for what he was about to do.

In a way, it would've been better if she hadn't told him. He'd been looking for a reason to end their relationship.

And she'd given him the ammunition.

Now he was going to load the pistol and shoot.

Eyes opening, he felt as if his chest had cracked wide open.

She swallowed, muscles in her cheeks twitching. "The longer I kept the secret, the harder it became to tell you, but I promise, I was going to. I never meant to keep it as long as I did. I know the timing was bad, but can't you see this as a good thing? You wanted to find your family and now you have."

He believed she would have eventually have told him. He wasn't even mad.

Just resigned.

He hardened his jaw—and his heart. "You've been lying to me," he said through gritted teeth.

She reared back as if he'd slapped her. Her bottom lip trembled. "To protect you."

Since the beginning, she'd gone above and beyond for him, risking her career and her life. But what had he risked?

Not a damn thing.

He'd selfishly taken everything she had to give. It was time for *him* to take a risk. The greatest risk he could ever imagine. Losing *her*. Because there was nothing in this world he wanted more. He'd promised not to hurt her, and once he broke that promise, she might never forgive him.

Call him weak, but he couldn't bear witness to the pain he was about to inflict. He thundered away from her, desperate to get her feminine scent out of his nose. At a safer distance, he stopped, keeping his back to her as he said, "I told you how Maddie manipulated me. I can't do that again. I won't be involved with a woman who lies to me."

It didn't matter that he couldn't see her pain because he could hear it in her voice. "What are you saying?"

"We had an agreement and I fulfilled it. I cured you of your phobia. Our agreement is done." He dropped his head to his chest. "And so are we."

Her loud footsteps neared. He braced himself for her tears, but instead, he got a slap to the chest. "You're pushing me away in order to protect me, aren't you?" Her eyes blazed with fury. "I'm not stupid, Cash, so don't treat me as if I am. I quit my job, so there's no need to hide our relationship anymore and now that the police are involved, you don't have to worry that my life is in danger. I told them everything about the threats and how it's all related to something you overheard the night of the accident."

She quit her job? He bit the inside of his cheek to keep himself from asking what had happened. "Of course, I feel protective of you—just like I'm protective of all women— but that's not what this is about." Steeling himself, he dug inside himself for all the resentment he'd kept bottled up about Maddie and channeled it toward Dreama. "This is about my inability to trust you. If you could keep this kind of a secret from me, what else will you lie to me about?"

She lifted her chin. "You're right. I am keeping another

secret from you. Something you need to know before I go."
She brushed the back of her hand across his cheek. "I love
you."

His heart took off like a greyhound in an open yard. He
was bleeding inside.

On her tiptoes, she kissed that same cheek, her soft lips
lingering. Then she turned her back on him and strode to
the door. "Goodbye, Cash."

He swallowed the lump in his throat. "Until the killer is
caught, I want you to stay at Jane's. You'll be safe there."

She stopped in her tracks. "You don't have the right to
tell me what to do." She peered over her shoulder at him.
"But I'll do it anyway. For you. Because I love you."

Watching her walk away nearly killed him. He suppressed his need to pull her back into his arms and tell
her the truth. That for the first time in his life, he was in
love too.

But he had to let her go. If he didn't, she'd continue poking her nose into his past. When the people responsible for
threatening her were in jail, he'd come clean and tell her
how he really felt about her.

He only hoped it wouldn't be too late.

TWENTY-SEVEN

Let me get this straight," Detective Henry said, leaning back in his chair. "Eight years ago, you overheard something that led to one or more people bribing an attorney to convince you to take a plea deal." He laced his hands together and rested them on his protruding belly. "Do you have any proof that this attorney, Browner, took a bribe?"

Frustrated as all hell, Cash slid a glance at Finn before answering. "No."

"And you don't remember what you overheard or know for certain who you overheard," Detective Henry said. *Again.*

Cash drummed his fingers on the table. He didn't give a fuck if his nervous habit made him appear guilty. "No."

In the past couple hours, they'd gone over this at least four times already. The police weren't going to do a damn thing, so what did any of this matter? If they weren't going to do their job, then Cash would just do it for them. He'd continue his own investigation. Unlike the good detective, he wouldn't lean back in his chair and waste time repeating the same questions over and over again while innocent lives were at stake. Cash had to finish things once and for all—without Dreama's help.

Detective Henry scratched his head. "While I admit the photograph and the baseball bat sent to Ms. Agosto have me intrigued, you have no proof that they're connected to the murders of Ms. London or Ms. Balsom. Maybe you and your lover concocted this whole story just to throw us off your trail. Is that it? Let's go over your alibi again."

He'd had enough. Time was running out. Dreama and Rebecca were safe for the time being, but he couldn't keep them locked away forever.

Cash slammed his fist on the table. "You already confirmed my alibi with the guard at Dreama's apartment. My answers aren't going to change even if you ask your questions in the form of a statement, so let me cut you off now. I've told you everything. Now are you going to do something about it or not?"

His attorney made a choking noise, covering his mouth with his hand.

The guy was...laughing?

Detective Henry sighed. He'd made it clear he didn't believe anything Cash had to say. The only reason he was letting Cash go was because he had an alibi, but Cash had no doubt as soon as he left here, whoever was responsible for the other murders would be doing their best to frame Cash for another one.

"Listen, if Ms. Agosto files a report about the incident in front of Club X and brings me the photograph and baseball bat, I can open up an investigation into it," the detective said, reluctance evident in his tone. "It's not much to go on, but at least I can use it to question"—he looked down at his notes—"Sanders, Moran, Browner, and Lundquist."

His attorney sat up in his chair. "Detective Henry, you're no rookie. Surely you must have found it odd that you received two anonymous tips, both of which incriminated my client."

Cash had to hand it to the guy. He was smart. He hadn't outright accused the detective of lazy police work, but instead had wrapped the insinuation in a compliment.

Detective Henry no longer appeared so smug. "We get dozens of anonymous tips for crimes every day, but I can see your concern."

"Good. Then you and I see eye to eye. Next time you try to arrest my client, you better make damned sure you have an identity behind your anonymous tip. Because if my client did hide a bloody baseball bat in his trunk, you can bet he wouldn't be stupid enough to do it in front of a witness. Now, unless you can give me a reason why I can't, I'm going to walk out of this station with Cash Turner beside me."

Detective Henry stood, his jaw tight. "No. He's free to go. For now." The cop shot Cash one last contemptuous look and walked out of the room.

There was a long silence.

Unsure of what to say, Cash turned to the man sitting

next to him. Normally, a quick thank you would suffice, but nothing about this situation was normal.

"So...apparently, you're my brother," Finn said, tapping his fingers on the table.

"That's the running theory, but sharing DNA doesn't make us brothers." Although, Cash had to admit that it was a little freaky that Finn appeared to have the same finger-tapping habit as him.

"You have a problem with me in particular?" Finn flashed him a smile. "Tell the truth. It's because I'm better looking than you, right?"

Cash let out a snort and shook his head. Other than his gray eyes, Finn didn't resemble Cash at all. Finn was slighter in build and of average height with a paler complexion and reddish-blond hair. It was hard to believe they were brothers.

"Come on. Let's get out of here," Finn said. He typed a message on his phone, then popped up from his chair. "We can go across the street and grab a cup of coffee."

Not seeing any choice, Cash followed Finn down the hall toward the exit. A part of him wanted to stay inside the police station, knowing that as soon as he walked out the front door, whoever had set him up would set their sights on the next target. "I really should get home."

Finn smacked him on the back. "Hey, just one cup. It's not every day you meet your long-lost brother, right?"

Cash rubbed the back of his neck, still feeling the sting of Finn's hand on his back. For a smaller guy, Finn really packed a punch. "Yeah. Okay." Cash could use the caffeine.

He was currently running on the last legs of his adrenaline, and he had to figure out his next move. "Let me call my sister and let her know I'm out."

After his arrest, he'd made Rebecca promise to stay with a friend until the killer was caught, and unlike Dreama, he knew his sister would actually listen to him.

Since she'd walked out the door, Dreama's parting words had played on repeat in his mind. She loved him. *Him.* An ex-con, a widower with nothing to his name. Maddie had claimed to love him, and maybe she had in her own way, but that love had been toxic to them both. Dreama's love was as pure as the snow falling from the clouds.

And he'd destroyed it.

He pulled out his cell and dialed his sister. As he and Finn crossed the two-lane road to the coffee shop, he told Rebecca that he'd been released and would stay in touch. Understandably, she wanted to come and get him. When he explained he was having coffee with his attorney, he tried not to feel like a hypocrite for keeping the secret that Finn was also his biological brother.

Inside the coffee shop, he followed Finn to the back. As they approached, a man got up from his chair as if he'd been waiting for them to arrive. Cash noticed there were three cups of coffee on the table.

The stranger stuck out his hand. "I'm Ryder."

Finn's text must have been to let him know they were on their way. That's why Finn had been so insistent that Cash join him for coffee.

"Is this an ambush?" Cash asked. This was the man who'd

found Dreama after her attack and had saved her life. He owed Ryder more than a simple handshake, but for now, it would have to suffice.

"I called Ryder and asked him to meet us here," Finn admitted.

Another decision had been taken from him. "Listen, Finn, I appreciate you coming down to the station to represent me, but I can't deal with this brother shit right now." Not until the murderer was no longer a threat to Dreama or his sister.

"I'm not here as your brother," Ryder said. "Okay, maybe I was a little curious to meet you, but Finn and I are here as Dreama's friends. We came to help."

Where Finn was fair-skinned and fell somewhere on the ginger scale, Ryder had a darker complexion and brown hair. Only a few inches shorter than Cash, Ryder towered over his clearly older brother. The three of them couldn't look more different, and yet if Dreama was right, they all shared the same biological father.

Finn dropped into a chair. "If we're being honest, I was willing to let you hang until Dreama dropped the biology bomb on me."

"Really?" Ryder glared at Finn as he and Cash both joined Finn at the table. "You couldn't just keep that to yourself for now?"

Finn shrugged. "I don't want to start our relationship off with a lie."

Ryder and Finn might not look alike, but the fact that they were brothers was apparent in the way they interacted with one another. If he didn't have Rebecca, Cash might have been envious of their relationship.

Cash drummed his fingers on the table and glanced out the window. "Amusing as this is, I'm tired. I just want to go home, eat a pizza, and watch a little television."

"Sounds like a good plan," Ryder said, adding a couple packets of sugar to his coffee. "You're full of crap, but it sounds good just the same."

"You don't know me," Cash said, annoyed by Ryder's assumption.

Ryder lifted his coffee cup off the table but didn't drink it. "First, Dreama has told us all about you. I highly doubt that a guy who's spent the last couple of weeks looking into his past is going to give up now that everything has hit the fan." Ryder smiled smugly. "And if you're anything like us, you're going to leave here and go confront the son of a bitch you think is responsible for the murders. You might not want us as brothers, but that doesn't mean you're not one of us anyway."

Damn it. Ryder was right. Not about him being one of them, but about everything else. "Okay. What if you're right about my plan. Are you going to try and stop me?" he asked both of them.

"Hell no. You need backup," Finn said. "Oh, and someone who can legally carry a gun."

Finn had a point. The terms of Cash's parole prohibited him from having a gun. He supposed it wouldn't hurt to work with Ryder and Finn to bring down the killer. They'd been helping him these last two weeks anyway.

"You would do that for a complete stranger?" he asked.

"You're not a stranger," Ryder said as if Cash was an idiot. "You're family. But even if you weren't, Dreama is like a sister to Jane and for all intents and purposes, that makes you my brother-in-law."

Hearing Dreama's name brought all of his guilt and regret back to the surface. "Well, I doubt Dreama would care whether you helped me. We broke up."

"Judging by the tears on her face as she left the police station, I'm assuming you're the one who broke it off," Finn said matter-of-factly.

How could he act so cavalier about Dreama's pain? "What if I did?" Cash asked.

Ryder stood, put both hands on the table, and leaned forward, getting in Cash's face. "Then you're a fucking idiot. You don't throw a woman like Dreama away."

Finn flinched. "Ryder, it's not our place to—"

"The hell it isn't," Ryder said, not taking his eyes off Cash. "It's terrifying to love a person so much you want to lock them up in a padded room and throw away the key to keep them safe. But you can't cheat death, so don't even try. It's no way to live. Don't underestimate Dreama."

"You're saying she can take care of herself."

"Fuck no," Ryder said so loudly that the people at the tables around them all stared. "You need to watch out for her. And she'll watch out for *you*. That's a relationship." He lowered his voice. "That's love."

Was it? Normally, he might agree with the guy, but when it came to this fucked-up situation, he wasn't as certain. Had he made the wrong call? He rose from his chair. "I should go."

Finn stood and threw his arm around Cash's neck. "Not without us, lover boy. Where to?"

Although the decision to find his biological family had been taken from him, he made the decision to accept his brothers' help. He nodded to Ryder. "I need you to make a phone call."

* * *

"Men are assholes," Jane said around a mouthful of ice cream. Otis the pug sat at her feet, drooling as he waited for her to drop some food his way.

Dreama dipped her spoon into the creamy goodness but she just couldn't manage to find her appetite. Is that what love did to a girl? Cash hadn't only broken her heart. He'd stolen her ability to soothe her feelings with junk food. "Uh-huh."

On the other hand, Jane couldn't eat enough. But her combo of pork rinds, peanut butter, and chocolate chip ice cream wasn't helping Dreama's appetite either. "Not my Ryder, of course, but in general... yeah, they're all assholes."

In an hour, Dreama had gone from weepy to pissed off to wistful to numb and back again. "Cash isn't an asshole. He's just..."

"An asshole." Jane remained firmly lodged in the pissed-off stage.

Dreama was going to say *confused*, but maybe Jane was

right. Cash had bailed on their relationship the minute things had gotten hard. Well, harder.

"And scared," Jane said, grabbing a handful of pork rinds from the bag. She tossed a couple of them to Otis before grinding them up with her hand and dropping them into the jar of peanut butter. "He's afraid of losing you."

Sighing, Dreama folded her arms on the table and rested her head on them. She knew exactly why Cash had done what he had. He was terrified that something would happen to her if she continued digging into his past. But instead of being honest and talking to her about it, he'd done what he considered to be the valiant thing. *Well, fuck valiance.* It was overrated. "Well, he sure picked a funny way of showing that since he lost me anyway."

"But at least you're alive," Jane pointed out, eating a spoonful of peanut butter pork rinds.

What good was being alive when she wasn't even living? She'd thought it had only been in the past year, since the assault and her subsequent anxiety attacks, that she'd been living in fear. But in truth, she'd never lived life to the fullest before meeting Cash. She'd never risked her heart.

She'd promised to stay at Jane's. Wouldn't it be a giant *fuck you* to Cash if she didn't? A part of her wanted to rebel against Cash in the name of women everywhere. But there was a killer on the loose and she wasn't suicidal. This was his idiotic way of protecting her. Because he loved her. She knew he did, no matter what lies he told her. She just wasn't sure she could ever forgive him for breaking up with her.

Maddox's babbles came through the baby monitor. "Mama Otes."

Otis must have recognized his name. He ran off toward Maddox's nursery. And speaking of dogs...

As much as Dreama would love to lavish all her affection on Maddox, she needed to let Butch outside before he had an accident. He was currently in his doggie crate in her bedroom.

Noticing Jane struggling, Dreama helped Jane get out of her chair. "I'm going to go pop home, pack a bag, and grab Butch."

"You're not supposed to leave," she reminded Dreama.

Then maybe Cash shouldn't have adopted a dog for her. He wouldn't expect her to neglect Butch, right? She didn't have a choice. "It's the middle of the day. No one is going to come after me in the next thirty minutes."

The second the words left her lips, it hit her. Her assault last year had occurred in the morning.

Bad things didn't always happen at night.

Sometimes, monsters attacked in the light of day.

TWENTY-EIGHT

As much as Cash looked forward to getting to know his brothers, he didn't need to see them naked on day one.

"Apparently, we have more in common than our eyes," Ryder said with a smile, thankfully wrapping a towel around his lower half.

Finn shook his head at his brother. "Really? You couldn't have kept that thought to yourself?"

"What?" Ryder laughed. "Like you weren't thinking it too?"

A phone call by Ryder to Stephen Browner had led them to Detroit's oldest and only bathhouse. Eager to nail down the McKay account, Browner had let Ryder know where to find him.

Browner was their strongest lead into finding out the truth about Cash's case eight years ago. While Cash still couldn't prove that Browner was bribed into convincing Cash to take a guilty plea, there was at least enough evidence to suggest it and his gut told him Browner was the missing link to finding the person responsible for the murders of Cash's coworkers. The plan he and his brothers had concocted was a Hail Mary pass. If Browner wouldn't talk, or if Cash's gut was wrong and Browner didn't have any information to give, the killer could go free.

According to the attendant, Browner was waiting for Ryder in one of the steam rooms and had paid extra for privacy so that Ryder and he could talk business uninterrupted. It didn't hurt that Browner would be caught unaware and without a weapon.

"You ready?" Cash asked them, ready to confront the son of a bitch who had ruined his life.

Knotting the towel at his waist, Finn nodded to Cash. "Lead the way."

They walked down the hall to where the attendant had instructed they'd find Browner. At the door, Ryder peered through the small window to confirm Browner was alone. "He's in there. I don't see anyone else."

Finn opened the door and Cash stepped inside. It was like entering the bowels of hell. Visible steam floated in the room like clouds and his skin immediately beaded with sweat. The next few minutes would be miserable.

But worth it.

Through the mist, Cash spied the man he'd come to see sitting on the wooden bench. "Excuse me, this room is reserved," Browner said. His words were polite, but his tone was not. "You'll have to use another one."

"Yeah, I don't think so, Browner," Ryder said, coming into the room with Finn behind him. The door closed.

Browner stumbled to his feet, his towel slipping. "What the fuck is going on?"

Cash moved closer, getting a better glimpse at Browner. His hair was a much darker brown than it had been eight years ago. If Ryder hadn't verified it was him, Cash would've never known who he was if he saw him on the street. In fact, he hadn't known.

"I saw you," Cash said, things coming together. "I was in the lobby of Lundquist Animal Health, waiting for Thomas to finish his previous appointment. You were that previous appointment."

Cash had to hand it to him. Browner didn't flinch. Then again, he was an experienced liar. "I have no idea what you're talking about."

Cash wiped the sweat from his brow. "You had your phone up to your face to block my view and you were looking away. Your hair threw me off. Lundquist Animal Health is one of your clients, isn't it?"

The dickhead had the audacity to puff out his chest. "I'm ethically bound from revealing the identity of my clients."

"That's a lie," Finn said. "A client's identity isn't privileged information under the attorney-client privilege. Why don't you try again?"

Browner huffed out a breath. "Fine. I've represented Lundquist Animal Health on a few legal matters. So what?"

Were Lundquist and Browner working together to frame him? "You tried to set me up for my coworkers' murders, but you messed up. I have an alibi."

"Murder? You're out of your mind." Browner strode toward the exit. "I'm getting out of here."

"I don't think so," Ryder said as he and Finn blocked the door. "Not until you finish answering our questions."

Seeing he was trapped, Browner started to look a bit more nervous and returned to sit on the bench. "Fine. I'll answer your damned questions."

Having eaten nothing all day and losing about a gallon of water through his sweat, Cash felt a little dizzy on his feet. "Tell me about Laci London and Nancy Balsom. They were both beaten to death with a baseball bat."

Browner shook his head. "I heard about it on the news, but I swear, I had nothing to do with it. I don't know those women."

Shit. Either he was a better liar than Cash thought or he was telling the truth.

"How long has Lundquist been your client?" Ryder asked, taking the questioning in another direction.

Not answering, Browner shifted on the bench.

"You know when he sues, we can subpoena your records," Finn said. "If you help us out right now, maybe we won't take all of your money."

Finn had spoken the magic word. *Money.*

Browner swore under his breath. "Eight years."

"How much did he pay you to ruin my life?" Cash asked, his fingers curling into the palms of his hands. It was a good thing Ryder and Finn were there to keep him from pummeling Browner's face in. While it might feel satisfying, assaulting his ex-lawyer would be a return ticket to prison for a parole violation.

"He didn't pay me anything." Browner's sweat continuously dripped off his chin. "He promised to provide me with some major accounts to help me get into the law firm of my choice."

Even hearing Browner's confession, Cash still couldn't believe the man he'd considered a father had betrayed him. "And in return?"

"I had to bury your Breathalyzer and toxicology report and convince you to accept the plea deal," Browner admitted.

Cash stumbled, the room spinning as if he was drunk. "Did he tell you why?"

Browner wiped his cheek with the back of his hand. "Not in so many words. But it had something to do with some study results."

"Study results," Cash repeated.

A light flashed in front of his eyes as the floor seemed to tilt beneath his feet. His legs buckled and his knees slammed onto the hard surface. An intense pressure banded around his skull. He heard his brothers calling out to him, but he couldn't respond. Memories flickered through his mind like an 8 mm film reel of his life and when he got to the end, he realized India had been right.

Once he'd been ready to face them, his repressed memories had returned.

Cold water spilled down his throat. Realizing his eyes were closed, he opened them and took stock of his location. He was lying on a couch in the locker room. From above him, Finn held the rim of a water bottle to his mouth. "Drink up. You passed out in the steam room."

Grabbing the bottle, Cash sat up just as Ryder entered the room.

"We might have a problem," Ryder said. "I just spoke with Jane. Dreama went to her apartment."

Cash's chest filled with dread.

He'd finally remembered everything from the night of the accident, but what good did it do him if he couldn't keep Dreama safe? He should have never made her believe he was angry with her. He should've kept her by his side.

Because of him, Dreama was in danger.

He just prayed he got to her before it was too late.

* * *

Positioning her key between her fingers as a makeshift weapon, Dreama hurried through her apartment lobby to the elevator. She passed by the guard desk, a little surprised it was currently unmanned. It wasn't uncommon—after all, they worked twelve-hour shifts and had to use the bathroom a couple of times a day—but it raised a red flag nonetheless. Until she was safe behind her locked door, she'd remain extra vigilant. Because despite what Cash believed, she could take care of herself.

Once on her floor, she eyed the hallway to ensure no one was lurking, and upon determining it all clear, she quickly unlocked her door, stepped inside, and slammed it shut. She slid to the carpet and closed her eyes, resting her chin on her knees.

She appreciated having Jane to comfort her, but at the

same time, she needed space to mope alone. There were times a woman needed to ugly cry without an audience, and this was one of those times.

Cash loved her. He might not have said it, but he wouldn't have broken things off with her if he didn't. The stupid thing was if he'd only asked her to stay at Jane's for a couple days until the real killer was caught, she would've done it. He hadn't needed to lie to her. There was a reason she'd always been drawn to BDSM. The key principles of communication and consent were essential in every Dom/sub relationship. In Cash's obsessive need to protect her, he'd violated both. It was ironic he'd accused her of acting like Maddie when he was the one who'd tried to manipulate her with his lies. She loved him, but until he learned that he couldn't control her outside of the bedroom, she couldn't be with him.

At the knock on the door, she snapped up her head. *Cash.* She got to her feet and peeked through the peephole. Disappointment swept through her. It wasn't Cash.

She had never seen this man before in her life, but judging by his uniform, he was a police officer.

"Can I help you?" she asked.

He held up his badge. "I'm looking for Dreama Agosto. I'm here to get some more information from her regarding Cash Turner."

She opened the door and waved him inside. "I'm Dreama. I'm not sure what else I can tell you, but you're welcome to ask your questions."

"Thank you. I promise not to take too much of your

time," he said, stepping into her apartment. As she closed the door, something sharp, like a bee sting, poked her neck. Rubbing the spot, she flipped around.

Gray-haired with wrinkles around his eyes and mouth, he looked like he could be friends with her father. He wasn't more than a few inches taller than her and definitely skinnier. If she walked by him on the street, she wouldn't look twice, and if he offered her candy, she wouldn't hesitate.

But monsters came in all shapes and sizes. Hitler had been slightly shorter than the average height for a man and he'd been responsible for the murder of millions. The man who'd beaten her to within an inch of her life had been tall and beefy. Meg was shorter than herself and rail thin.

Judging by the baseball bat that was now in his hands, there was no mistaking that the man she'd invited inside her apartment was also a monster.

She tried to scream but her vocal cords weren't working right. The noise that came out of her throat was too quiet to be heard by anyone. From within her purse, her cell phone was ringing.

The adrenaline coursing through her made her dizzy. Her chest felt tight as if there was a heavy weight sitting on it and her heart was sprinting a mile a minute. She wobbled as her vision started to darken.

No, no, no. She couldn't have a panic attack. Not now.

She reached behind her for the door handle, but before she could escape, the monster grabbed her and tossed her to the floor as if she were a rag doll. "Who are you?" she asked, her words coming out slurred and whispered.

"Haven't you guessed?" he asked calmly.

Her tongue felt as if it had swollen to ten times its normal size and her limbs tingled. Her gaze landed on the syringe sticking out the top of his pocket.

That sting on her neck. Had he injected her with something?

She wasn't having a panic attack. He'd drugged her.

Based on her final conversations with Cash, she took a guess at his identity. "You're Thomas Lundquist."

He tipped his head. "I am."

If her life wasn't in peril, she would feel badly for Cash. Out of all the possible suspects, she'd never thought it would turn out to be Lundquist. "What happened to the guard?" Because she knew Lundquist had to be responsible for his disappearance.

"I pulled the fire alarm in the parking garage," he said matter-of-factly. "When he came to investigate, I jabbed him with the same thing that I just gave you, although a much higher dose. He's currently sleeping it off between a Lexus and a Ford. He won't remember a thing about how he got there or understand why all the security tapes are blank when he checks them."

Her body trembled violently. "You killed Cash's co-workers."

"You're not only beautiful, but smart too. I see why Cash fell for you."

Her limbs were becoming less useful by the second. It was as if they were filled with gelatin. If she couldn't get out of her apartment, she needed another plan. There was only one thing she could do to help herself. She just hoped she didn't pass out before she achieved it. She slowly scooted backward toward her bedroom. "If you're going to kill me, at least tell me why."

He placed a hand on the gun in his holster. "Do you know how expensive it is to bring a drug to market? Ten years ago, I had to borrow money from some very questionable people in order to stay in business, but I knew I was onto something special with Dosothysomine."

"Doso..." Her lips were numb, making it difficult to speak.

"Dosothysomine. It's a dissociative anesthetic used to induce a trancelike state in animals for surgery. I promised my financial backers that the drug would make them millions. Everything was going according to plan. The studies went perfectly. The drug showed no adverse effects like the other drugs on the market. Then my research scientist discovered the drug didn't work quite as we believed. While it caused catatonia and amnesia, the brain EEG tests detected that the animals still felt pain. I had no choice. If I didn't bring the drug to market, my financers would've killed me."

Catatonia and amnesia.

She had a feeling that he wasn't talking with her out of the goodness of his heart. He was just biding his time until the drug took full effect and she became catatonic. Then he'd bash her head in with the baseball bat. "That's what Cash overheard that night. Wasn't it?"

"Sanders and Moran were discussing it. When Cash came

to me with what he'd heard, I put some of the drug into his champagne during our toast."

That's why Cash couldn't remember what happened that night. The drug had given him amnesia. It also explained what had caused the accident.

She continued slowly crab-crawling toward her bedroom. She was almost there. "I don't understand why you killed Cash's coworkers."

"When Browner came and told me that you'd contacted him about Cash's case, I initially planned on just scaring you into dropping the issue with my car and the photograph. Once I realized you and Cash weren't going to give up, I decided to go after his coworkers. I'd read all about your attack. I figured killing those women with a baseball bat would send Cash the message to stop digging into his past. But then he told me he'd started to remember things." He lifted his bat in the air. "Your murder and his suicide will tie up all the loose ends."

Her strength ebbing, she got to her feet and lumbered the last couple of lengths to her bedroom. The second she crossed inside, she fell flat on the floor, pain blasting through her chin and head. She couldn't move. Her legs were useless. She was going to die here and there was nothing she could do to stop it. A rough wet tongue licked her finger.

Harnessing all her energy, she managed to lift that finger to unlatch the door to the dog crate. Butch's growls and shouts from behind her were the last sounds she heard.

Then everything went black.

TWENTY-NINE

Cash rushed into the lobby of Dreama's apartment building with Ryder and Finn following close behind. When Dreama hadn't answered her phone, Cash had comforted himself with the thought that she lived in a secure building and had Butch to defend her.

But comfort turned to dread as his gaze fell upon the unmanned desk. "Damn it. The guard isn't here." He shot past where he normally signed in, raced toward the elevator, and hit the button on the wall.

Finn's hand wrapped around Cash's arm. "You shouldn't assume—"

"Make the call," Cash said to him. They had made a contingency plan on the way over and it looked like they were going to have to use it.

He didn't know what happened to the guard. Thomas could have paid him off or he could've just gone to take a piss. Either way, the guy wasn't there to do his job and that gave Thomas a chance to gain access to the building.

He turned toward Ryder, who sat behind the guard desk. "Are you ready?"

"I need about...three minutes," Ryder said, typing on the computer keyboard.

Cash stepped onto the elevator and prayed he wasn't already too late.

The doors slid closed and each second that followed felt like an eternity.

He wouldn't be able to live with himself if...

No. He bit his cheek so hard he tasted blood. He couldn't bear to finish the thought. Suffused with rage, Cash kicked the elevator wall. How could he have been so naïve as to trust Thomas? Eight years ago, sure. Cash hadn't known any better. But after prison? He'd practically hand-fed Thomas the details of his and Dreama's investigation. He'd admitted his memory of that night was returning. If he'd only kept his mouth shut, Dreama would be safe right now.

As soon as his foot hit Dreama's floor, he heard Butch's vicious growls coming from Dreama's apartment. Cash tore down the hallway, his heart beating so fast, he was sure it would kill him. And if Dreama was dead, he might even welcome it.

A pitiful yelp resounded as Cash flew through her unlocked door. He moved farther into the apartment, unsettled by the unexpected silence. Dressed in a police uniform, Thomas stood with his back to Cash, holding his wooden baseball bat high in the air.

"Wait!" Cash shouted. "Don't do it, Thomas. Put the bat down."

Thomas turned around. Behind him, Dreama lay prone on the floor, her arm outstretched toward Butch's cage. Both legs of Thomas's pants were torn and bloody, making Cash wonder if Butch had been responsible. But other than Thomas's injuries, there was no sign that the dog was even there. Cash tried not think about what that meant.

Cash had expected to look at Thomas and finally see the man behind the mask. But from the outside, Thomas was still the same man Cash had always known, the man he'd once revered as a father figure. The man who'd inspired Cash's love of animals. How could a person like that hide such evil inside of him?

"Cash." Thomas lowered the bat to his side. "You're early."

He covered the area over his heart with his hand. "And you're a serial killer." If he was early, did that mean Dreama was still alive? There was no blood on the baseball bat, but from far away, he couldn't tell if she was breathing. "Is Dreama alive?"

Thomas's gaze darted wildly from side to side. "She is, but not for long."

"Let her go, Thomas. You don't want to take another life."

Thomas pulled his gun from its holster and aimed it at Cash. "You're right. I don't. But sometimes we have to do things we don't want for the greater good."

Thomas's actions no longer surprised him.

"And what greater good is that?" Cash asked, putting out his palms to show Thomas that he wasn't armed. "Money?

Because you obviously care nothing about the animals you allege to be helping."

A muscle in Thomas's jaw ticked. "You remember."

"Everything," Cash said, enunciating the word. "Stephen Browner told me how you bought him off and it's just a matter of time before Moran and Sanders start talking. Even if you kill Dreama and me, it's all over for you, Thomas. I've told two other people, two men with more money than you. They'll make sure to take you down."

Thomas's didn't blink but there was a tremor in the hand holding the gun. "You're lying."

Cash didn't respond, but he did take a step toward Thomas. He tried to act as if he wasn't scared, but the truth was he'd never been more terrified in his life.

Thomas shook his head and laughed bitterly. "The night of the party, you were never supposed to get behind the wheel. I had expected the drug to take effect much quicker than it did. I suppose I didn't factor in your size. It took you longer to metabolize. I thought you'd pass out at the party and everyone would assume you had drunk too much."

Hearing Thomas admit the truth wasn't as gratifying as Cash would've expected. "I overheard a conversation between a couple of your scientists. They found evidence that Dosothysomine paralyzed the animals but that they could still feel pain during the surgery." He looked his old family friend right in the eye. "I told you and you said you'd *take care of it*."

Thomas had taken care of it all right, by covering his tracks. "Higher doses of Dosothysomine cause memory loss."

"That's why I couldn't remember what happened at the party or even before it," Cash said, putting it all together. "Why I had so much trouble communicating after the accident. The police thought I was drunk or high."

"They tested you, but as you know, Dosothysomine doesn't metabolize in the kidneys or liver, so it doesn't show up in blood tests. I bribed Browner and a lab tech at the hospital to switch your results with another patient. I didn't want you to go to prison, but if you realized you weren't intoxicated, you would've started asking questions. I couldn't risk losing FDA approval for Dosothysomine."

"By drugging me, you set off a chain of events that ended up with my wife and unborn son dead!"

"It was an accident," Thomas said, a bead of sweat rolling down his cheek. His hair stuck up in all directions as if he'd been pulling at the ends. He looked out of control and for a man waving a gun in his hand, that was a dangerous thing. "I never meant for anyone to get hurt. All I ever wanted was to help animals. Since Dosothysomine came to market, thousands of dogs and cats that would've otherwise died during surgery survived. My company has developed three other drugs that greatly improve animals' lives. I have thousands of employees who depend on me for their livelihood. If you expose me—expose Dosothysomine—the company won't survive. All those people will lose their jobs. I love you like a son, Cash, but you really shouldn't have poked your nose into all this."

Cash didn't know whether to laugh or cry. "You can't believe you're actually making animal lives better. Animals feel pain. Just because they don't have the ability to communicate that fact or remember it later doesn't make it right."

Nothing Thomas did was for the animals.

It was greed, pure and simple.

Thomas's fingers twitched on the gun. "I never wanted animals to suffer, but like I said before. It was for the greater good. The animals live longer, healthier lives because of me."

"And what about Nancy and Laci? Did they also die for the greater good?" Cash asked, needing to get Thomas to admit his role in their deaths.

"Do you know how easy it was to get them each to accept a date from me just because I'm wealthy? Their deaths were your fault—yours and Dreama's. If you had only stopped meddling, I wouldn't have needed to kill them and frame you for their murders."

Cash blew out a breath. "Did you get what you needed?" Cash asked.

The voice in his ear applied in the affirmative as the stomp of several people came up from behind him.

"Put the gun on the floor, put your hands in the air, and step back from the weapons," Detective Henry ordered. "Thomas Lundquist, you're under arrest for the murders of Laci London and Nancy Balsom."

"You were wearing a wire?" Lundquist looked at Cash as if he'd betrayed him. "It doesn't matter. There's nothing that my money can't fix. I'll be out of jail by the end of the day."

"I wouldn't count on it," Ryder said as he entered the room with Finn, who'd been the one to call Detective Henry. "Since I just sent your confession to all the major news outlets across the country." A gifted techie, Ryder had used Cash's phone to record the confession and through the guard's computer, had downloaded it from the cloud and mass emailed it to over one hundred news organizations.

Once the police had Thomas in handcuffs, Cash hurried toward Dreama. Not far from where she lay, a panting Butch rested on his side with blood dripping down his chest. Someone called out for medical assistance for the dog as Cash took in the sight of Dreama.

Eerily pale, she was now on her back as two female EMS workers hovered over her. He didn't see any blood, but she was way too still.

It took him three tries before he could get the words out. "Is she alive?"

The EMS worker with her fingers on Dreama's pulse point met his eyes. "I can't find a pulse."

Cash fell to his knees.

His heart felt as if it were being ripped apart. This was all his fault. It was because of him that Thomas had set his sights on Dreama. He'd thought he'd been doing the right thing in pushing her away, but in the end, he couldn't save her.

He'd made plenty of mistakes in his life, but the biggest one was not telling her how much he loved her.

And now he'd never get the chance.

THIRTY

Dreama awoke to a familiar steady beeping and the scent of disinfectant. Before she even opened her eyes, she knew she was in the hospital. She just didn't remember why.

Her body felt heavy, much like she had when she'd had the flu last year. She catalogued the sensations of her body. She had a headache and the typical aches and pains leftover from her attack, but nothing else. And she didn't have the numb feeling that morphine gave her.

The last thing she remembered was leaving Jane's house to go get Butch. Had she gotten into a car accident on the way home?

"I think she's waking up," her mother said on a loud whisper.

Oh shit. Her mother was there.

Dreama's eyes fluttered open. Her parents stood on the right side of the bed, both of them looking haggard. It was last year all over again, only this time she couldn't even remember what had put her in the hospital.

"Thank God. We've been so worried about you," her father said. He reached out as if he was going to touch her, then snatched back his hand. "You've been unconscious for twelve hours."

"Hi," Dreama said scratchily, her throat terribly dry. "What happened? How did I get here?"

"An ambulance brought you over from your apartment. Thomas tried to kill you," Cash said from the other side of the bed.

She turned to look at him. If she wasn't so confused, she might have freaked out that her parents and Cash were all in the same room. "Why don't I remember?" she asked him.

He curled his fingers around the bedrail. "He gave you a drug that causes amnesia. Dosothysomine. The same drug he gave to me the night of the accident."

Her head pounded. That Doso...damned drug left her with a massive hangover. "You saved me?" Had they reconciled? Because she *did* remember him breaking up with her.

"Actually, you can thank Butch for that," he said. "He attacked Thomas, buying us enough time to get to you."

"Us?"

"Ryder, Finn, the police, EMS...It was a team effort." He shrugged as if it was no big deal.

But it *was* a big deal. Because the Cash who'd broken up with her wouldn't have accepted anyone else's help. He would've insisted on saving her alone. "Butch got a little hurt in the battle, but Rebecca patched him up. He'll be back home with you in no time."

"I'm sorry," her mom said. "Who's Butch? Dreama, I thought you didn't have a roommate?"

Dreama bit her lip to keep from laughing. "Butch is a dog, Mom."

"You have a dog? They carry germs, you know." Her mother leaned over and tucked Dreama's hair behind her ear. "No matter. Your father and I have talked and we think in light of what's happened, you should move back home. With your dog, of course."

Oh no. She should've known this would be coming. Still a bit weak, she hit the button on the bed's remote so that she could sit up. "I'm not moving home."

Not unless she wanted her mom to drive her insane.

"Honey, you've been through too much." Her mom took her hand and squeezed. "You need someone who will take care of you."

"You're underestimating your daughter," Cash said. "She can take care of herself just fine."

That's not what he'd implied at the police station. When did he have a change of heart? Had she forgotten a conversation with him?

She really wished her parents would take a hike so she could talk to Cash in private. This amnesia thing was freaking annoying.

"I'm sorry," her mother said sarcastically. "I'm her mother. I think I know her better than some friend she's never mentioned."

Dreama sighed. A little morphine could've really come in handy right now. "Mom. He's more than a friend, but even if he wasn't, he has every right to voice his opinion."

Her mother frowned. "You didn't even tell me you were seeing someone."

If her head didn't hurt so much, she'd be banging it against the wall. "There's a lot I don't tell you. Not because I'm hiding it, but because it's none of your business. I know you worry about me and that's fine, because you're my parents, but I'm an adult. You need to accept that I'm capable of taking care of myself."

Her mom's eyes grew watery. "I just wanted to protect you from getting hurt."

Dreama was so tired of everyone wanting to protect her. "I know, but it's not your job anymore. It's mine and I'm going to make choices that you may not agree with. Sometimes, I eat ice cream for dinner. I quit my job. I mix my darks, whites, and colors all together in the washing machine." She wrung her hands together. "I just wish you guys believed in me."

"You quit your job?" her mom asked.

It shouldn't have surprised her that her mom had glommed onto the part about her quitting her job.

"Honey, that's not important," her father said, throwing his arm around her mother's shoulders. "Dreama thinks we don't believe in her."

"That couldn't be further from the truth." Her mom's eyes turned watery. "We're so proud of you." She nodded, dabbing her tears with a tissue. "You're right. It's your life. You should be free to live it the way you want. But know that no matter what happens, we love you. We support your decisions. And we'll always be here for you if you need us."

Dreama wasn't sure if her mom would hold to that promise, but it didn't matter, because she was through letting it affect how she lived her life. Quitting her job had only been the first step. From this point on, she lived life on her own terms.

She shifted on the bed, angling toward her parents. "I'm sorry I haven't been home since I moved out. I've missed you guys so much."

Then she did something she'd wanted to do for a long time.

After hugging her mother, she held out her arms to her father. He stood from the chair, hope lighting up his eyes, and leaned over the bedrail.

For the first time in more than a year, she hugged her father. Engulfed in his warmth, she closed her eyes and breathed him in. He and her mother didn't need to do more than this to make her feel safe.

"Well," he said as he pulled back. "Your mother and I have been up all night. If you've got a ride home..."

She glanced at Cash. "I'm good. Go home."

Five long minutes passed before they finally left. Cash had been awfully quiet. She had no idea what was going through his mind.

"So..." Cash lowered the bedrail and scooted his chair closer. "That's twice now you've mentioned quitting your job. What happened?"

Her hackles went up. If he thought he could swoop in

and make everything better, he had another think coming. "Yeah, I quit. Although Meg will write it up as a termination due to misconduct." He motioned for her to continue. "Someone—I'm assuming Thomas—sent the photograph of us at Club X to Meg. After admitting she'd been yanking my chain about the promotion, she offered to give me a promotion for real if I broke things off with you."

"And you chose me."

She sidestepped his assumption. "Meg wanted to keep the competition going and I decided I didn't want to play anymore. Anyway, there's a chance there will be department hearing to determine if charges should be brought against me."

"Whatever you need from me, let me know." His eyes bulged out a little and the muscles of his neck grew taut. But to his credit, he kept his cool.

"You're not going to tell me what to do about it?" she asked.

"No."

"Or rush to the department of corrections and take the blame for everything?"

"No." He gave her a little smile. "You can handle it."

Maybe she had a head injury. "I don't get it."

He took her hand. "I thought I'd lost you."

She yanked it back. "What makes you think you haven't?"

"You're alive," he said as if it was obvious.

She rubbed the sides of her head. "If you've already groveled, I'm sorry, I have amnesia. I don't remember it. You'll have to do it again."

Cash climbed onto the mattress. "Move over."

"You're being bossy." But she shifted herself on the mattress to give him some room anyway.

"You're in bed." He settled beside her and took over the role of massaging her temples. "You know the rules. I *am* the boss."

Ooh. Those large hands of his felt good on her. "I seem to remember you breaking up with me. That means you no longer have bossing rights in bed."

"What if I tell you that I was wrong?" He stopped his massaging just long enough to tuck a lock of hair behind her ear. "That I had made a horrible mistake and I was sorry?"

He paused, but she didn't speak, sensing he had more to say. "I never talked about it, but my mom fell apart after my dad died. For months, she didn't get out of bed, and even when she did, she was a walking zombie. Rebecca was only a year younger than me, but I thought it was my responsibility to take care of things. And I did until, finally, Thomas convinced my mother to get professional help."

How ironic that the man who'd once been Cash's savior had later become his greatest enemy.

She wanted to give Cash a second chance, but she was scared. If she felt this deeply about him now, what would it be like in six months or a year? She wouldn't survive the heartbreak if she was forced to walk away. "How do I know you're not going to try to make a decision for me again? You heard what I told my mother. It also applies to you. I might make choices you don't agree with, but you need to accept that right or wrong, they're mine to make."

He kissed her forehead. "I can say I learned my lesson, but you deserve more than empty promises. That's why I'm going to ask India for a referral." As if he couldn't stop touching her, he swept her cheek with the back of his hand. "It's time I dealt with everything else that's happened."

If she was on her feet, she'd swoon. "You'd go to therapy for me?"

He lifted her on top of him, so that they were eye level, and cradled her face in his hands. "Don't you know? I'm in love with you, Dreama. There's nothing that I wouldn't do for you. You're the first woman I've ever loved—and if you'll have me—my last and only."

She could make him grovel some more, but then again, she had made the decision to start living her life and there was no time like the present. She smiled. "I love you too. And when I get out of here, I plan on showing you how much."

THIRTY-ONE

Spread out on her couch, her feet in Cash's lap, Dreama tossed the empty bag of potato chips onto the coffee table. For the second night in a row, they were watching television. And while she appreciated he had eight seasons of *Supernatural* to catch up on, there was something she'd rather be doing right now. *Him.*

Two days out of the hospital, Dreama was ready to grab the bull by the horns. Or rather, she was ready to get laid by one. Since bringing her home, Cash had been super sweet. Too sweet. He'd been treating her as if she were made of glass. Whenever she'd tried to initiate sex—a kiss, a grope, or anything remotely sexual in nature—he'd give her a chaste kiss on the lips and ask if she wanted a glass of water.

The answer was no. It was always no.

What she wanted was his tongue in her mouth and his dick in her pussy.

Tired of giving hints, she climbed onto her knees and turned to him. "There's something I need from you." She whipped off her blouse. Her nipples protruded from the lavender lace covering them. "Your cock. I want you to fuck me."

Not make love. Not have sex. She wanted their boundaries pushed and their fantasies realized. She craved a no-holds-barred fucking with Cash in control and her at his mercy.

He swallowed hard. "Are you sure? If you're not ready, I'll wait until you are."

"I'm so ready, if you don't fuck me, I'm going to empty the entire box of sex toys onto my bed and have an orgy for one with them."

His gaze didn't leave her breasts. "I don't want to scare you."

She smiled wide. "I want to be scared."

Not the kind she'd experienced during her assault. That was like falling out of an airplane at ten thousand feet without a parachute.

But being scared by Cash? Not only was he the one pushing her out of the plane, but he was also her parachute, keeping her safe.

Cash held his hands out, midway between their bodies, at level with her rib cage. "Tell me your safe word," he said hoarsely.

"Marathon." She couldn't stop staring at his hands—those blunt fingertips, those thick digits, the light dusting of hair. "Don't hold back."

His lids grew hooded. "You don't know what you're asking for. I might hurt you."

Magic words for a masochist. "Cash, I want to be scared. I want to be hurt. I want to feel you inside of me with nothing between us." They didn't need condoms. They were disease-free and there was no chance of her getting pregnant.

Her heart was sprinting a mile a minute. She watched his hands moving closer. Roughened fingertips swept across her skin. She shivered, feeling it not only wherever his fingers made contact with her skin, but *everywhere*.

There was no fear. No pain. No flashbacks.

Only immense pleasure and heat—so much heat in that whisper of a touch. She was burning alive from it.

He groaned and wrapped his hands around her waist, yanking her to him. "Fuck. Fuck. Fuck."

"That's the general idea," she teased.

His hands skimmed up her sides, roaming until they settled on the middle of her back and unclasped her bra. Then he slowly peeled each strap down her arm, taking his time as if he was savoring the moment. "Your skin is so soft." His lips caressed her naked shoulder. "Softer than I ever imagined." He kissed her other shoulder as her bra fell to the mattress. "How does it feel to have my hands on you?"

She slid one of her hands up his chest while she curled the other around his neck. "It feels as if they belong there."

And then his mouth was on hers, crushing and demanding. Taking everything she had to give without restraint. He tasted like a man who not only knew what he wanted but refused to settle for anything less. This was the Cash who'd been buried beneath his civility. The Cash who'd been waiting to be released from his shackles. And now that he'd been freed, he was wild in his abandon, hungry for that of which he'd been deprived.

There was nothing for her to do but surrender to it.

Her mind went fuzzy, as if all her thoughts were blurry around its edges. She was drunk on Cash's passion, his bruising lips, and powerful tongue. She reveled in the capable hands that were desperate in the exploration of her body.

One hand gripping the back of her neck, he held her tight to him, while the other hand pinched and stroked her breast. He twisted and pulled her nipples until she moaned into his mouth. She held on for dear life, bright white stars dancing in front of her eyes.

"Clothes off," he said against her lips. His frantic hands moved to her waist. "You have ten seconds to get these fucking clothes off before I rip them off you."

She'd never hated cotton more.

Her trembling fingers went to the button of her pants. It took her three tries before she finally got the damned thing through the opening.

"Time's up," Cash growled by the time her pants were down to her knees.

In one swift motion, he had her on her back and her pants off. On a loud rip, he tore her panties clean off her body and his head descended. Before she could process that he'd managed to tear her panties using only one hand, he maneuvered her on the couch, lifted her legs straight into the air, and threw her feet over his shoulders. Then without pause, he positioned his face between her thighs and speared his tongue into her soaking channel.

And he wasn't gentle about it either.

Spreading her past the point of comfortable, he used his tongue, fingers, lips, and teeth to completely consume her. The rough hairs on his chin burned the inside of her vulva. The sensation of it was like lighting a match against her skin. Her thighs shook from the intensity and from having this carefully controlled man out of control with want for her.

There was no holding back from the approaching climax. If she was supposed to ask for permission to come, she'd have to take the punishment. She was incapable of speech or rational thought. She was simply *his*. A moaning, writhing, woman on the precipice of something too big to name or deny.

Her fingers curled into her palms as she burst into violent flames. Over and over, her pussy clamped down on Cash's thrusting tongue as spasms wracked her sex and flowed outward, bathing her in liquid heat.

Cash raised his glistening mouth from her pussy, his chin soaked with her release. His gray eyes had turned dark, the pupils blown to the size of a full moon in the midnight sky, and his nostrils flared. He almost looked possessed. "Run," he warned.

Slow to process, she blinked.

"Go. Run!" he commanded.

She quickly rolled off the couch and sprinted toward her bedroom. Her thighs were slick with her climax and his saliva, but she couldn't allow it to slow her down. Heeding his warning, she raced away, growing more aroused with every step she took.

Outside her room, she looked both left and right, not sure which way to turn. She heard a growl and a rustle as Cash removed his clothes. With mere seconds to decide, she darted inside her bedroom. Before she could close the door, Cash caught up to her, wrapping his arms around her waist, then throwing her onto the mattress.

He covered her naked body with his own, pinning her to the bed with his weight. His hand plunged into her hair, tugging on it hard enough to tilt her chin up and expose her neck. "Did you honestly think you could get away from me? There's not a place you could run where I wouldn't find you."

"Fuck you," she spit out, torn between fighting and surrendering.

He yanked her hair harder, hard enough to make her eyes water and her pussy clench. "That kind of language isn't going to help your case. I'm going to hurt you." He lowered his mouth to her ear as if he didn't want her to miss what he was about to say. "The only question is how much."

"Please don't hurt me," she said, playing her part. "I'll be good. I promise."

"Words aren't enough." He released his grip on her hair only to flip her onto her stomach and turn her around to face him. "Prove it to me." He curled his fingers of one hand around the base of his cock and the other cradled her skull. "Suck it, baby. Show me how much you want it."

Last time she'd had his cock in her mouth, he'd been cuffed to the bed, but tonight, he was the one in control. She opened her mouth wide in submission. His cock slipped between her lips and over her tongue. He tasted like a salty treat and she savored the flavor. With his hands on both sides of her face, he worked himself in and out of her mouth, going farther and farther each time until he hit the back of her throat. Tears leaked from her eyes as she gagged.

He laughed darkly. "Gagging and crying only makes me harder. If you knew how many times I've made myself come thinking about you choking on my cock while your mascara runs down your face, you would've run a lot faster."

Even as he said those nasty words, he was easing his cock back.

She looked up at him, giving him her silent consent to continue.

He lovingly brushed his hand down her face. Then he fucked her mouth as if it belonged to him.

Cash's act of dominance gave her permission to surrender. Her mind went blank and her muscles relaxed as she sank into that place where her only goal was to please him.

Suddenly, he ripped his cock out of her mouth. "I'm not ready to come yet. Not until I'm in your pussy."

He moved to the other side of her body and slid his hand between her thighs. "You're drenched, baby."

His fingers grazed her throbbing clitoris, causing her to shudder. A moan spilled from her lips as he shoved his fingers into her pussy. She couldn't stop from squeezing around him. "Fuck, you're tight." He pulled out and rubbed her clitoris before plunging inside of her again. "That's three. You're ready for me." He lowered his mouth to her neck. "I can't wait any longer. I need to fuck you."

For all his threats of hurting her, he'd made sure that she was ready for his cock. "Please," she begged. "I need you too."

Holding her in place with a hand on her hip, he drove himself inside of her on one hard thrust. Even with his preparation, her pussy burned as his cock stretched her. It had been more than a year since she'd last had sex and none of her previous partners or even her vibrators could compare to the length and thickness of Cash's cock. He filled her completely, igniting every sensitive nerve inside of her and sending pulses throughout her pussy. Even if he didn't move, she didn't doubt that she could come just from him inside of her.

He didn't allow her the chance to confirm it. Clasping her waist, he slid almost all the way out, then yanked her back onto his cock, driving himself farther, deeper, and harder into her, hitting that spot inside of her that made her eyes roll back in her head and senseless pleas spill from her lips.

Cash's sharp bites pierced her neck and her shoulders until pain and pleasure blurred together. Like the love she felt for Cash, her climax crept up on her fast and without warning. It was so overwhelming, she was sure it would blow her apart.

"Let go, Dreama," Cash said against her ear. "I'm right there with you."

His permission pushed her off the ledge. She shook as liquid bliss blasted through her core. Over and over, her pussy clenched and released in blinding climaxes that knocked her world off its axis.

On a loud roar, Cash came, his cock jerking and twitching inside her and the heat of his release bathing her channel. Exhausted and boneless, she fell to her stomach. Cash followed her down, collapsing beside her. As they both caught their breath, he turned her onto her side, so that they were chest to chest.

She had only one thing to say to him. "When can we do that again?"

EPILOGUE

Cash threw his keys on the entrance table and walked down the hall toward the back of their house. Surprisingly, it was silent, which was a rare occurrence these days. Since moving to their farm last year, he'd grown used to the noisy chaos and pitter-patter of little paws on the linoleum.

"Dreama?" he called out, peeking into the master suite.

Their white calico cat slept contently curled on Cash's pillow, the sheets and blankets tangled together at the foot of the bed. His groin tightened as he thought back to what he and Dreama had been doing in that bed a few hours earlier, things that would make that poor pussycat blush if it had been allowed in the room at the time.

There were advantages to living with someone you loved. He hadn't wanted to leave their bed this morning, but he'd promised to meet Ryder and Finn in the city for breakfast. Sunday pancakes had become a weekly tradition for them, as were the Friday night dinners that rotated between their three houses and Rebecca's. They had become more than his biological brothers. Other than Dreama, Ryder and Finn were his closest friends. He couldn't imagine his life without them.

Becoming a multimillionaire overnight hadn't come as easily for Cash. He figured most people dreamed of having that kind of money, but he was never going to be one of those people. Turned out, neither were his brothers. They were both shockingly normal for guys who'd grown up in a mansion not wanting for anything. Well, not anything. Because while Cash had been adopted by a loving couple, Ryder and Finn had been raised by their mutual father, a man without a moral compass or time to devote to his sons. Cash would always be grateful to his birth mother for protecting him when it was clear she could have used him as a bargaining chip for millions of dollars.

Barking from the backyard gave him a hint as to where to find Dreama. He should've known she'd end up there this morning.

With a smile on his face, he headed toward their living room, passing by the open doors of the three additional bedrooms. Their house wasn't very large, but it was theirs, and it was more than enough to suit their purposes.

Millions of dollars could buy New York penthouses, Connecticut mansions, and French châteaus, but he and Dreama had bought only one property, a charming farmhouse on ten acres of grassy land, an hour outside Detroit. They had spent hours renovating the interior themselves, changing it from a traditional farm-style home complete with rooster-covered wallpaper to a bright, eclectic modern-style home, much like Dreama herself. He'd bet the previous owners had never imagined using the space in the cellar as a sex dungeon.

Cash opened the living room sliding door and stepped out onto the deck. Right away, he spotted Dreama, running around the yard with ten barking dogs racing behind her. Butch was by her side, where he always remained. Normally, they'd have nearly two dozen dogs at any time, but in the past month, they'd been able to place fifteen of them in permanent homes.

"Trying out a new training method?" he called out to her.

She laughed and changed directions so that she was now running toward the deck. The sight of her was a punch to his chest. He didn't know how he'd gotten so fucking lucky.

Her hands were folded across her chest where she wore a baby carrier that she'd designed and sewn herself. A head of black hair poked out of it. Dreama's lips moved and he knew she was probably singing to the little guy.

She climbed up the deck stairs, her pink-tipped hair whipping around her face, and jumped into his waiting arms. "Missed you," she said, before planting her lips against his.

He took over the kiss, putting his palms on her cheeks (she still had her fetish for his hands), and angling her head to get deeper access into her hot mouth. She tasted like coffee and maple syrup and smelled like sex and fresh air.

A yelp came from between them. Cash pulled his lips away from hers and looked down. The black pit bull puppy yawned sleepily before resting his head against Dreama's breast.

Smart dog.

"How's he doing?" Cash asked Dreama as she slid down his legs to stand on her own two feet.

"Milo's great. He's already made friends with Princess Peach."

"Milo?" he asked. When he'd left this morning for break-fast, they hadn't named him yet.

She petted the top of the puppy's head. "After the actor from my favorite television show."

"Oh, you mean the one you have a crush on?"

"Why, are you jealous?" she taunted.

"Crush away. Maybe I'll just have to name our next dog Mandy."

Milo had come to him from his sister, who had per-formed emergency surgery on the poor thing after someone had thrown him from a moving car into oncoming traffic. He'd lost one of his legs as a result. The combination of him being a pit bull with the loss of his limb made it less likely he'd be adopted.

He and Dreama fostered as many animals as they could. Dogs. Cats. Rabbits. Even the occasional hamster. When-ever an animal was due to be euthanized at the county shelter, his sister transferred that animal to Cash's farm, and he or Dreama would find permanent placement for it.

After the truth had come out that Cash had been un-knowingly drugged the night of the accident, the judge who had presided over his case overturned his conviction, clearing Cash's record. Lundquist pled guilty to a long list of crimes, including conspiracy and murder. He was currently serving a life sentence. Stephen Browner admitted to taking bribes and had been disbarred. Jay Moran and Kevin Sanders had both received three years for their part in falsifying the Dosothysomine study and lying to the police about Cash's drinking. They hadn't known anything about Laci's or Nancy's murders.

Even though Cash had more than enough money, he sued all of them in civil court and unsurprisingly, they quickly settled. He'd donated the money to the Innocence Project, a charity whose mission it was to free the innocent from prison.

Dosothysomine had been removed from the market. Lundquist Animal Health had filed for bankruptcy after it was hit with a class action lawsuit. Cash's heart went out to the employees who'd lost their jobs, but he didn't feel guilty. The blame fell squarely on Thomas's shoulders.

In the end, the department of corrections hadn't recommended filing criminal charges against Dreama for her relationship with Cash even though they'd determined she had engaged in misconduct. Dreama had reported Meg's behavior, but like Dreama had predicted, the department did nothing more than give Meg a figurative slap on the wrist.

He and Dreama used Cash's newfound money to fund the Dream a Little Dream Foundation. Not only did the foundation save animals from euthanasia, but it also rehabilitated dogs that others had considered a lost cause. Several of the animals came from dog-fighting rings. Others had been abused and neglected, and rather than being aggressive, they no longer had the will to live. Some were crippled or required medical care. Here on the foundation's farm, Cash, Dreama, and several others retrained the animals so that they could have the chance they deserved. Dreama utilized her parole officer experience to supervise the PAWS program. With Dreama at the helm, the PAWS program had expanded to nearly every jail and prison in the state.

"I'm glad you're home," Dreama whispered in his ear. "I left you a surprise in the barn."

He immediately went hard.

He'd been fantasizing about her playing the farmer's daughter since they bought this place. And he definitely had something for her to milk.

The sun's rays glimmered on the silver collar around Dreama's neck.

"What are we waiting for?" he asked, removing Milo from the sling and placing him gently on the ground before sliding his arm around Dreama's waist and pulling her toward the barn.

Dreama's laughter and the dogs' barking filled his ears.

His life was nothing like he'd imagined it would be.

It was so much better.

About the Author

A sucker for a happy ending, Shelly Bell writes sensual romance and erotic thrillers. She began writing upon the insistence of her husband, who dragged her to the store and bought her a laptop. When she's not working her day job, taking care of her family, or writing, you'll find her reading the latest romance.

Learn more at:
    ShellyBellBooks.com
    Twitter @ShellyBell987
    Facebook.com/ShellyBellBooks